SEAGARDEN

Grow a Revolution with the other books
in the **PLOTTING THE STARS** series:

1: *Moongarden*

PLOTTING ❧ THE ❧ STARS

SEAGARDEN

MICHELLE A. BARRY

PIXEL+INK

PIXEL✚INK

Text copyright © 2023 by Michelle A. Barry
Jacket illustration copyright © 2023 by TGM Development Corp.
Jacket illustration by Sarah J. Coleman

Pixel+Ink is an imprint of TGM Development Corp.
www.pixelandinkbooks.com
Printed and bound in August 2023 at Lake Book Manufacturing, Melrose Park, IL, U.S.A.
Book design by Jay Colvin

Names: Barry, Michelle A., author.
Title: Seagarden / Michelle A. Barry.
Description: First edition. | New York : Pixel+Ink, [2023] | Series:
Plotting the stars ; 2 | Audience: Ages 10 and up. | Audience: Grades
4–6. | Summary: Forced to hide her new-found magic, Myra enrolls in an
interplanetary academy exchange program to dig up more about the
government's many conspiracies.
Identifiers: LCCN 2023023459 | ISBN 9781645951292 (hardcover)
ISBN 9781645951308 (ebook)
Subjects: CYAC: Magic—Fiction. | Schools—Fiction. | Student exchange
Programs—Fiction. | Gardens—Fiction. | Food supply—Fiction. | Venus
(Planet)—Fiction. | Conspiracies—Fiction. | Science fiction. | LCGFT:
Novels. | Science fiction.
Classification: LCC PZ7.1.B37277 Se 2023 | DDC [Fic]—dc23
LC record available at https://lccn.loc.gov/2023023459

Hardcover ISBN: 978-1-64595-129-2
E-book ISBN: 978-1-64595-130-8

First Edition

1 3 5 7 9 10 8 6 4 2

To Julie ("Auntie"), who gives everything for everyone.
This book is for you, with all my love.

—M.A.B.

CHAPTER ONE

Second Month, 2449

I STAND IN THE DOORWAY, SCANNING THE ROWS AND rows of seats surrounding the hoverball court. A sudden gasp from the crowd, followed by a cheer loud enough to shake the moondust off the school's roof, echoes in the brightly lit space.

"Great shot, Canter!" someone nearby shouts, and I turn to squint at the players in their cyan jerseys. Canter's tousled blond head emerges from a huddle of one-armed hugs and backslaps. He must have just gotten a point. Good thing, too. The score's close, with the Scientific Lunar Academy of Magic just barely in the lead. The letters *S.L.A.M.* are projected into the air, glowing over the center of the hoverball court, and next to it, a golden 95 rotates slowly in place beside L.S.S.A.'s 93.

The Lunar School of Scientific Applications is a

non-Creer school on the outskirts of the capital. Even though they're down, the players look confident. They should be. Usually, we'd be up fifty by this point. Plus, non-Creer schools always take special pleasure in beating magical ones.

"Myra, over here!"

I turn toward the voice and grin as Lila gestures to the seat she's saved beside her, then make my way up the stairs to where she's sitting with Sloane. My seat, floating in midair, bounces as I flop into it, then gradually settles into place.

"This game is too close," Sloane says, chewing the end of her blond ponytail. "We always crush L.S.S.A. What is happening?"

"Canter's off today," Lila says, giving me a sideways look.

"He just got a point," I remind her, then lean toward the court. The canary-yellow floor is divided by red and blue stripes, marking off the boundaries of where players can hover, fly, and swoop to score. The two teams line up opposite each other on the court. L.S.S.A.'s players in their maroon jerseys look eager to retaliate.

"Yeah, but it was kind of a lucky shot," Lila counters. "Canter tripped, and the ball went sailing, then hit the rim and bounced in." She winds a strand of dark hair around her finger. The rest floats loosely above her shoulders, framing her golden-brown complexion and dark eyes. Her gaze flicks to mine. "Do you think he's okay? He seems distracted."

Resting my elbow on my knee and my chin on my hand, I watch Canter take his normal starting position in the center of the brightly colored floor. When the buzzer sounds, the players streak into action, aided by the low gravity of the court. Half the players propel themselves into the air, eye level with the stands. The ball flies through the air. A S.L.A.M. player somersaults after it, then smashes it with his elbow, sending it careening in Canter's direction. He makes a wild catch, turns as he touches down, and pushes off again, flying toward the lime-green hoop. But then the ball bounces off the rim and back into play.

"Ah, c'mon, Canter," a deep voice somewhere behind me calls over the crowd's grumbling. "You had that."

I turn, stiffening as I meet the eyes of Director Weathers, then quickly turn back around.

"See," Lila whispers, nudging me. "He *always* makes those shots."

He does, but I'm not surprised he missed. Canter hasn't been himself. Not since everything that happened in the moongarden last year. And I can't really blame him. Finding out your dead mother is actually alive but imprisoned, and your dad knew and hid it from you, is bound to take a toll.

Add to that discovering you have forbidden Botan

3

magic (like mine), and I'm amazed Canter hasn't floated off into orbit.

The crowd groans as L.S.S.A. steals the ball and scores again. By halftime, they're beating us 109–97.

A bell chimes overhead and I brace myself, clutching the arms of my seat.

"Halftime swivel," Lila says, gripping her own chair tightly. As the teams prepare to switch sides, our hovering chairs give a sudden jolt and slide sideways, gliding along until we're on the opposite side of the court, near L.S.S.A.'s net.

The buzzer sounds again. S.L.A.M. has possession. Canter snags the ball, cartwheeling midair, and lobs a shaky pass to his teammate . . . who drops it. A maroon-clad player scoops it up easily, leaping down the court and scoring another two points.

Sloane moans, covering her eyes. "I can't watch this anymore. The whole team is off today."

I exchange a look with Lila. Canter, usually the star the rest of the players orbit around, has become a black hole, sucking his team down with him. Missed passes. Slow reflexes. Wide shots.

"I guess we were due to have an off day," I say to Sloane. Then more quietly, so only Lila can hear, I add, "I hoped hoverball would help distract him."

"It's not working," Lila whispers back.

"I know what might, then."

"Where are you going?" Sloane asks as I rise.

"I really can't watch this." I shoot Lila a look, and she stands, too.

"Me either."

"Tell us the score later," I say to Sloane, but she's already animatedly rehashing the last play with a boy on her other side. "Let's go," I murmur to Lila, and we carefully pick our way down the stands.

But when we reach the door, it's blocked by a tall man with a Chemic Creer pin on his collar glinting under the harsh court lights. "Leaving so early?" Director Weathers asks, eyeing us suspiciously. More creases frame his eyes and forehead than the last time I saw him. His blond hair is darker, with hints of gray. "You need to support your school, win or lose."

"We're going to make a sign for Canter," Lila says quickly.

Director Weathers sighs. "I don't think he needs more distractions."

"Must be a lot on his mind," I say before I can stop myself. Heat rushes to my cheeks. "Usually, he has laser focus on the court."

"Maybe it's all the reporters nosing around about the food controversy leak that got the Chemic rep kicked off the Governing Council," Director Weathers replies, his voice icy.

5

I shrug, ignoring Lila stepping on my toe. "I wouldn't know anything about that."

For a pair of heartbeats, we just stare at each other, accusations scorching my throat as I swallow them down.

"We'd better make that sign if we're going to get back by the last quarter, Director Weathers," Lila says, pressing down so hard on my foot my sneaker dents like a moon crater.

He nods, his gaze still fixed on mine. "I suggest you be careful," he says, then relaxes slightly as his attention shifts to Lila. "No running in the halls."

We scoot by him, not daring to say a word until we're through the gym doors. "You need to watch what you say to him, Myra," Lila chides. "He's still the school director."

"What's he going to do? Expel me?" We're not going to have much time now if we have to make a sign and get back before the game ends. I'd bet Bin-ro that Director Weathers will be watching for our return. "This is all his fault, anyway. If he doesn't want me to remind him of last year, he should try leaving me alone."

We slip into a darkened room where cooking equipment is scattered across the countertops, and cabinets line the far wall. A thin layer of dust has settled over everything. We're careful not to disturb it.

"Kind of ironic that we're doing this in an abandoned, kitchen, isn't it?" Lila asks as we tiptoe farther inside.

Before Jake Melfin and MFI started using the *imitation method* to produce our food (if you can call it that), Chemics used their magic on plant samples from the Old World to create ingredients for the galaxy. But now that the samples are too old to be used in the plant cloning formulas, all that's left are the jiggly squares of slime MFI is force-feeding us.

With nothing to cook, the kitchen's been deserted for months, which fortunately has worked to our advantage.

I open a cabinet, smiling as a familiar glimpse of emerald peeks out from the shadows in the back corner. Spilling out of a couple of old pots and pans we found in the otherwise empty cupboards is a tiny herb garden. Small grow lights dangle over the containers, courtesy of Canter's Elector handiwork. I pull a shiny metal bowl closer, then frown at the wilting leaves. "They still aren't looking good."

"I thought Bernie said parsley does well in low light," Lila says, leaning closer.

I wince. Even though Bernie's been gone for months—*retired,* on Director Weathers's orders—hearing his name sends a fresh, sharp pain through my chest. "He did," I reply, forcing my throat to unclench. "I was able to mimic his fertilizer formula, too. At least I think I did. But it's doesn't seem to be helping."

"What about your magic?" Lila asks, gently brushing

the leaves, which are tinged a muddy brown, with her fingertips. "If we can get some of them blooming again, it'll definitely cheer Canter up. Especially if we lose this game to L.S.S.A."

I close my eyes and lay my hand over the top of the plant, then imagine it thriving, the air full of its spicy scent. My palm warms as love for this little plant fighting to survive in the dark cupboard washes over me. A memory follows.

Leaves from a patch of parsley unfold over the ground speckled with the same silvery dust piled at its roots. Bernie hunches down, carefully pruning the dead leaves, humming as he works.

Just as quickly, the sensation disappears. My fingers, icy and stiff, curl into fists as I pull my hand back.

Lila's gaze shifts from the plant to my face. "What's wrong? It won't work?"

"I think it's too far gone," I say quickly, trying to force the old moongarden from my mind.

"Oh," Lila replies. "Should we check the rest?"

Together, we inspect the cilantro, chives, and even a spindly tomato plant, hidden away in various cupboards. None are faring much better than the parsley. Each time, I close my eyes and let my hand hover above their brittle leaves.

"Any better?" Lila asks.

"A little," I lie. "I think they'll be okay." I carefully tuck the pots and pans back into their hiding places. "I'll ask Canter to check on them tomorrow."

Lila nods. "He's always in a better mood after he's used his plant magic."

Thankfully, that's true. I can't bring myself to say it out loud, but I know the only reason our new little garden is alive is because of Canter's magic, not mine.

"We'd better hurry if we're going to make that sign," I say. We pause in the doorway, glancing up and down the empty corridor.

Relief floods through me as we rush down the hall. In the past, I'd always been sad to leave my secret garden behind, but lately I can't lightspeed away fast enough.

CHAPTER TWO

THE NEXT DAY, I STIFLE A YAWN, FORCING MYSELF TO sit straighter behind my workstation. S.L.A.M. Chemic professor Mr. DeGraf, a stocky, gray-headed man with more eyebrows than hair, rests his elbows on his desk and his chin on the edge of his palm. A glass jar sits on his workstation, filled halfway with translucent gray gelatin. A gritty substance the color of ash has settled at the bottom. Mr. DeGraf's dark eyes wander the room as if considering which of us is the snack he wants to devour first.

At least that's what it looks like, but I know otherwise.

"Miss Hodger," he says lazily, his gaze settling on my face, just like I figured it would. "Care to demonstrate today's lesson?"

I force a polite smile. "Sure, Mr. DeGraf," I answer, then make a show of rolling up my sleeves. A few kids lean over to steal glances at the Chemic Inscriptions scrawled up my forearm (thanks to Lila's artistic skills).

"Did you review today's syllabus?"

"Of course, Mr. DeGraf," I lie. I haven't looked through our lesson plan since the first day of class almost a full lunar orbit ago, but I know Mr. DeGraf only pulls this charade on days we're working with edible extracts, the one area where I demonstrate the faintest Chemic abilities.

"Let's get started, then." Mr. DeGraf tilts his head toward the glass container, though he remains hunched over, leaning on his elbows.

I take a deep breath, and this time it's no act. Sweat beads at the back of my neck as I focus on the contents of the jar, willing them to fuse together.

As I concentrate, they start to swirl, turning into a tiny tornado, and then a whirlpool. After a hundred or so rotations, the gritty sand binds together, forming a solid strand poking through the slimy surface. On its tip, a tiny bud forms.

"Well done, Miss Hodger," Mr. DeGraf says, peering closer to inspect the jar. "With more advanced Chemic magic and the proper tools, this could turn into an actual food source."

The class around me *ooh*s, but I can only grimace at the hideous shadow of a plant I created.

"Mr. DeGraf?" the boy beside me calls, waving his hand

in the air as if our teacher might not see him in the crowd of eighteen students.

"Yes, Mr. Wakefield?"

"How can Myra do plant cloning magic if the food cloning formulas are broken?"

I can't help but roll my eyes. I've only been a "Chemic" a little while, but it doesn't take a master's in magic to understand the basics. Plus, Mr. DeGraf explained this all a moment ago.

Our teacher sighs. "Let's think on this, Mr. Wakefield. Miss Hodger did an excellent job demonstrating the initial bonding of the elements that spur artificial plant growth, but you wouldn't want to eat that, would you?"

"You should eat it, Gavin," a girl next to him whispers.

"Eat it, eat it, eat it," chants another boy from the opposite corner of the room.

I slouch, dropping my head into my hand.

"All right, all right. Settle down," Mr. DeGraf says, standing up with a groan. "You wouldn't want to eat it because it's not edible. Not yet. As I was saying before your, er, insightful question, the food creation process requires a great deal more magic, and many more phases, to transform elements into anything edible. And it's during those phases of the process that the cloning formulas break down."

"Why do we have to learn this if it doesn't even work?" the boy from the corner calls.

"So that when the problem *is* solved, we have Chemics capable of producing food," Mr. DeGraf explains, raising the specimen to eye level. "So we don't *starve.*" He grunts as he turns and deposits the jar on a shelf behind him, then loads the day's theory lecture onto the screen.

"My parents think this whole thing about food formulas breaking is fake. A publicity stunt or something," Gavin whispers to the girl next to him. "Maybe the anonymous tip about the MFI cover-up was from one of their competitors. My dad said that in a few months, food cloning will miraculously start working again."

"Well, try growing your own vegetables then if it's so simple," I snap, then immediately wish I hadn't.

Gavin's eyes narrow. "Maybe *you* should. All you ever seem to do in this class is plant magic."

Ignoring him, I spin and face the board, then slide my messenger out of my pocket and onto my lap, checking my inbox for the hundredth time today. *Still nothing.*

When the bell rings after what feels like an eternity, my eyes are still glued to the screen. I jump at the screech of sneakers and stumble backward to avoid a collision. My messenger flies through the air before clattering across the tile.

I stoop to grab it, but so does the boy I swerved to avoid. "Ouch!" I yelp, rubbing my head. The boy eyes me wearily as he runs his hands through his dark hair.

With a start, I stare into familiar, icy blue eyes. *How do I know him?* I glance down at his clothes, looking for a clue, but instead of the brightly colored Creer jumpsuit most Slammers wear, I take in gray Rep coveralls.

"Sorry, miss," the boy mutters, turning to go.

"Wait." I step in front of him. He must be only a couple of years older than me, and I've never met a Rep that young. Still, I can't look away. And there's something about his voice, too. . . . "What's your name?"

"Why do you need to know that?" he asks, his expression a mixture of curiosity and suspicion.

"So . . . so I can apologize properly," I sputter. "For knocking into you."

"No need," he says, sidestepping me and walking away.

"Well, er, how about so I can tell Director Weathers how helpful you were?" I ask, turning to follow him.

He glances over his shoulder but doesn't stop. "Helpful, how?"

"You tried to pick up my messenger for me."

He shrugs and turns back around. "Courtesy isn't worth reporting."

"Please," I say. "Please, just tell me your name."

"Why?"

"Why not?"

He keeps walking and my shoulders sink. Just as he's about to turn the corner, he calls back over his shoulder.

"Bernard. Just call me Bernard."

CHAPTER THREE

"I'M TELLING YOU, IT WAS HIM!" I REPEAT FOR AT LEAST the twentieth time. I try to spear a bite of my dinner, but it's so hard, it bends the prongs of my fork.

"Just because his name was Bernard doesn't mean it was Bernie," Canter says, not looking up from his dinner tray. "Besides, we don't even know if Bernie's full name *was* Bernard."

"Pretty big coincidence, though. Don't you think?" I slide my carefully sliced pieces of artificial food around my plate, not eating any of it. And not just because it's disgusting. My appetite vanished the moment Bernard disappeared around the corner. "Plus, he looked just like Bernie. He had the same blue eyes—"

"Lots of people have blue eyes. *I* have blue eyes." Canter waggles his brows.

"And his voice was the same, too. Younger, obviously, but he called me 'miss' and everything."

"That just sounds like he was being polite."

I slap my hand down on the table, and several kids glance over just as the square of food I'd been poking at bounces off my tray and onto the floor. "Canter. It was *him*. If we can find him, I'll prove it to you."

Canter looks at me, his gaze serious, but his voice is gentle as he says, "That's impossible."

"Bernie was a *clone*. It's not impossible."

"Clones have accelerated aging, but the process isn't that fast."

"We don't know how long he's been around, though, do we? Have you found out anything about Rep life cycles on the open network?"

Canter shakes his head. "Nothing new."

"Then that kid could have been around for a while before they sent him here. Your dad said Bernie was due to be retired." I wince as the words leave my mouth. So does Canter. "Look, it's not your fault your research hit a wall."

"I thought I'd be able to figure out what was blocking Reps from using their magic," he grumbles.

"Maybe if we can find Bernie, we could ask him. It can't hurt to try."

"Well, dissapointment hurts more than pretty much

anything," Canter says quietly, staring past my shoulder toward the back of the cafeteria.

I turn and follow his gaze. Director Weathers is talking with Mr. DeGraf as he collects his dinner tray.

"Any luck finding anything more on your mom?" I ask, my voice low.

Canter shakes his head. "No, but I've got a plan."

I take a deep breath. Canter's plans have gotten riskier with each passing week.

"I'm going to call the prison's control center on Mercury," Canter begins, and I cover my face with my hands. "No, seriously. This could actually work!"

"Do you think she's got a video pod in her cell?"

"I'm not trying to *talk* to her. Not yet, anyway. . . . But seriously, listen. So I call and pretend to be my dad—"

"Because you sound just like him."

"—and I tell them, as her husband, I want a well-being check on her. You can demand that. I read it on the open network."

"Well, if it was on the *open network,* it must be true . . ."

"After that, I can start slipping her messages to let her know it's actually me. Then she'll know that I know."

I raise a hand and Canter finally stops rambling. "That won't work for about a hundred reasons."

He crosses his arms. "Name one."

"No one is going to believe you're your dad. No guard is going to pass on a message in a well-being check. Besides, you can only request one check per year—I read about the Mercurian prison system on the open network, too. And"—I drop my voice to a whisper—"your mom isn't just a plant offender. She's a *Botan* prisoner. They'll probably deny she's even there. She's supposed to be dead, remember?"

Canter opens his mouth and then shuts it.

"Whoever you end up talking to at the prison is going to call your dad and tell them you're pranking them, or worse." When Canter doesn't say anything, I nudge his arm with my tray. "We'll think of something, though."

He sighs. "At least we have our little *project* to distract us." His voice drops to a whisper. "I checked on the plants this morning and gave them a little boost. They seem to be doing much better."

I resist the urge to rub at my arms. "We need more space. It's too tight in there to get anything going."

"And we need a new plan for what to do with the garden."

The silence stretches between us like a vine.

"What we need is a fresh perspective," I say, sitting up straighter.

Canter frowns. "From who? You know we can't tell anyone about all this."

"No one *new*," I say, raising my eyebrows.

18

"That wasn't Bernie, Myra. It couldn't have been."

I stare at him, defiant. "Prove it."

He scoops his tray off the table as he stands. "Fine. But only so you stop pinging me. I can't eat this junk, anyway. It's worse than the last version."

He's not wrong. MFI has been *enhancing and expanding* their imitation line, and now we have three versions of inedible food: jiggly, super jiggly, and cement. I follow him out of the cafeteria. Director Weathers is still lingering near the back, deep in conversation with Mr. DeGraf. His head turns toward us as we pass, but I quickly look away.

"You know I don't like these," I say through gritted teeth as Canter leads me to an Anti-Grav Chamber.

"Would you rather wait for my dad to come marching down the hall insisting he needs my help with another one of his made-up projects?"

"Just hurry up so we can get this over with."

Canter presses the button for the top level of the school. The floor falls away and we're shot up the shaft, jostling each other as we float up through the center of the spiral structure. Despite the queasiness flooding through me, I manage to smack both elbows on the sides of the chamber.

Finally, the doors slide open, and I tumble out, gritting my teeth as Canter strides forward as if he's stepping off a sturdy ledge.

"You really had to pick the top floor?"

He shrugs. "If you want to do a proper search for this *Bernard,* we might as well start at the top and work our way down. Besides, it's as far from my father as we can get."

Unfortunately, he's right.

We make a loop around the top level with no sign of Bernard. Just before we walk down the ramp to the floor below, I pause to glance out a window. The view from up here is the best in the school. Maybe anywhere on the Moon.

The silvery-gray landscape stretches below us, the chalky dust sparkling in the school's glow. Sometimes, S.L.A.M. feels suffocating, more like a prison, but right now a wave of fondness for it sweeps over me and I can't help but smile.

Off in the distance, a cluster of lights marks the edge of Apolloton. I notice a slow-moving cloud heading toward the city—it must be a Crawler. For a moment, jealousy flares in my chest as I imagine the people sitting inside, traveling into town for dinner, or shopping, or a meeting, without any worries about secret gardens or secret magic churning inside them. Overhead, a million stars glitter like snowflakes frozen in time, and hovering among them is the Old World. Beneath its haze, I know plants cover the surface from coast to coast, free to grow wild—unchecked—spiraling off wherever they please, however they please, twisting and climbing over everything in their paths. Despite the fact that they're poisonous and deadly, I long to see them. Ever since I found the moongarden, it's like a piece of me belongs back on the Old World. Like the plants are calling me home.

"Did you give up already?" Canter asks behind me.

"No. Just thinking," I say before trotting down the ramp. "I wonder what it's like to live in a place where plants can sprout up anywhere and everywhere."

"Meanwhile, we're stuck shoving them into nooks and crannies."

"Exactly. I wonder if our magic would be stronger there." I hesitate, rubbing my arms. "I think my magic was stronger in our old moongarden."

Canter's eyebrows shoot up. "You never told me that before."

"Then it's not that way for you?"

He shakes his head. "My Botan magic feels the same. Maybe even a little stronger."

"Really?" I wilt, then quickly stand straighter so Canter doesn't notice.

If he does, he doesn't say anything. "Remember how Lila told us emotions impact her Mender magic?"

I nod.

"Well, my Botan magic makes me feel closer to my mom, maybe because I know she's alive. Has your magic been affected?" Canter asks after a pause. "By your Chemic classes, I mean?"

The potential responses pile up on opposite ends of *Truths* and *Lies*. My Chemic classes are about as dull as my Number Whispering ones were, but I can't help but feel like everything is simple in Mr. DeGraf's classroom. Unlike everywhere else. Before I can decide which side tips the scales, a flash of gray down the hall catches my eye.

"A Rep just went into that classroom," Canter says slowly. "He looked young."

Without another word, we speed up to follow him.

CHAPTER FOUR

"WHERE'D HE GO?" CANTER PANTS, HIS EYES DARTING around the space.

"I don't know." The classroom, an upper-level Elector one by the looks of the tools and contraptions scattered across the workstations, is deserted. "The lights are on, so he definitely came in here."

"No kidding. We saw him walk through the door. Unless you think we were both hallucinating."

Before I can reply, a crash behind the teacher's workstation makes us both jump. We exchange a look, then quietly make our way around the desk from opposite sides.

A brown-haired boy in Rep coveralls is stooped over, scrubbing the floor behind the workstation. He doesn't glance up.

"Uh, hello?" I say. "Bernard, right?" His eyes meet mine

for a second. *It's him.* I shoot a triumphant look at Canter, but from where he's standing, he can't see the young man's face.

The Rep returns to his cleaning. "Did you need something?"

Canter frowns. "Sort of. Couldn't you hear us talking when we ran into the classroom?"

"My ears work fine."

Canter still can't see Bernard's face, but even he can't deny how Bernie-ish a reply that was. His eyes widen. "Why didn't you come out, then?"

"Didn't know you were looking for me." Bernard gives the spot a swipe with his cloth, then stands, turning toward Canter. "Did you need my help?"

"Y-you're B-Bernie," Canter sputters.

The young man's expression darkens. "It's Bernard, actually."

"But we always called you Bernie," I blurt out, and he gives me a puzzled look. "We knew you. Back before . . ."

"You were our friend," Canter clarifies. "Your, er, the old you."

Bernie—Bernard—eyes us curiously, his expression softening slightly. "You knew my prior Repetition?"

"Yes!" we say in unison.

Bernard's quiet for a moment. "Interesting," he finally says, then returns to his duties.

Canter and I exchange a confused look.

"We're so glad we found you!" I try.

Bernard glances up. "Why? Did you need help with something?"

"No. I mean, yes. Um, not like that. You were our friend. You helped us with the—with a project. A special project." I bite my lip, unsure of how much to say. "You taught us so much . . ."

"About what?" he asks, pushing dark hair out of his bright blue eyes.

"Well, plants, for one thing," I say carefully.

"We're not supposed to speak of those," he replies, looking scandalized. "Only those with approved Creer abilities are able to process materials associated with the study of flora." It's like he's reading from a textbook.

"But you were a gardener once," Canter counters. "A master gardener. You told us."

"I did?" Bernard looks confused, trying to make sense of this new information. "And that's what got me here," he replies coolly. "Well, my original, anyway."

"That's not the plants' fault," I snap, frustration burning into anger. "And that's not how you felt before. You taught us that plants are good. That they can help us. All of us. Just like on the Old World, before they turned poisonous."

"Ancient history. Just like my past Repetition. It's just me now. And I've got to get back to work."

25

"But—" Before I can say anything more, Canter grabs my arm and steers me away.

"We need to regroup," he whispers, and I reluctantly agree. "Okay, Bernie, I mean, Bernard. We'll see you around."

Bernard nods but doesn't look up.

Disappointment bubbles inside me as Canter and I make our way out of the classroom and back into the hall. "Now what do we do?"

Hours later, I flop back on my bed in the room I share with Lila (and thankfully, *only* Lila), while she hunches over her computer. She's lost in her notes and doesn't look up.

"Do you study the effects of sleep deprivation in your Mender classes?" I ask after watching her for a few minutes.

She glances over at me, startled. "Of course. Sleep is critical to physical and mental wellness. Why?"

"Just wondering why you don't take your own advice," I reply, and she groans. "I woke up in the middle of the night, and you were *still* studying. It's already past curfew. You haven't looked up for *hours.*"

"That's not true," Lila says with a smirk. "I listened intently for fifteen minutes when you came back from dinner and went on and on about you and Canter finding Bernie."

"Bernard. And he's nothing like Bernie. " I pick at my blanket. "What are we going to do?"

"Keep trying?" Lila says with a shrug. "Maybe he just needs to warm up to you guys again."

"That's possible. I'll just keep bugging him until he likes me."

Lila laughs. "That's not exactly what I meant. But you could try working your charm on him. I will, too." She glances back down at her screen and rubs her eyes. "It'll probably have to wait until after my next test, though."

"When's that?" I ask, pulling my messenger out of my pocket and grimacing at the blank screen. No new notifications.

"Tomorrow," she says, stifling a yawn. "But I actually meant the one I have next week. I'm ready for tomorrow. It shouldn't be too bad. Next week's is going to be an asteroid of an exam." She sighs. "After that, I'll be able to be a regular human again. At least for a little while."

I take in the dark circles under her eyes. "Is everyone in your Creer this stressed out?"

"Some of them," Lila answers, losing her fight against the yawn. "But Mending is a really complicated Creer . . . and very competitive. The university you end up at can have a major impact on what sort of job you get after you graduate."

"I thought you wanted to work at the Lunar Mending Institute in Apolloton."

"I do." She stretches, rolling her head from side to side. "Still, the Lunar University Mending program isn't as highly regarded as the one on Mars, so that's where I want to go. If I can get in."

"Lila, we're thirteen years old. We don't graduate for four more years. You've got plenty of time."

"I can't think that way." All drowsiness has disappeared from her face. "If I'm going to give myself my best chance, I've got to stay focused now."

"Okay," I say, giving up the fight (for the moment). "Just don't work yourself into the Mending wing."

"I won't. I promise," she says with a grin. "Besides, you should talk. Tell me you're not obsessed with your Botan powers. You've been checking on our little garden every day since we found a place to hide it." She turns back to her screen. "If you're not careful, you'll have Botan Inscriptions covering your ears."

"I wish," I say softly, but Lila doesn't hear. She's lost again deciphering the differences in Mending techniques for transverse bone breaks versus spiral.

For a moment, I consider repeating myself, but decide against it. Instead, I sigh and roll over. Light from my messenger bathes my arm in a soft glow. After dinner, I took a shower and scrubbed off the fake Inscriptions Lila had carefully drawn over a layer of concealer this morning, leaving behind only my real ones.

I trail my finger over them, tracing the branches of the giant oak tree covering my forearm, and the vines, leaves, and flowers winding around my wrist. All the Inscriptions I earned last year in the S.L.A.M. moongarden. And not a single new one.

Well, that's not entirely true. I follow the outline of a tiny Inscription nestled in the crook of my elbow, right over what was previously a heart-shaped leaf. At first, I wasn't sure what it was. A new oddly shaped flower, maybe? But then one afternoon in Chemic class I saw it glowing on Mr. DeGraf's screen: an illustration of a hydrogen isotope.

Also known as a Chemic Inscription.

CHAPTER FIVE

A COUPLE OF DAYS LATER, I CLIMB ABOARD A NEARLY deserted school Crawler bound for Apolloton and lunch with my mom. Usually, students aren't allowed to go to town except on S.L.A.M.-sanctioned outings, but when your mother not only knows the director but also shares a galaxy's worth of secrets with him, exceptions can be made.

Bracing myself for the upcoming interrogation disguised as Mom trying to be more *engaged and attentive this year*, I stare out at city lights glowing brighter and brighter. What seems like a nanosecond later, I'm passing beneath a sign that reads OLD-FASHIONED BURGER DISCS—VOTED BEST SPUD STICKS ON THE MOON!

The tables inside are round, surrounded by shiny, cushy red booths. Amazingly, Mom's already here and waves me over. Once I free myself from her hug (maybe I'm imagining it, but they seem to get tighter as I get older) and sit down beside her, I surrender to the barrage of questions about my friends, my dorm room, and of course, my studies.

"I don't see why you aren't tutoring first-year Chemic students, too." She sniffs. "If Ms. Goble finds your knowledge useful for younger students, why doesn't Mr. DeGraf?"

"Mom, I'm barely even a Chemic. Besides, I thought you said these lunch dates were supposed to be fun. If you keep raining questions on me like a meteor shower, I'm going to have a *big project due* the next time you want to meet."

"Okay, you win," she says, holding up her hands. "What do you want to talk about?"

I consider being honest and saying nothing, but instead I point to the illuminated menu screen on the table. "How about which flavor of MFI junk we're going to order?"

We tap in our selections, and I escape to the bathroom. After I stall for as long as I can without inviting a whole conversation about whether I should visit the Mender wing, I head back into the main dining room and freeze. A familiar form is standing beside our table.

"Val, I'm so glad I caught you here," Mom says. "I've been meaning to vid-call you."

"Not to talk about our upcoming S.L.A.M. reunion, I assume?" Ms. Goble asks, taking my seat in the booth.

"Oh, for Pluto's sake, no," Mom replies, with a brittle laugh. "Twenty-five years. After graduation, time seems to move faster than a Warp Bubble."

"It certainly does." Ms. Goble presses her lips into a tight, polite smile. "Did Myra already leave? Her return Crawler wasn't due for another hour."

"Oh no." Mom waves her hand. "She's in the bathroom trying to avoid conversation. Or interrogation, as she'd probably call it."

Ms. Goble chuckles.

"But I'm glad she is, because I'd rather she didn't hear this. I don't want to worry her."

I step farther into the doorway's shadow.

"What can I do for you?" Ms. Goble asks.

"I need to know what happened to Fiona Weathers," Mom says, dropping her voice.

I frown. I already filled my parents in on my conversation with Ms. Goble at the end of the school year. What else is there to know?

"I told Myra before she left for break what happened to Fiona," Ms. Goble says.

Mom leans forward. "What I want to know is how exactly Fiona got caught with the seeds in the first place. Who knew about the *special arrangements,* and whose idea was it?"

"Wouldn't your husband have heard most of this already?"

Mom shakes her head. "Jake Melfin never said a thing to us about it, and it's never been discussed by the Council. At least not that Joe's heard. But I'm sure Jake knew, since his father was the one who supposedly caught her."

"Jake definitely knew," Ms. Goble says, a bitter edge creeping into her voice. "It was his fault Fiona was caught in the first place."

My head whips around so fast my ponytail smacks my cheek.

"Myra didn't tell me that."

"I didn't think it was appropriate to share with her, especially since Jake's son and Fiona's son are classmates."

On one hand, it's not Kyle Melfin's fault that his father did whatever he did to Fiona. On the other, Kyle's such a smug little space cadet, I can't imagine it'd be a good idea for Canter to know about this particular detail.

"Robert," Ms. Goble continues, "was very friendly with Jake at the time."

"I remember them being good friends in school, too," Mom adds.

"Jake had just started at MFI and was on track to take over the company when his father retired. Robert thought it would be the perfect partnership. It would give Fiona

33

a legitimate way to use her . . . *talents*. If MFI publicly supported the use of Botan magic, it could have changed everything."

"But he didn't agree," Mom finishes, her voice tight.

"No, he did," Ms. Goble says slowly, gazing out the restaurant window. "Jake said he did, anyway. But he wasn't in charge of MFI. His father was. Bradford Melfin. Director Weathers wanted Jake to wait. Hold off until he controlled the company. Apparently, Jake was sure he could convince his father."

"Or it was a ploy, and Jake and his father were in on it together," Mom says.

Ms. Goble gives a small nod. "That's what Sandra Curie thought, too. Robert disagreed."

Mom looks my teacher right in the eye. "What do *you* think?"

"I think it's mostly irrelevant. Whether the end result was intentional or not, Jake told his father that Fiona had seeds, his father reported it to the rest of the Council, and Fiona was charged and convicted."

"Is it irrelevant, though, whether or not Jake meant for Fiona to be arrested or it was an accident? Intention is everything: in magic and in life. If Jake meant for Fiona, his best friend's wife, to be imprisoned rather than reveal her Botan magic to the galaxy, doesn't that make him all the more dangerous to Myra?"

Ms. Goble sighs. "That's entirely possible."

They slip into silence, and I'm about to make my reappearance when Mom says, "I still can't believe they convinced Sandra to blow up Fiona's shuttle."

"Not they," Ms. Goble corrects. "Fiona. Sandra wouldn't have done it for anyone else in this galaxy or beyond. But Fiona insisted it was the best way to protect Canter and Robert."

Mom glances toward the bathroom and I press my back against the wall. "That was the other thing I wanted to talk to you about." She's speaking so quietly I have to strain to hear. "I know of another family in similar circumstances. They have two daughters, and Myra was close friends with their youngest."

I gasp, then slap my hand over my mouth, peering around the corner. Thankfully, they don't seem to have heard. What could Mom have found out about Hannah that she doesn't want me to know?

"I checked to see where the younger daughter enrolled on Venus, and . . . it's non-Creer."

"What?" I demand.

"Oh, Myra." Mom's cheeks go red. "Look who I bumped into! So, Val, is Sandra still teaching on Venus?"

"Oh yes." Ms. Goble glances sideways at me. "At a non-Creer school."

"*Mom.*" I plant my hands on my hips. "I *heard* you.

Hannah qualified to come to S.L.A.M. as a Tekkie! Why wouldn't she be at a Creer school on Venus?"

"Myra Josephine Hodger!" Mom sears me with a glare. "Were you eavesdropping?"

"You're the one keeping secrets, and you're accusing me of being sneaky?"

"You didn't answer my question."

"And you didn't answer mine."

"I think Myra's may be the more important of the two," Ms. Goble says quietly. "And unless you know some magic I'm not familiar with, I don't think you can make her unhear our conversation."

I slide into the booth beside Ms. Goble. "Well?"

"I don't know why she isn't at a magical school," Mom says with a sigh.

"What about Meredith?"

"I didn't find anything on Hannah's sister. It's like she doesn't even exist."

My heart sinks to my sneakers.

"There's more." Mom clears her throat. "I reached out to Hannah's parents. They're both working at an MFI factory."

"As Chemics?" In my bones, I already know the answer, and Mom's sad look only confirms it.

"It was a brief, chilly conversation, and Mrs. Lee refused to tell me anything at all about the girls. She said it's clear that the Council ranks above friendship in my book, and her girls are no longer my business."

I wince.

"When I asked about work, she said something about her and her husband losing their passion for their Creers, but it was like she was reading from a script. Just before she ended the call, she blurted out something about the Councils becoming too powerful."

"What do you think she meant?" Ms. Goble asks.

"I'm not sure, and I can't remember her exact wording, but it was along the lines of the Council stealing her daughter and her magic."

"Can the Councils take away people's Creers?" I ask.

"Not that I'm aware of," Ms. Goble replies. "Over the years, I've heard of a few others caught with seeds, but the only one I knew well was Fiona. It was always hushed up pretty quickly. The families moved to another Settlement. I thought it must have been the shame, but now I wonder. . . ." She taps her fingers on the table. "If members of the Governing Council were stripping people of their Creers, there'd be an uproar if word got out."

"It would explain why plant crimes are kept relatively quiet," Mom suggests.

Ms. Goble shakes her head. "But how would the Council prevent people from accessing their magic?"

"They stop Reps from using theirs," I say. "Bernie's

original was a gardener back on the Old World. The garden could never have existed without him. If anyone should have had magic, it was him."

Mom puts her hand on my shoulder, and for once, I don't shrug it off.

"Was he the one who helped Fiona?" Ms. Goble asks.

"Until Director Weathers . . ." I can't finish the sentence. Anger flares inside me, burning away the sadness that always seems to cling to my bones lately. "It's not right what happens to Reps. How they're treated. How they're bound by contracts they never even signed."

"I don't disagree." Ms. Goble's eyes are softer than I've ever seen them. "And I'm sorry for the loss of your friend, Myra."

I don't answer. I can't.

No one speaks, all of us deep in our own thoughts. After a while, Ms. Goble gets up to leave, and I groan silently at the lecture I'm about to receive.

"Why don't you stay?" Mom asks. "We just ordered."

Ms. Goble's gaze flicks between us. "I don't want to intrude. I'm sure you both have lots to catch up on."

"Oh, I think we've probably covered the main points," Mom says. "My interrogations are efficient and thorough."

Ms. Goble settles back down, and I sigh, relieved. Even Mom looks more relaxed.

As Ms. Goble taps in her order, a thought occurs to me.

"Is Ms. Curie really teaching at a non-Creer school? Or were you just trying to cover up what I heard?"

"She really is," Ms. Goble says. "She said she needed a change. That the magic reminds her of . . . things she'd rather forget."

I know the feeling.

Our food arrives, but I'm not hungry. Luckily, Mom's so engrossed in talking with Ms. Goble about the new teaching standards proposed by the Lunar Governing Council, she doesn't notice my fully intact slimy square. I tune out, picking up my messenger to check my inbox. No new messages.

She's not going to write back, Myra. Give it up. Hannah never replied to the apology message I sent last term. Based on what Mom's discovered about her family, I don't blame her.

I switch to my news feed, scrolling aimlessly until a familiar face in a looping video snippet catches my eye. Jake Melfin.

I tap the Play icon, and my breath catches as the footage rolls. The video quality isn't great. The picture bounces and shakes, as if the person holding the camera was nervous, or trying to conceal it, or both, but there's no mistaking Melfin standing in the middle of a deserted restaurant, cosmic cuff links reflecting like a million spotlights.

"I have no idea who contacted the media, Mr. Melfin. I

told you that," a man barks off-camera. "Just like Liam at the Diner told you last week. And Devi at Classic Venusian the week before. It wasn't any of us. Our business is hurting as much as yours."

"Well, it had to be *someone,* and only a handful of people knew about those codes," Mr. Melfin growls back. "I don't take betrayal lightly. Once I find them, whoever talked to that reporter will wish I *had* fed them poison."

He storms past the camera toward the exit, pausing in the doorway. "And if it turns out it *was* you, all that'll be left of your Creer will be faded Inscriptions and a vacant storefront."

The shot fades to black as words flicker across the screen just before the video ends: *If Jake Melfin cares that the galaxy found out that the food codes are broken, then shouldn't we? What else is MFI hiding?*

Mom and Ms. Goble are talking animatedly now, something about course prerequisites, but they fall silent when I shove my messenger in their faces. "You need to see this."

Their eyes go wider as the video plays. "Well, it doesn't look like Jake Melfin's buying into the pro-MFI spin," Ms. Goble says quietly when the words scroll across the screen.

"No, it doesn't appear so." Mom's paler than I've ever seen her before. "And someone else isn't, either."

CHAPTER SIX

THE VIDEO OF JAKE MELFIN WAS TAKEN DOWN BY THE time I boarded my Crawler.

Scrubbed from any news feed, like it never existed. Even Canter with all the tricks he's picked up from Tekkie friends couldn't find a trace of it on the open network. I told him and Lila about Hannah's family and Jake Melfin's sonic meltdown the second I got back to school, but something stopped me from sharing what I'd learned about how Fiona was caught with the seeds. I know I should tell them, especially Canter, but I also know it won't lead anywhere good.

Later that week, as I'm walking to my next class, a flash of dark hair and blue eyes disappears around a corner. Without hesitating, I hurtle after him, skidding down the hall and into the empty cafeteria.

"Bernie! I mean, Bernard! Hey, Bernard!"

He stops, hand still stretching toward the door leading to the kitchen. "You again?"

"Yup!" I say cheerfully. "Third time this week!"

"Fourth," Bernard grumbles. "You're going to get me in trouble. You almost made me late for an assignment yesterday. I'm due in the kitchens in five minutes."

"Then you should probably just talk with me. I'll only take four. I swear on my lucky meteor."

He raises an eyebrow. "Meteors don't stay in one place. How can you have a lucky one?"

I shrug. "Who says your lucky meteor can't change?"

He sighs. "What is it you want, miss? Whatever it is, it must be pretty important if you're following me all over the school."

"Listen, Bernie."

"Bernard."

"Okay, fine. *Bernard.* Look, I know you don't remember me, but we used to be friends."

"That wasn't me. That was my prior Repetition."

"I know, I know. But it's still you in there somewhere. The Bernie I knew is the same Bernie you'll grow to be someday, right?"

"That's not necessarily true," he says stiffly. "There are a lot of variables. I'm him, but I'm not *him.* We're not a hive mind, you know."

"See!" I yell, pointing at him, and Bernard takes a step

backward. "You said that exact same thing to me before!"

"Well, apparently you need to hear it again."

I grin from ear to ear. "*Now* you're sounding like you."

"You've got about one minute left."

"One and a half," I correct. "All I wanted to say, or ask, is that we be friends."

He studies me for a moment. "Why would you want that?"

"Because . . . because . . ." I know the answer. I know it in my bones. But how do I say it so he'll understand? "Because I miss you. You . . . you meant a lot to me. You taught me so much. About myself. About the galaxy. About . . ." I study those familiar blue eyes in their less-familiar form. "How old are you?"

He shifts uncomfortably. "Fourteen."

I open my mouth and then shut it.

"What? Spit it out."

"It's just, you were so much more, I don't know, fun before. No offense. I would have thought a younger you would be even more carefree. But you're so serious."

"Like I said, lots of variables make up a personality." He looks me up and down with that now-familiar skepticism. "You might have to wait a long time to find the friend you knew. He may never come back."

"I'll take my chances. Do we have a deal? Can we be friends?"

"I don't know what that means."

"We talk. Hang out—when you have time. I know the school keeps you busy. C'mon, don't you want a friend your age? You must be the youngest Rep here."

He gives a small sigh. "By decades."

I wait.

"Fine," he mutters, turning back toward the kitchen. "We're friends, and I'm late. See you later, miss."

"It's Myra!" I call after him. He doesn't reply, but I know he heard me. For now, that's enough.

That night, I sit cross-legged on a stool in the modulab while Bin-ro rolls back and forth in front of my feet, his wheels whirling over the hard floor. Canter's sprawled on a putty lounger nearby, tossing a hoverball over his head and catching it.

"Do you have to do that?" I ask, grimacing. "I'm trying to find more on whatever's suppressing Rep magic and I can't concentrate."

"You're wasting your time."

"You wouldn't be saying that if you knew what it was like to worry about losing the magic you have or wondering if you even have any magic," I fire back. "That's what Reps live with every day. And apparently other people, too, if Melfin's threat was real."

Smack! "I get it, but I told you, you won't find anything

else." *Smack!* "I couldn't even find a lead on where Reps come from." *Smack!* "Just some references to a *facility.* Not so much as a sentence on what it's called, where it is, or what they do there." *Smack!*

The next time Canter tosses the ball, I lean over and slap it away. It bounces off the wall and rolls under a table. Bin-ro beeps and zips after it.

"Your reflexes are pretty good," Canter says, surprised. "You should think about trying out for the girls' hoverball team."

"Then who's going to do all the work?" I ask, groaning when Bin-ro pushes the ball back to Canter.

"Thanks, buddy," he says. Shockingly, he doesn't start throwing it again. Nope, he's discovered a new game. He rolls the ball across the floor, and Bin-ro chases after it and sends it spinning back. *At least it's quieter.*

"Whatever's blocking Rep magic could be located at the same place Reps come from," I say.

"And if we can figure out how to undo it, the Reps will have their magic back, and who knows what could happen."

"'The whole system would crumble,'" I murmur.

"Sounds good to me." He folds his arms behind his head. "Do you think Melfin was serious when he threatened to take away the restaurant owner's Creer?"

"It didn't sound like a bluff."

"I've never heard of someone being stripped of their magic."

"Tell that to Hannah's parents," I say quietly. "Or her sister." We agreed that Meredith must be on Mercury, maybe locked in the cell next to Canter's mother.

"What's Lila doing?" he finally asks. "I thought she was meeting us here."

"Studying. What else?"

"But we're in the modulab." Canter bats the ball with his foot so it goes zooming across the room. "Can't she study here?"

"She says we're too distracting," I answer wearily as I watch Bin-ro send a stool flying. He whistles as he finally captures the ball and guides it back to Canter. "I have *no* idea why."

"Me either." He smirks and bounces the ball off another putty lounger across the room. Bin-ro chirps and spins after it.

"This is useless." I moan, waving the hologram keyboard away. "How can we find a way for Reps to use their magic if we can't figure out what's stopping it?"

"Welcome to my galaxy." Canter shakes his head. "I hit so many dead ends searching over break."

After another few minutes with no luck, I pull out my messenger, scrolling through the screens, not expecting to see anything since the last time I looked. My mouth falls open when an alert pops up in my inbox.

Hannah replied!

I tap the message and frown. It's not from Hannah. It's from someone named Indra.

> You're not the only ones who want to unleash Rep magic and take a weapon out of Jake Melfin's arsenal. Celebrate the progress of the rogue Rep settlement by baking a Venusian three-layer cake.

> Indra

Below the message is an embedded video. I tap the play icon and gasp.

"Canter, look at this," I say, passing him my messenger. "It's the video of Melfin threatening the restaurant owner."

He watches the video and skims the message, then looks up at me. "Who's Indra?"

"No idea." I lean over and we both reread the message. "A free settlement of Reps? Have you ever heard of one?"

"Never," Canter says. "I haven't heard of a Rep going rogue, much less a whole community of them. Breaking a Rep contract has serious consequences. And spying on

Melfin on top of that." He shakes his head, reading the message again. What's that bit about a cake?"

"I don't know." With another wave of my hand, I reactivate the hologram keyboard and type *Venusian three-layer cake* into the search bar. Dozens of recipes populate. "Look," I say, pointing at one. "This one was posted a few weeks ago, but the rest are years old."

"Why would someone post a new recipe now? There are no ingredients to cook with."

"Good question." I tap on the link. The contents of the page are what you'd expect from a baking post. Ingredients and instructions.

"Try the comments," Canter suggests.

I scroll down. A couple of posters have left messages about the cake sounding good, and wanting to try it out when the ingredient supply picks up again. A couple of others are more interesting.

"Skip the cream and try a pinch of sugar instead. Bake at two hundred twenty degrees for three minutes and thirty seconds." I look up at Canter. "Those are really strange instructions. That temperature for so short a time? No cake could cook that fast."

"It must be a code. Hey, today's the twentieth day of second month. The oven temperature could be a date."

"For a meeting . . ." I look up at him. "And the cooking time is the time of the meeting!"

"That would make sense!" Canter bounces up on the putty lounger. "But where is it?"

I scour the recipe for clues. "Might be something to do with the pinch of sugar comment?"

"It can't be a coincidence that this is a Venusian recipe," Canter says, swiping his hair away from his face. "What did that message say again?"

As we both reread Indra's note, I notice something else. "The person who posted the comment! Look at their username."

"Indra031533," Canter reads aloud.

I'm bouncing in my seat now. "Let's try searching for other Venusian recipes." Lots of results come up for breads and cookies and pies. "Try the ones posted in the last two months."

Canter adds a filter, and this time only a handful of results fill the screen. We click through them and find similar comments—strange suggestions with modifications to times and temperatures, but a few words are the same from post to post—*pinch of sugar*. It must be the location. And every recipe is some sort of Venusian cuisine.

"What does all this mean?" Canter asks, shaking his head.

"There's an underground settlement of free Reps on Venus," I answer excitedly. "And they're trying to accomplish the same things we are. If we could find them, maybe we could help." I shake my head. "But who is this Indra, and how did she know what we're up to?"

"Someone could have cross-referenced our searches and traced you," Canter says, running a hand through his hair. "We haven't been that careful lately, and the school network isn't the hardest system to hack."

"But how would they even know to look?"

"I don't know." He leans over to scoop his ball up off the floor and then throws himself back into his seat. "But it's the best lead we've got."

Buzzing with excitement, I open the message again and tap out a reply:

Who are you?

I hit Send, and immediately, my messenger pings with a response: THIS USER DOES NOT EXIST.

Canter glances at the screen, then shakes his head. "They must have deleted the account after they sent you that message."

My excitement fizzles out. "Sounds like we might be able to find answers on Venus."

"Too bad we don't have a way to get there."

"A way where, Weathers?" We both jump. Kyle Melfin stands smirking behind us, a modulab screen tucked under his arm. "The annual hoverball championship? The way you've been playing, you'd better buy a spectator ticket."

"Says the guy who couldn't even make the team," Canter replies coolly, spinning the ball on his fingertip.

"Nice trick." Kyle leans toward our computer screen. "What are you two so absorbed in? You didn't even hear your metal shoe box beeping that someone was coming." Bin-ro blows a loud raspberry before zipping away under Canter's chair.

"A research project on why some kids annoy the moon-dust out of their classmates," I snap, quickly closing our search and logging out. "Want to be interviewed for it?"

"Why don't you ask your dad?" Kyle fires back, jutting his chin at Canter. "He must know all sorts of tips for *interviews*."

"Go dunk your head in a Chemic solution, Melfin," Canter says, pushing to his feet. "Let's get out of here. I think we've got enough data for our project."

I shoot Kyle my best glare as we leave the modulab, Bin-ro beeping and chirping angrily behind us.

"What did he mean about my dad?" Canter asks when we're a few halls away.

"I bet he thinks the director has something to do with the story about MFI. And if Kyle thinks that, his dad must, too."

"Is that bad?"

"Nothing with the Melfins is ever good."

CHAPTER SEVEN

THAT NIGHT, I SIT CROSS-LEGGED ON THE FLOOR IN THE abandoned kitchen prep room watching as Canter tends to the plants. He opens one cabinet door and removes a large silver pot filled to the brim with scarlet begonias, then fluffs their petals, his hands glowing. Before long, a new layer of ivory flowers is poking up among the red.

Although the new blooms are nothing like the lily of the valley we had in our old moongarden, the white petals of the begonias remind me of one of the first times I ventured into the garden and thought the bell-shaped blossoms might actually jingle when I touched them. A familiar ache clangs inside me as I turn back to where Lila is perched on a countertop, fully absorbed in her bookpod.

"I don't understand how you have more to study," I say

after a while. "You must've read every Mender textbook in the modulab by now."

"I'm not reading Mender theory," Lila says, looking up. "I'm scrolling through articles about MFI."

"Why?" Canter asks, tucking the begonias back in their cabinet and shutting the door, careful not to smoosh the plant. "What are you looking for?"

"I'm not really sure." Lila chews her lip. "I was curious how MFI got so powerful. They've been around forever, even back before everyone left the Old World, but there used to be lots of companies making food." Her gaze skims the screen. "Looks like they bought out their last big competitor almost three decades ago."

"If they don't have any real competition, why does Melfin care who leaked the story?" Canter asks. "MFI isn't going anywhere."

"Even if they are trying to poison us," I add pointedly.

Lila tucks her bookpod into her bag. "Canter's right. If the story didn't matter, why would he bother threatening that restaurant owner? It doesn't make sense."

"Maybe it doesn't have to," I say. "To us, anyway. People like Melfin make their own rules."

"I don't know how my dad's still friends with that guy," Canter mutters.

"Maybe he's loyal to him because of what happened after your mom . . ." Lila says, then stops herself.

I still haven't told either of them the real reason Fiona Weathers got caught with the seeds, and given the way Canter is narrowing his eyes, now's not the time. "If he wasn't so well connected, you and your dad's Creers could have been taken away, too. Like Hannah's family."

And like mine, if I'm ever caught with Botan powers.

For a moment, I try to imagine my parents as anything but Number Whisperers, but I can't separate them from their magic. The two are as closely fused as a planet's orbit around its sun.

Canter glowers. "I'd rather lose all my magic than take anything from the Melfins. And if Myra's right and he's somehow involved in taking away people's Creers, that's even more of a reason to figure out how to undo whatever's stopping the Reps from accessing their magic."

Lila frowns. "It can't just be Melfin. If people are being stripped of their magic, the Councils would have to be involved."

"Not officially," I say. "And not all the members. My dad's on the Lunar Council, and it was news to my mom that taking someone's Creer away was even possible."

"It can't be legal," Canter agrees.

Lila twists a strand of hair around her finger. "Melfin doesn't seem like the type to make empty threats, though."

"Or," I add, "like someone who cares about rules or laws."

The next day, I'm sitting in Ms. Goble's Number Whispering theory class, fiddling with my messenger, obsessively checking my inbox while other kids trickle into the room. Maybe Hannah only checks her messages every three and a half months. Or maybe she only sends messages during the third Lunar orbit of every year. Apart from mysterious Indra's message, my incoming folder remains frustratingly empty. I've got a new letter message waiting in Drafts, though.

Dear Hannah,

I'm sorry to be pinging you again. I assume you're ignoring me, which, if I'm honest, is totally justified. But I really do need your help. I don't expect you to want anything to do with me. But I think if you help me, we might also be able to help your family. At least I hope so. Anyway. If you can stomach the idea of using me to fix things for them, please write back.

Myra

I hit send without reading and rereading it a thousand and a half times, then power off my messenger and tuck it into my pocket as Ms. Goble stands.

"Before we begin, I'd like to share an exciting new opportunity with you."

Most of the kids around me sit straighter in their seats, but I know better. When a teacher says *an exciting new opportunity,* that usually translates to *a whole lot of extra work.*

"S.L.A.M. is developing an exchange program with the Venusian Academy of Magical Arts."

"V.A.M.A.? Really?" I blurt out. Ms. Goble raises an eyebrow. "Who can participate?"

"Second-years or above, as long as their grades are acceptable and they are generally well-behaved and trustworthy."

My stomach does a flip like I'm on a hover coaster. If Canter, Lila, and I were accepted into the exchange program and spent the next term on Venus, maybe we could see if we were right about the recipe posts' code and find the group of Reps there. And we might have more freedom to raise a new garden without Director Weathers breathing down our necks. After all, who would ever suspect three exchange students of using supposedly extinct Botan magic to build an impossible garden?

"When does the program start, Ms. Goble?" the girl next to me asks.

"After Family Weekend. But the deadline to submit your application is the end of next week."

"Are there a lot of spots available?" I ask, trying to force my voice to sound casual.

"Only two per grade," Ms. Goble answers. "We may expand the program next year, but as this is a trial, we've decided to keep the numbers small."

Only two per grade. That means Lila and I would need both second-year spots and Canter would have to get one of the third-year openings. My friends and I are going to have to work some serious magic. Still, a familiar determination bubbles in my chest. This chance could solve so many of our problems. Maybe all of them. Hannah's on Venus, too, and she'd have to talk to me if I showed up at her door.

Ms. Goble directs interested students to her class page on the academia network for the details and application, then turns to the holo-board.

"Ms. Goble?" I ask, raising my hand before she can start with her lesson. "Who'll be choosing the kids who get to participate in the program?"

She eyes me as if performing an advanced calculation. "I will. Along with Director Weathers."

I don't know if this news helps or hurts our chances, but a plan starts to form in my mind.

CHAPTER EIGHT

"CANTER, IT COULD WORK," I ARGUE, FIGHTING FOR HIS attention as he blasts space aliens in the Rec hall. "Can you pause that stupid game so we can talk about this?"

"I'm almost to the final level, and I've never gotten this far before," Canter answers, stabbing at a button. "And I told you fifteen times already, I'm not asking my dad to give us a recommendation for the exchange program. Besides, Ms. Goble told my class she's choosing who gets to go."

"Her *and* Director Weathers." I plant my hands on my hips. "If your dad asks her to include his son and his friends, do you really think she'll say no?"

"Yes," Canter replies, blowing up another spaceship. "Have you *met* Ms. Goble?"

I stomp in front of the screen. "If you give him a good reason, and then he passes along the good reason to her, then *bam!* We're in. And we can find that Rep settlement on Venus!"

"It's not going to work that way," Canter insists, dodging to see around me. "My dad will never go for it. Lila, back me up, please."

She glances away from the computer she's been lost in all evening. A half dozen holo-texts are scattered around her. "I think Myra's plan could work, actually."

I shoot her a grin. "See!"

"On what planet or moon?" Canter asks, dancing back and forth as he aims the controller. "Move out of the way, Myra!"

I cross my arms. "Not until you agree."

"Emotions are one of the strongest motivators humans have," Lila explains. "That's what I'm studying right now, actually. How emotions play into decision-making when it comes to well-being, and how to overcome negative reactions to produce the best possible patient outcomes."

Even Canter looks away from his game to gape at her. "Are you possessed by your Mender textbook, or did you really just recite all that from memory?"

Lila rubs her eyes. "I have the whole unit memorized."

I frown. I can't remember the last time Lila came to dinner with us. "Why are you working so much this year? Is there a secret second-year Mender test I don't know about?"

Lila makes a sound like she's trying to laugh, but really

she's choking back a sob. "No. At least I sure hope not. Now that I'm officially on the Mender track, my mom's been checking my grades on the academia network on a daily basis. She even spoke with my Mender professor last week because my test score was two points lower than my quiz the week before."

"Has she been hanging around with my mom?" I ask, and Lila laughs, a real laugh this time. "Sorry. I know what that's like. Maybe talk to her and tell her she's stressing you out?"

"She's just excited I'm going to be a Mender like her. She'll calm down soon," Lila says, waving her hand dismissively, but her eyes don't look so sure. "Anyway." She reaches out and flicks away some of the hologram texts hovering around her. "Mender theory about emotions playing a role in decision-making would back up what Myra's saying. Your dad's got to be feeling guilty about last year: destroying the garden; Bernie; getting caught lying to you about what happened to your mom . . ."

"I doubt he feels much of anything," Canter says, savagely blasting an alien ship to bits. "I'm sure all he cares about is that after everything that's happened, he'll never be Chemic rep on the Governing Council. Not with half the galaxy thinking he was wrapped up in Melfin's scheme."

"He didn't get blamed for that, though," I remind Canter. "Melfin told the press your dad wasn't involved."

"That's what they said publicly, but I heard Dad on the phone yelling about his reputation getting sucked into a black hole." Canter glances sideways at me. "He mentioned your dad by name."

"Yeah, well, my dad is definitely not his biggest fan, but there's no way he told the other Council members anything about last year. If he did, I'd be on the next shuttle to Mercury." I cringe as soon as the words leave my mouth, then dart a glance at Canter.

"Besides that," Lila quickly adds, "I find it hard to believe that your dad doesn't feel bad about hurting you. And we should use that guilt to get into the V.A.M.A. program."

"How?" Canter demands. Thankfully, he doesn't notice his ship being blown up by an alien starship.

"You could tell him that the bad memories are making it too hard for you at S.L.A.M. The garden, your mom, Bernie. It's all too much."

"That's not really a lie." Canter drops his controller and flops onto the putty lounger beside Lila. The remaining holo-books bounce and wobble as the lounger stretches to accommodate him.

"Exactly," Lila says. "A kernel of truth makes most lies easier to believe. Then you tell him you need a fresh start."

"With your best friends," I add.

"At V.A.M.A.," Lila finishes, beaming at me. "It's kind of genius, Myra."

I blush. "What are the odds that this exchange program opens up the same year that basically everything we're trying to accomplish is centered around Venus?"

"It's pretty lucky," Canter agrees; then his expression darkens. "Is it too lucky, though?"

Lila frowns. "What do you mean? Like did someone set this up for us?"

"That's impossible," I say. "No one knows what we're up to."

"I guess not." Canter runs his hand through his hair. "There's still no guarantee my dad'll buy it. And even if he does, we have Goble to convince."

"She knows a lot of what happened last year already," I remind him. "The same guilt trip might work on her."

"Okay, let's say I agree." Canter crosses his arms. "How do we do convince my dad to recommend us?"

Lila and I exchange a look. "Well, the first step is you have to talk to him . . ." I begin.

"What's Plan B?" Canter asks, glowering at us.

Lila turns to look him straight in the eye. "You talk to your dad."

"Plan C?"

"YOU TALK TO YOUR DAD!" Lila and I yell together. A few kids in the far corner turn to glare at us.

Canter sighs, dropping his head into his hand. "All right, fine. But if this works, you two seriously owe me."

I grin. "If Director Weather agrees, I'll fill out your application myself."

"Can you do mine, too?" Lila asks, taking in the shimmering wall of textbooks surrounding her.

"Sure." She looks at me, surprised, and I shrug. "I'm your roommate. I can see you're drowning in schoolwork."

Canter lifts his head, settling his chin on his hand. "I'm not your roommate and even I know that."

"Correction," Lila says, throwing her arms around me. "You're the galaxy's *best* roommate."

I awkwardly hug her back before untangling myself. "I'll start on the applications tonight." Then I turn to Canter. "And you talk to your dad."

He flops back on the putty lounger, which stretches to catch him before he hits the ground. "If I'm going to do this, you guys are going to have to coach me on what to say."

Lila and I exchange a grin. "Deal," I reply. "Start taking notes."

Later that night and two hours deep into completing the exchange program applications (and regretting volunteering to do them all), my messenger glows with a response from Canter. It's only four words, but it makes the endless pages I still need to fill out slightly more bearable.

I talked to him.

"Phew," I say to Lila as I hold out the screen for her to read. "I was worried he'd back out."

She smiles, looking almost as relieved as me. "Hopefully, Canter convinced him. We're going to need all the help we can get. I overheard a bunch of kids at lunch today talking about applying. They said they wanted to go because the food might be better there."

"Not likely. MFI controls Venus's food production, too. They control almost everyone's." I glance back down at my messenger. "Why isn't Canter telling us how it went?"

Lila taps out a group message:

Did you convince him?

A minute passes, then two. She shifts nervously at her desk while I refresh my screen so many times my finger starts to cramp.

CANTER!

I finally type, and hit Send.

He wants to talk to us about it.

I groan. "That does *not* sound good."

"He didn't say no, though," Lila says, chewing her lower lip. "Maybe Director Weathers just wants to make sure we're applying for the right reasons."

"And make sure we're not up to anything."

Lila shoots me a sly look. "Well, we're not, right? We want to expand our magical knowledge and forge intersettlement bonds."

I smirk. "Yes, exactly. It's a chance to broaden our horizons and see more of the solar system."

"And definitely not start a new garden," Lila says, her overly proper tone punctuated by giggles.

"Or meet up with a group of Reps living on the outskirts of galactic law."

"And help them unleash their magic on the galaxy."

I gasp and clutch my chest. "Never!" Still chuckling, I tap out another message to Canter:

We can handle that. When does he want to see us?

My messenger pings almost immediately. Lila and I read the message at the same time, our laughter dying in our throats.

Tonight.

CHAPTER NINE

FOR THE SECOND TIME IN MY LIFE, I LINGER OUTSIDE Canter's apartment, my heart pounding as my hand hovers over the bell. At least this time I have reinforcements.

"We've got this," Lila murmurs, eyeing the entry like it's the door to a dungeon. "Just stick to the story and it'll be fine."

I nod, take a breath, and slap my hand on the buzzer. The door opens, revealing a nervous-looking Canter. He's in sweats and a T-shirt with the name of his favorite hover-ball team, the Martian Meteorites, across the front. His hair's standing on end, like he tried to electrocute something and the magic backfired.

"Quick, give us the scoop," I hiss as he waves us in. Being summoned to speak with Director Weathers makes me want to hide in the Anti-Grav Chamber.

"Lila can talk about how beneficial it would be to study Venusian Mending techniques in person. You stick to how it's too hard to be here since Bernie and the garden."

I glance over at Lila. "But Lila's not supposed to know about the garden."

Canter shuffles his feet. "Uh, did I mention he wants to talk to you separately?"

"No, you did *not*," I whisper-yell.

"Myra, it's okay," Lila says, slipping into Mender mode, what I've started calling the tone she uses to soothe me like I'm a hysterical patient. I take a deep breath. "Just go in and talk about your friendship with Bernie and how much you miss him. That's true. It's no big deal."

"It's a big deal for *me*! I've barely spoken to Director Weathers since he destroyed the moongarden and threatened to send me to Mercury, and now I have to go in there and relive the whole thing alone."

"Not alone," Canter says, nudging me with his elbow. "I'll be there, too, to back you up."

I take a deep breath, my face so hot it feels like it's been scorched by a sun flare. "You'd better."

"Why did he want to talk to us tonight?" Lila asks. "Is he interviewing all the applicants?"

Canter shakes his head. "He said since I'm his son, and you're my friends, he wanted to speak with us before we submit our applications. Something about not showing favoritism. He says he'll disqualify us if he doesn't think our reasons for wanting to go are good enough."

"Canter, are your friends here?" Footsteps echo down the hall, and it feels like my spine has turned into Neptune ice as Director Weathers steps into the room. He forces a smile when he sees us. Canter glowers at him. "Hello, Miss Crumpler," he says, his tone genuinely warm. "How's the star second-year Mender?"

Lila blushes, beaming down at her feet. "Hi, Director Weathers. Thanks for talking with us so late. The exchange applications are due in a few days, and I have a feeling there'll be a lot of kids applying."

"That's exactly my concern, and why I wanted to talk to you. All three of you." His gaze sweeps over Canter and me, and though it's only for a second, I swear his cheerful mask drops. "This is the first time we're trying a program like this, and selecting the inaugural participants is not something I take lightly. If I'm going to make a recommendation, I need to be certain your interest is genuine." His icy gaze shifts to me. "Hello, Miss Hodger. I've been hearing positive reports about your recent academic performance. It appears you've become quite the example for your peers."

My eyebrows spring up. "Mr. DeGraf said that?"

The director narrows his eyes. "You're asking me to reveal my sources?"

My stomach swoops.

"Actually, it was Ms. Goble. She mentioned you've been tutoring some classmates."

I shrug. "Some good should come from all those years of my parents drilling me on mathematical theory."

Director Weathers clears his throat. "Well, it's getting late, and I don't want you kids out past curfew. Let's get started, shall we? I'd like to speak to each of you about what you hope to gain from this experience. Why don't we start, Lila? We can chat in my office. It should only take a few minutes."

"Sure. No problem, Director Weathers." I study her easy confidence as she brushes her curls away, smiling as she bounces through the doorway.

Trying to mimic her movements, I skip over to the couch, brushing my brown hair out of my face, and accidentally knock my glasses off in the process, sending them clattering to the floor.

"What are you doing?" Canter whispers sharply.

"Trying to look confident and comfortable and not like I'm about to be interrogated," I snap as I bend to scoop up my glasses before flopping down.

"Well, it's not working. This whole thing isn't going to work."

"Why? What happened when you talked to him?"

Canter runs his hands through his hair. "He knows

something's up, but I think he also bought what I was saying. It's like he's at war with himself. He sees that I'm struggling, but he also knows that's not the whole story. He asked me a zillion questions about the garden."

"Stop doing that," I hiss, jumping up and pulling Canter's hands away from his head. "What *about* the garden? He can't know we've started a new one."

"No, but he did straight-up ask me if I was hiding any seeds."

My mouth falls open. "What'd you say?"

"No, obviously. I don't think he's convinced, though." Canter starts pacing, then freezes midstep. "*You* have to convince him, Myra."

"Oh, sure. No problem. Because he trusts me so much. I'm sure we'll have a fun little catch-up. Maybe he'll recommend some cool Venusian tourist spots while he's at it."

"Wait, that's perfect!"

"What is?"

Canter snaps his fingers. "The attitude. If you're telling the truth, he'll expect you to act like having to reexplain everything I already told him is ridiculous. A waste of time. Just be your usual sarcastic self and he might buy it."

"Is that meant to be a compliment?"

"Today it is," Canter says with a grin.

The door behind us whooshes open and Lila practically

skips into the living room. "Thanks, Director Weathers. I'll be sure to check out the Venusian Museum of Magical Arts if I'm selected for the program."

I shoot Canter a look—*See, my impersonation wasn't so bad*—but he just rolls his eyes.

Thank goodness Lila is as likable as a rainstorm in a Martian desert. I smile at her and raise my eyebrows, and she gives a double thumbs-up.

"Miss Hodger," Director Weathers calls. "Come on in."

Trying not to appear like I'm marching to my own execution, I cross the living room and then into the boring beige room with its too-large desk. Canter's close on my heels.

"We've already had our discussion, son," Director Weathers says, jutting his chin toward the door as I settle into a chair. "I told you I wanted to talk to your friends individually."

Canter closes the door behind him. "I'm not going to let you bully Myra because you don't trust me."

Director Weathers's jaw muscles twitch. "I don't want you coordinating your stories."

"This isn't an interrogation, Dad," Canter says, dropping into the chair beside me. "It's a school exchange program. Myra needs to get out of here for the same reasons I do."

"I'd like to hear that from her."

I squash down my nerves and slouch back in my chair,

one shoulder raised. "Then ask. I'm sure Canter told you everything, but I'm an open browser. What do you want to know?"

"I want your answers. Not the ones Canter feeds you."

"What does it matter?" I ask, heat rising in my cheeks. "We have the same ghosts. The garden. Bernie." I pause. "Fiona." Director Weathers flinches, and I lean forward. "Even though I never met her, I can still feel her here, haunting me, just like Canter does. He might not remember her, but that's because of *you*."

I hear a sharp inhale beside me, but I don't dare turn. Instead, I hold the director's gaze as it shifts from fire to ice and back again.

"Don't you dare—"

"Tell the truth?" I lean in even closer so there's only a foot separating us. "I thought that's why you brought me here. Didn't you want me to tell you how I can't walk down the halls without imagining the flowers and plants and trees that used to grow beneath my feet? That I can't pass by the Fiona A. Weathers Auditorium without wondering what she thinks of you, what you did, and what you've done while she's locked away in her Mercurian prison cell? How I can't see a Rep working away inside the walls of this school without wondering if Bernie was scared at the end? If he knew what was coming? If he tried to fight?" I settle back and glance sideways. Canter's gaping at me. I might have gone a little overboard. "Isn't that what you wanted to hear?"

The director's features are like stone. "Why V.A.M.A.?" he finally asks.

I shrug. "Why not? It's far from here. My parents won't care because it'll look good on my university applications. And floating on a Venusian sea—it's nothing like the Moon or S.L.A.M." I sigh. It would actually be a relief to get away from S.LA.M., the Moon, all of it. "After all, seas don't have gardens."

Director Weathers opens his mouth to respond but turns away instead. "Thank you, Miss Hodger. You may go."

I study his profile, the urge to ask what he's decided burning inside me like rocket fuel. Instead, I force myself to rise. Without a word, Canter follows me back into the living area.

The adrenaline drains from me as soon as I walk into the hall. *Did I do enough? Too much?* I twist strands of my hair around my fist. I might have just blown our entire plan. Gathering my courage, I glance over at Canter, but I can't read anything as he settles onto the couch and rests his chin on his hands.

"Well?" Lila whispers eagerly, her gaze bouncing between us.

A grin stretches across Canter's face as he meets my eyes across the room. "Myra nailed it!"

CHAPTER TEN

Third Month, 2449

DAYS PASS WITH NO NEWS, OTHER THAN MS. GOBLE commenting that my application was thoughtful and thorough, probably thanks to all of Mom's suggestions. She reads applications for the Number Whispering program at the university all the time, so I'd pinged her for advice.

Ms. Goble mentioned that Director Weathers had confirmed our eligibility, but since he feels he has a conflict of interest, he's leaving the ultimate decision to her. Hopefully it's enough. The list of accepted students hasn't been posted yet.

After my sixth or seventh trip to Ms. Goble's classroom, she banned me from asking her about anything not related to Number Whispering. "One more question about the program, Miss Hodger, and I will remove you from consideration," she said before snapping her computer shut, whisking it off her desk, and disappearing out the door and down the hall.

"I just wanted to know how many kids applied from our year," I muttered at her retreating back.

Lila has an exam tomorrow, so she's evicted me from our room until just before curfew—she said my fidgeting was too distracting—and Canter barred me from his hoverball practices ages ago, probably because I heckle him every time he misses. I told him if I'm not allowed near the hoverball court, he had to at least drop Bin-ro off at my room.

"This beats waiting around for Canter to get back, right?" I say, smiling at my robot friend as we roam the halls.

He whistles and turns in figure eights.

"Keep your scanners alert, buddy," I say, peering through a classroom window. "He's got to be around here somewhere."

Between our V.A.M.A. mission and Bernard's busy schedule, it's been ages since I've had time to chat with him. Bin-ro and I finally find him in one of the Chemic labs, where he's organizing containers of chemicals and sorting test tubes, glass jars, and various instruments.

"Hi!" I say, sliding behind one of the workstations.

He looks up, brown hair falling across his eyes. "You again?"

"Me again," I answer brightly. "And Bin-ro. He's an old friend, too."

The little robot scoots over, whistling as he spins circles around Bernard's feet.

"My last version knew him?" Bernard asks, eyeing the robot with a mixture of curiosity and wariness. It's the first time he's asked me anything about Bernie, and I nearly fall off the chair in my rush to answer.

"Yes," I say, hoping the excitement coursing through my veins isn't making me unnaturally loud. "You knew Bin-ro way longer than me, actually. You worked together."

"Around the school?" Bernard asks, returning to organizing the glassware.

"You could say that," I reply carefully.

"What sort of projects?"

I bite my lip, remembering how he reacted the last time I mentioned plants. "Er, something to do with your old skill set. Your original's."

Bernard's hand slips and a glass rolls off the counter, smashing on the floor, shards scattering like a starburst. With a sigh, he unclips a brush and dustpan from his belt. But before he can kneel down to start cleaning up the mess, Bin-ro scoots over. A tube emerges from his metal hull, and with a soft whirring noise, he sucks up the debris.

"Thanks, buddy," Bernard says, his eyes softening as he watches Bin-ro work. But his guard snaps back into place the moment he returns his attention to me. "Why would the school approve that sort of—that kind of project? Were those *things* allowed back then?"

"Not exactly," I say, toying with the buttons on the workstation. "Someone in charge gave you permission. You were helping them."

"Who?"

I weigh how much I want to tell him against how much I should. "Do you remember the boy I introduced you to? Canter?"

"The school director's son."

I raise my eyebrows. "How'd you know that?"

He looks away, his cheeks slightly flushed. "I did some research after we met." He pauses, and I don't say anything. "We're not allowed to, you know. Reps, I mean. Not for anything other than work-related queries. So I'd appreciate if you . . . if you didn't—"

I snort. "I'm not going to *tell* on you!"

His cheeks flush darker. "I can't ask you to go against school rules."

"I break rules all the time," I say, laughing.

He glowers at me. "That's not something to brag about."

"You're sounding like Bernie again. Anyway, it's not like it's a secret that Canter is Director Weathers's son."

Bernard turns back to his work, the tops of his ears still pink. "What did you want to tell me about him?"

"The person you were helping with Bin-ro—it was Canter's mother."

Bernard jerks around so fast, he nearly knocks over another jar. "The director's wife? The auditorium is named after her."

I nod. "She's gone now," I add quietly.

He stares at me, gears turning behind his eyes. "Not hard to guess why. Those *things* are dangerous."

I shrug. "The whole thing is pretty complicated. Anything with plants is complicated." My words echo in the room, and for a moment, it feels like there's someone else here with us.

"You shouldn't talk like that," Bernard hisses, peering anxiously at the door. "Why are you so interested in all this, anyway? You're a Chemic."

Now it's my turn to blush. "Sort of."

He raises an eyebrow. "*Sort of?* What's that supposed to mean?"

I trace the buttons again. "It's more like a disguise. For the reason you're thinking."

Bernard doesn't answer. Even Bin-ro falls silent.

"And that's what all this is," Bernard finally says. "I helped you before, to create . . . what you created. And you want my help again." His hand clenches around the handle of the brush. "Because Reps are expendable, right? You don't want a friend. You saw the kid version of the

Rep who helped you hide your . . . your *abnormality,* and figured that was the best route to continue your *project.*"

"What! No! My *abnormality*? What are you—" I sweep sweaty hair out of my face. "That's not what this is!"

"Then what?" Bernard demands. "You don't expect me to believe you *really* wanted to be friends with a Rep? No, this makes so much more sense. You've got forbidden magic. It's enormously risky to use it, so who better to help you cover it up?"

"That's not what this is at all!" I insist, scrambling to my feet. Bin-ro zips out into the hall. "I want to be friends with you. Bernie wasn't some secret worker in my evil plan to build a deadly garden to set loose on the galaxy! I found it. And when he figured out I had, he tried to scare me away. But I convinced him I needed his help, and—"

"Why? Did you know him? Were you already friends?"

"N-no," I stammer. "I wanted him to help me because he'd already known it was there. He understood the plants, and I thought he could teach me about them."

"Aha!" Bernard points at me. "Exactly like I said. You needed *help,* and you needed someone who would have to keep it quiet so they wouldn't take the fall with you."

"It wasn't like that! Well, at first, but . . ." I wring my hands. Old memories come flooding back, and guilt flashes through me as I realize he's right. Sort of. But it's not that simple. I take a steadying breath. "That may be what first drew me to Bernie. I realized he must have helped whoever first created the garden—Fiona—and I figured maybe he'd be able to help me, too. Help me get the plants to grow, and also keep it secret."

Bernard opens his mouth, ready to call me out again, but I rush on. I need to make him understand.

"I've learned so much since then. About him. And myself. And the galaxy." I walk around the workstation so I'm standing right in front of Bernard. "Bernie was my friend. And he was my teacher. And I cared about him. Not because he could help me hide my secrets—I've got a lot of them, in case you haven't figured that out. But he was so much more than that." I pause, looking into those familiar blue eyes. "Please believe me."

Bernard stares back, some of the anger melting away. For a moment, his eyes soften, then his mouth presses into a thin line.

"I don't," he says. And then he turns and leaves.

CHAPTER ELEVEN

I FIND MYSELF HOVERING OUTSIDE THE ABANDONED kitchen, but I can't convince myself to go inside. This moongarden is a chilly shadow of our old one, and I have no idea how to fix it. Footsteps echo down the hall, and I grin, expecting Lila or Canter to round the corner. Instead, I find myself face-to-face with Kyle Melfin.

He smirks when he sees me, slowing to a stop a few feet away. I force myself not to glance at the kitchen, setting off in the opposite direction.

"Going to interrogate Ms. Goble again? I heard you badgering her last week about the V.A.M.A. applications." He leans back against the wall. "Did Weathers apply, too?"

"Why do you care?" I demand, turning to face him. "Are you going?"

He shrugs. "I applied, like pretty much everyone else. I've been to Venus loads of times, though."

I roll my eyes. "Aren't you special."

"My dad likes to drag me along on his business trips. He goes every chance he gets. Him and my grandfather like the concerts there." Kyle's gaze wanders to the kitchen door. "Didn't that used to be one of the meal prep rooms? They should turn it into another Rec hall or something. What's even in there now, anyway?"

He steps closer, his hand reaching for the door panel, and my breath catches.

"Wait!" I throw up a hand just as a buzzing reverberates through the hallway. Kyle and I both look down at our pendants.

"The list of kids picked for V.A.M.A. just posted," Kyle drawls. "Guess I should go see who scored a ticket off this dusty rock." He takes two steps, then stops. "What were you saying before the pendants went off?"

"I, uh . . . Just that the door is locked. I tried it earlier to dodge Mr. DeGraf."

Kyle smirks. "Smart. I'd rather scrub that old kitchen than have to hear him go on and on about the different classifications of matter." Kyle looks like he wants to say something more, but instead he turns and heads back down the hall.

I watch until he disappears around a corner. Once the

sound of his footsteps fades, too, I snatch up my messenger, shoot Lila and Canter a message to meet me at Goble's classroom, and take off the same way Kyle went.

There's already a crowd around Ms. Goble's door when we skid into the hall. Canter and I elbow through the pack while Lila murmurs apologies.

"Are we on the list?" Lila asks, bobbing on her heels behind me.

"Jupiter Jackpot!" I say, punching the air and nearly clipping Canter's chin in the process. "You are, Lila!"

"What about us?" Canter asks.

I scan farther down. "You are, too!"

Canter whoops so loud, the rest of the crowd falls silent for a moment before the excited babble swells again.

"What about you?" Lila asks. "You were accepted, too, right?"

I read the list a second time. And then a third.

"Myra?" Canter prods.

I look back at them. "I'm not there."

It's no use going to Ms. Goble. Lila and Canter have begged, bribed, and threatened me to make me try, but I know it wouldn't change her mind in a hundred million light-years.

What's even worse is that the second spot in our grade—

the one that should have been mine—they gave to Kyle Melfin.

The next morning, I get up even earlier than Lila and slip out of the room. I don't know where I'm going, but old habits kick in, and I find myself moving through the halls like I'm on a mission, just like last year, when my feet led me to the moongarden. I slip inside the abandoned kitchen and slowly cross to the row of cabinets, gingerly opening one, as if there's a monster lurking inside. Instead, I only find a wilted plant. It's a tulip, but with no bud. In fact, it looks like it's struggling to keep its leaves from shriveling to nothing.

I sit cross-legged on the floor, cradling the metal pot in my lap. "I'm sorry," I whisper. "I'm sorry I haven't taken better care of you. I meant to. I mean to. But every time I try . . ." I draw in a steadying breath, finally ready to speak the words I've known in my heart for weeks. "It reminds me of my old garden and how it was taken away. How it took so many people with it."

I look down at the scraggly little plant, and a tear trickles down my cheek. I catch it on my fingertip before it can fall.

I can help it, though. What happened in the old moongarden doesn't change that. I can still help this tulip now.

I watch the clear droplet for a moment, holding it up in the dim light, marveling at the tiny prism created by the speck of salty water. And then I let it fall. As I do, a wave of warmth rushes through me. Inside the pot, the leaves glitter with gold, and a bloom the color of sunshine bursts from the top of the stem, opening into a beautiful yellow tulip.

I smile at it waving at me from its metal home, and instantly, another yellow flower flashes across my mind, pushing its way through dust and ash. Its goldenrod petals eaten by inky blackness until it is nothing but ash, too.

Pain sears through my chest and I almost drop the pot. The blossom quickly tucks back into itself as if rewinding to a bud, its color mostly hidden inside its evergreen enclosure.

I stand and sigh, setting the plant carefully back on its shelf.

"At least it looks better than it did when I got here," I mutter, rubbing a fist over my eyes.

I don't take any more pots out of the cabinet. Instead, I perch on the counter, scrolling through my messenger screens until an alert catches my eye. A new message.

It's from Hannah!

But my excitement fades as quickly as the tulip when I take in the three short words.

Leave. Me. Alone.

Each period thuds in my brain, like a hollow, unanswered knock. For a moment, I wilt, hope leaching out of me like water seeping through gravel. And then I slowly raise my messenger, tap out a few sentences, and hit send.

It's not addressed to Hannah, though. It's to my parents.

CHAPTER TWELVE

A FEW HOURS LATER, MS. GOBLE ESCORTS ME TO THE
school hangar. "I know you're disappointed, Miss Hodger,
but I couldn't justify sending all three of you together. It
would be unfair to the other students."

"I understand, Ms. Goble," I say dully.

"You've never requested a weekend visit home before,"
she says, her dark eyes tinged with concern.

I shrug. "Just need a change of scenery." In truth, I can't
bear the buzz that's sure to wash over the school the next
couple of days. And I don't want to spoil Canter's and Lila's
excitement. Add to that Family Weekend, and a trip home
seemed like the best possible decision.

"Well, if all goes well with this exchange, I expect there
will be another opportunity for you next year."

Next year. After Canter and Lila are back from Venus.

I haven't even had time to process that not only am I not going to V.A.M.A., but I'll be stuck at S.L.A.M. for the rest of term.

My stomach drops and I pick up my pace, reaching the hangar door before Ms. Goble so I have to wait for her to catch up. She scans me in, and we find the transport already there. It's not the bulky, spidery Crawler I'm used to, but a sleek train. I say a quick goodbye to Ms. Goble and board the silver tube.

Settled in, I watch the chalky gray landscape blur past, trying to forget the concerned expressions on Canter's and Lila's faces when I told them about my plans for the weekend. I assured them that yes, I was okay, and no, I didn't want them to drop out of the exchange program. At least they could still try to find the rogue Reps and help with whatever they're up to. And I promised my friends I'd be fine, even if I didn't believe my own words.

In what seems like no time at all, we're docking in a hangar flooded with people, mostly professionals with Creer pins gleaming on their collar.

I weave my way through the crowd and out into the street. My parents asked if I'd mind walking home from the station alone so they could finish some projects and give me their full attention during my visit. I agreed, but there's no way on the Moon they won't be working while I'm home.

Low, brightly lit buildings line the block, and the streets are crowded, even on a weekend. The capital is always alive with magic.

I duck under a misty list of numbers surrounding a man like a math tornado, and almost knock into a woman absorbed by a metal contraption in her hands. She drops it to the sidewalk with a clatter, shooting me a glare as she snatches it up and continues on, sparks trailing her.

I cut across a small patio to avoid a herd of Number Whisperers bouncing equations back and forth, and slam into a wall that wasn't there two nanoseconds before.

"Sorry! So sorry!" yelps a young man wearing a lopsided tie accented by a gleaming Tekkie pin, also askew. He clears away the barrier with a wave of his hand. "I'm redesigning the decorative enclosure and was experimenting with materials. Go on through. I can wait until you've passed," he says with a grin.

"It's fine," I mutter as I trot back onto the sidewalk and turn the corner. It's fine. I'm fine. Everything's fine.

At my building's entrance, I press my finger onto the DNA reader and the door slides open. I glance at the Anti-Grav Chamber, shudder, then opt for the stairs and climb the two flights to my apartment. As I pass Hannah's old place I wince, then hurry ahead. At the scanner to my apartment, I hold up my hand, and the door slides open.

Inside, it looks the same as always, everything precisely

(and mathematically) placed, as if my parents spent hours calculating the dimensions and measurements of every wall, piece of furniture, and accessory.

Spoiler signal: They did.

A sectional sofa forms a sharp right angle against the far wall, with a square table placed exactly to maximize space. Paintings and photographs hang on the wall, the distance between each precise to the millimeter. At the far end of the room sits a rectangular table with two chairs on each side and one at either end. While the rest of the room is neat and ordered, the pair seated at the table are anything but.

Projected holo-screens clutter the air above my parents' heads. The chaos almost looks like an art installation. Years of dodging equation projections allow me to decipher the contents: math, math, and more math.

"Myra!" Mom exclaims, spotting me a moment later. The projections wobble as she stands, and she quickly shoos them away. "You're here already?" She glances down at the pendant on her wrist and gasps. "For Pluto's sake, Joe! Look at the time! You were supposed to ping me fifteen minutes ago to remind me to clear this up."

"Fifteen minus what—" he murmurs, looking from my mother to his own pendant, and then to me. "Myra! When did you get here?"

"Just now," I say, already regretting my decision to come home.

"Joe, finish up!" Mom barks, brushing dark hair off her shoulder and crossing the room. "It's not often our brilliant daughter decides to ditch her friends to hang out with her parents for the weekend!"

I'm beginning to remember why that is when Mom captures me in a rib-cracking hug.

"Right. Absolutely," Dad replies, powering off bookpods and computer screens and waving away a long line of calculations he has stacked over his head.

"Dad, it's okay. You don't have to stop midcalculation. That looked like it took a long time to valuate."

"Nonsense." He flicks at the remaining magical numbers, and they zip into the walls and disappear. "It wasn't anything important. Just some musings about a new way to calculate taxes based on an individual's real-time net worth. The trick is to adjust the denominator to account for—"

"*Joe,*" Mom says in her sternest professor voice.

"Oh yes. Sorry. Getting carried away again." He removes his glasses and polishes them on his rumpled shirt. "So, Myra. What brings you home? Anything special? Or just in need of a change of scenery?"

"Maybe she missed us and wanted to see us," Mom suggests, beaming.

"Uh, honey. Didn't you see her a couple of weeks ago?"

Mom glowers, and I can't help but laugh.

"Is there a start clock for when a daughter can begin to miss her family?"

"No, of course not," Dad says with a mischievous grin. "But I expect you'd need to divide the normal time frame by the well-known tween-angst-diminishing factor in order to have any hope of calculating anything approaching accurate."

"*Teen*, Dad," I say, shooting him a faux-stern look. "I'm thirteen now, or can't you count?"

"It's not really my strong suit, no." He flops onto the couch, upsetting the pillows, which had been positioned precisely at the center of each cushion. Mom's eyes track their movement, but she resists the urge to adjust them.

"So, what really brings you home, Myra?" Mom asks, settling on the other side of the couch and patting the space next to her.

I glance over at the hall opposite the dining room table, which leads to the quiet and question-free space of my bedroom.

"We called and got you special permission to come home today," Mom reminds me. "Usually, you have to schedule trains to the capital a week in advance. At least give us the short version."

I sigh and flop down next to her, scattering more pillows. Surprisingly, neither of my parents even glances at them. "I didn't get picked for the V.A.M.A. exchange program."

Mom's mouth falls open, and Dad sits up straight.

"What?" Mom says. "Did you submit your application on time?"

"Of course," I snap. "And before you ask, I used all that wording you messaged me."

"Who was making the selections?" Dad asks, frowning. I may not be a Number Whisperer anymore, but any sort of academic slight is basically the galaxy's worst insult to my parents.

"Ms. Goble and Director Weathers," I answer, then wince, waiting for the explosion.

"Saturn's rings. Are you kidding me, Myra?" Mom demands.

I groan. "No one says *Saturn's rings* anymore."

She waves an agitated hand in the air. "That's beside the point. I thought things were improving between Val and me, especially after our lunch, but now this—"

"It wasn't just her, and she didn't do it to be unfair," I explain. "She said she couldn't justify taking all three of us."

"All three?" Dad removes his glasses and immediately puts them back on.

"Canter and Lila got in," I whisper, picking up a pillow and twisting the edge.

Mom's eyes widen. "And who got the other second-year spot?"

I look back and forth between my parents uneasily. "Kyle Melfin."

"Jake Melfin's son?" Dad's tone is colder than the Boomerang Nebula.

I nod. "Have you heard from Mr. Melfin since he was kicked off the Council?"

"No, and I'm not complaining." Dad settles back on the couch. "He was never particularly pleasant to work with. Arrogant to no end. And with what I know now, I'm not making any extra effort to reach out."

"What do you mean?"

My parents exchange a look but say nothing.

"What?"

"I've been talking to a former Council member who was serving when Fiona Weathers was arrested. She was on the Governing Council subcommittee that handles plant crimes. And it turns out the Melfins have a bit of a reputation," Dad explains carefully. "Whenever there's been chatter around criminal possession of seeds in recent history, Jake and his father seem to be tangled up in the story."

I should be surprised, but I'm not. "Did you ask her about the Council stripping people of their Creers?"

"I did. And at that precise moment she urgently had to take another call."

Mom huffs a laugh. "Sometimes the equation's value is zero."

"Exactly," Dad says.

I frown. "What does that mean?"

"It means sometimes no answer is an answer in itself." He straightens a pillow. "It explains why that subcommittee's so secretive. Their reports are always brief and vague."

"Clearly, they don't want it known that the Council has the power to take away magic," Mom says. "How do they even do it?"

Dad shrugs. "Same tech they use with the Reps, I'd imagine."

"So how would Jake Melfin be able to threaten that restaurant owner from the video with taking away his?" I ask. "He's not on the Council anymore."

"A bluff?" Mom suggests.

I scoff. "He seemed pretty serious."

"Melfin may not be on the Council, but he's still head of his company, which may be the more dangerous of the two positions."

"All that wealth along with his old Council connections." Mom shakes her head. "I'd be surprised if it was only plant offenders he's used his influence to silence over the years."

"Have you heard of anyone else turned in for plant crimes?" I ask my dad quietly. "Besides Hannah's family?"

"Only the subcommittee knows that. Prosecutions of plant offenders are handled by the prison system. The Council's responsible for referrals to the warden on

Mercury or relocation, depending on the details of the crime." He winces. "I only knew about the Lees because we were the ones who . . . reported the evidence."

I pick at the fabric on the couch, the silence weighing me down like a meteor resting on my back. "Part of the reason I wanted to go to Venus was because I was hoping I could talk to Hannah. Tell her I'm sorry."

Mom is quiet. "You are getting into that program, Myra," she finally says.

I raise my eyebrows. "I told you, it's done. There were two spots for my year. Two kids were chosen. Just not me."

"Who says?" Mom's focus is still fixed on the wall.

"Uh, me? Myra. Your daughter. Sitting right next to you."

"No," Mom says, chuckling. "That's not what I meant. Who says they can only send two students from your year?"

"Ah." Dad nods. "Good point."

I glance between them. "Ms. Goble said that V.A.M.A. would only allow two representatives from each grade."

"There you go!" Dad says, slapping his knee. "That's the answer."

"You know I hate when you say only half the thing you're thinking, whether it has to do with math or not."

"We mean that you need to go straight to V.A.M.A.," Mom explains, though from my expression, it's clear I still have no idea what she's talking about. She sighs and then gives me a small smile. "Write to the director there, or better yet, the Chemic teacher. Do you know who that is?" she asks, turning her attention to my dad.

He shakes his head. "Unfortunately, I don't know many of the folks at V.A.M.A. I've visited a couple of times. Different sort of place. But, oh, wait!" He looks over at the jumble of screens still piled on the table. "I think my old university roommate teaches Number Whispering there now. Matt Finch. I can give him a call and see who Myra should write to."

I hold up a hand. "Wait a nanosecond. Who am I writing to? And why? What's going on?"

"Listen, sweetie," Mom says, trying to sound soothing. "I accept and reject kids from the university Whisp program all the time, right?"

I nod, cringing at her slang, but bite my tongue.

"And, of course, as you expect, some of the prospective students I decline reach out to try to change my mind."

I'd actually never considered that once in my life. "People do that?"

She laughs. "All the time!"

"Do they ever convince you?"

"Of course. More often than you think. That they're determined enough to contact me again—politely, of course—to ask me to reconsider shows that they have the ambition and the drive necessary to be a successful Number Whisperer."

I turn all this over. "So you're saying I message the Chemic teach at V.A.M.A. and convince him to add me to the program?"

"Exactly." Mom beams. Then we all get to work.

It takes almost the whole weekend for my dad to track down the name of the Chemic professor, but his old college pal comes through and provides us the contact information for Mr. Kote. While Dad is busy getting the name, Mom and I work on writing my message. I've never been happier that my mom works at the Lunar University. She knows just what to say. By the time we're finished, even I'm impressed with the summary of abilities, passions, and ambitions we've assembled. Politely and modestly, of course. Just before my train back to S.L.A.M. arrives, we send it off.

And now all I can do is wait.

CHAPTER THIRTEEN

THE NEXT FEW DAYS AT SCHOOL ARE SO UNBEARABLE, I actually half wish I were back home with my parents. And I've never wished that. Not ever. But that all changes when I slip into Number Whispering theory.

"Miss Hodger, a word," Ms. Goble says as soon as I enter.

I approach her desk uneasily. My track record with her isn't good.

"I have an update for you," she says, picking up her messenger and tapping the screen. "I received a very interesting inquiry this morning from a Mr. Kote at V.A.M.A. Does that name ring a bell?"

I nod. "He's the Chemic professor there." May as well fess up. "I sent him a letter over the weekend."

"While you were home?"

I nod, sure she can see my mom's genetic imprint all over this.

"Well, it must have been quite the letter. He reached out to ask if S.L.A.M. could spare one more student. After reading your message, he appears desperate to have you in his class for the term."

My eyes widen. "Wh-what did you tell him?"

Ms. Goble glances down at her messenger before meeting my gaze again. "I said that in the spirit of intersettlement cooperation this program is meant to foster, I could not find a good reason to decline his request."

"So . . . so I'm going?" I ask, hardly daring to believe it.

"You're going," she confirms, smiling, before giving me a stern look. "So long as your academics and behavior meet school standards between now and then."

With a quick nod, I return to my seat, floating so high I wonder if the school's artificial gravity enclosure is malfunctioning. The rest of class, I daydream about what it will be like on Venus while trying to appear to be paying attention. I manage to tap out a quick message to my parents under my workstation, though, and they're almost as excited as I am.

After class, I sprint to find Lila, and then Canter, to tell them the news. They can't believe it, either, but immediately we start plotting.

I visit the deserted kitchen after school, opening and shutting cupboards as I peek in at the plants inside. With us headed to Venus, we have one big problem we need to still take care of before we go: What are we going to do about our new moongarden? We can't bear the idea of destroying it but know we can't leave it behind, either.

I open the last cabinet and lean in to look at the tulip plant, the one I helped bloom and then somehow made slip back to little more than a sprout.

A thought occurs to me as I study the bud, still curled in on itself. After a moment, I quickly shut the door, tap out a message to Canter and Lila, then scoot myself onto the counter to wait.

I'm still perched there when they arrive ten minutes later.

"So, what's the plan?" Canter asks, his face red from racing down the halls.

I take a deep breath, trying to channel calm confidence. "My plan," I say, hopping down and opening the cabinet doors, "is to reverse all this."

"What do you mean *reverse it*?" Lila asks. "Like destroy it?"

"No, the opposite. Remember when we used your magic last year to sprain my ankle?"

Lila winces, then nods. She hadn't been happy when I asked her to use her healing abilities to injure me, but it had been necessary to save the garden.

"I was wondering . . . what if we could do the same thing with our Botan magic?"

Canter looks skeptical. "What do you mean?"

"We know our magic can help make the plants grow, right? From seeds to sprouts to full-blown plants. But what if we tried to rewind the process? Bring them back to seeds?"

"Then we could take the seeds with us and use them somewhere safer," Canter says slowly. "If it works, it would be the perfect solution."

I shrug. "Can't hurt to try."

"How do we start?" Canter asks, hovering over a small shrub.

"I'm going to ask the plant to return to its original form," I say, brushing the petals of a daisy. Canter nods and returns his attention to the bush, resting his hands on top of it as he closes his eyes. It makes me sad, having to undo all the plant's hard work. I can imagine how difficult it must be to grow from a tiny speck to the beautiful, complicated plant at my feet. But I can't think of another way.

"Please," I whisper, flickers of magic vibrating from my chest through my fingertips. "Please go back. Back to how you were. I'll still take care of you, I promise, but I need to find you a better home. And I will. I swear. It just can't be here."

As I murmur to the daisy, silver fog seeps from my

fingertips, swirling around the stalk like dust motes, and then the plant starts to shrink. Petals curl in on themselves, tucking back into a bud. The stem retracts and the bud shrinks smaller and smaller until it disappears altogether. The leaves curl in, and soon they're gone, too. After a minute or two, only an empty pot sits before me. I gently press my hand into the dirt, feeling around until my fingers close over a spear-shaped seed.

I glance over and Canter is crouched down, cradling a cluster of dark brown seeds in his palm, the exteriors glistening under the dim lights. "Looks like your plan worked," he says with a grin.

With ten minutes to spare before curfew, we've managed to coax every plant back into seed form. I run my fingers through the small pile we've created, and my chest swells with relief that my Botan powers worked just as well as Canter's. Maybe even better. With a smile, I sweep half of them into my pocket. Canter hides the rest.

While we worked our magic, Lila zoomed around the room, clearing away all the evidence. By the time we hurry out the door for the last time, the room looks almost exactly like we found it all those weeks ago.

As I say a silent goodbye to the room, the memory of leaving behind the moongarden—the original one— washes over me. I hesitate in the doorway, waiting for a rush of sadness to drown me. But it never comes. Leaving this time doesn't feel as tragic. Our pockets are full of seeds. No ashes swirl behind us. I take a cautious breath and feel only excitement tightening in my chest. We're ready for our next chapter.

CHAPTER FOURTEEN

THE NEXT WEEK FLIES BY IN A FLURRY OF LECTURES, packing, meetings, itineraries, more lectures, and good-byes. Mr. DeGraf seems genuinely sad to see me go. If I'm honest, I'm a little sorry to leave his class, too. Ms. Goble's parting advice was less sentimental. If I hear the words *guests, good example,* and *S.L.A.M. ambassadors* one more time, I think I might need to visit the Mender wing.

Finally, only one last lecture stands between me and my trip, and it's the one I've dreaded most since I read my name on the short list of selected participants—our meeting with Director Weathers. It's supposed to be a send-off, but really, it's a last opportunity to impress upon us the importance of good behavior while we're at V.A.M.A.

My stomach flips. I haven't asked Director Weathers if

he's made any arrangements with the Chemic instructor at V.A.M.A., but I can't imagine he'd risk my secret getting out. Though I'm pretty sure Director Weathers would enjoy my inevitable humiliation, he'd never risk the blowback if it got out that he'd covered up my Botan powers.

It'll be fine, I tell myself again.

Director Weathers is meeting us a few at a time, so we wait clustered together on the bench outside his office. Groups of kids disappear inside, reemerging a short time later, grinning ear to ear. I have a feeling our session won't be that pleasant.

The lobby slowly empties, and the excited chatter fades to a soft buzz, punctuated by an occasional beep from Bin-ro as he zooms about in wide loops. It took some convincing, but Canter somehow got his dad to agree to let him bring Bin-ro to Venus. I think it might have had something to do with the little robot doubling as an alarm clock. Even Director Weathers knows that with Bin-ro's arsenal of show tunes, there's no way Canter will sleep through a single class.

I glance around. "Where's Kyle?"

My friends scan the remaining kids, then shrug. "Maybe he changed his mind," Lila says.

"Or," Canter mutters, "maybe he got kicked out for being a slimy space cadet."

Soon, we're the only ones left in the vestibule. I nudge

my packed suitcase with my toe, pushing it so it rotates in a circle. Bin-ro is rolling back and forth under Canter's seat.

"Stop fidgeting, both of you," Canter murmurs, glancing over at his dad's assistant, who's seated at a desk not far away. "You look suspicious. Like you're hiding something."

"I'm not, though," I say, patting my pocket. There was no way I was leaving our stash of seeds in my room, and at the last minute, I decided that packing them in my bag was too risky. What if Director Weathers searches it?

"I've got a bad feeling about this," Canter says, eyeing the slight bulge in the side of my jumpsuit.

"Why?" I lift one shoulder. "Your dad would never think I'd be dumb enough to have them on me."

"He might," Canter says, and I glare at him.

Lila worries her lip. "I don't like it, either, Myra. What if they accidentally fall out?"

"They won't," I insist. "Do you think I'm going to cartwheel into the director's office?"

Lila and Canter exchange a worried look.

"Listen," I say. "I'm more concerned he'll search Canter's bag and find the stash of reflector paper."

"Don't be," Canter replies with a smirk. "I've reconfigured the structure so the paper blends in perfectly with my jumpsuits. The strips are basically invisible."

A burst of raised voices coming from inside Director

Weathers's office interrupts our conversation, and then an older student—a fourth-year in an Elector jumpsuit—rushes from the room in tears, trailing her bag behind her.

Director Weathers emerges with two other students. One shakes his head, while the other appears shell-shocked. "I was very clear, as was Ms. Goble. Absolutely no magically enhanced pranking devices," Director Weathers says firmly. "V.A.M.A.'s stability is maintained by hydro-engines, and one stray pulse propeller could knock out the electricity and set the entire school adrift. It was exceedingly foolish of Miss Bask to try to smuggle contraband in her bag, and I'm sure she'll regret that decision for a long time."

My friends and I exchange panicked looks, and I anxiously tug my bag toward me, thanking every lucky meteor I decided to stow the seeds in my pocket.

The remaining students walk anxiously toward the hangar. Director Weathers watches them go. Once they turn the corner, he waves us into his office.

Canter seems even more nervous. He can't seem to stop fiddling with the closure on his bag. I force myself to take several slow, deep breaths as I follow him and Lila inside. Bin-ro trails silently behind us.

"Where's Kyle?" Canter asks once he's seated.

Director Weathers clears his throat. "Kyle Melfin's father was planning a visit to V.A.M.A., so he took him to the school yesterday."

"That's not fair!" Canter glares at his dad. "So he slithers out of your speech about behaving or else."

"I spoke with him yesterday," Director Weathers replies coolly, folding his hands on the desk before launching into a lecture he's already delivered many times today.

At first, his instructions are exactly what I predicted—we are to preserve S.L.A.M.'s pristine reputation while we're guests at V.A.M.A. and impress the Venusian professors and students, and will suffer grave consequences should our behavior come up short.

After a Lunar cycle, it seems he's run out of threats and demands, and I'm just starting to wonder if he'll skip the search when he turns and looks me dead in the eye. "All right," he says, rubbing his chin. "That's enough of that. Turn out your pockets."

I feel my jaw start to fall open but instantly snap it shut, forcing my expression into one of calm indifference. My insides, however, are going supernova.

"What?" Canter's eyes widen. "You searched the other kids' bags!"

"Which is precisely why I am asking you to turn out your pockets," Director Weathers says evenly. "Since you're so upset by this, Canter, you can go first."

Canter stands and makes a great show of pulling items out of his pockets slowly and dramatically.

While Director Weathers is distracted, Lila nudges me

in the ribs. Without moving my head, I shift my eyes just enough to catch her mouthing *Trust me*. I give her the smallest of nods.

Lila's eyelids drift down so low, it looks like she's about to fall asleep. I'm so focused on watching her that, at first, I don't notice that my hand is getting hot. *Really* hot. All at once, the palm and fingers on my right hand are burning like a sun flare. I'm about to jerk it out of my pocket, where it was shielding the seeds buried deep inside, when Lila nudges me again, shaking her head.

I leave my hand where it is, grimacing as the burning shifts to a feeling that my skin is being scraped with sandpaper. It's not sandpaper, though—it's the seeds. I brush my fingertips over my palm and realize, with a sickening jolt, that the seeds are embedding themselves *in* my hands. Or, more accurately, since Lila's magic only works on the human body, my skin is absorbing the seeds.

Longing to see if my skin looks like it's covered with a hundred tiny seed-shaped bumps (because that's exactly how it feels), I press my hand deeper into my pocket and grit my teeth.

Just as Canter draws the last objects from a compartment in his jumpsuit—an old sock—the tingling, burning, gritty feeling in my hand suddenly stops.

"Care to explain that?" Director Weathers asks, eyeing the sock with a mixture of revulsion and curiosity.

Canter shrugs. "Sometimes my foot gets sweaty at practice, so I keep a spare on me."

Director Weathers raises his eyebrow. "Just *one* foot?"

"Yeah, usually the left one," Canter says, grinning sheepishly as he tucks it, and the rest of the random fuses, wires, and batteries, back into his pocket.

"All right, next," Director Weathers says, shaking his head before turning to Lila and me. "Miss Hodger, how about you?"

"Are you even allowed to search our things?" I ask, forcing myself to sound relaxed and annoyed. "Don't you need permission from our parents?"

"You're correct," he says evenly. "And I have it. The form your parents signed to enroll you in the program stipulates that either school is allowed to search the property and person of any participating student."

Well, it was worth a shot.

From the corner of my eye, I can see Canter wince as I slowly stand and reach into my pockets. My hand still feels strangely bumpy, but not as much as it did a moment ago. I can only hope the seeds are hidden well enough. And that I don't throw up on Director Weathers's desk.

I grab the lining of my pockets and tug. They're completely empty. Not a single seed falls to the floor. I dare a glance at my hands, and while my right one looks a little pink, otherwise it's no different than my left.

I give my pockets a little shake, raising my eyebrows. The director studies me for another moment, then shifts his gaze to my face. I bite my tongue, not trusting myself to breathe normally. After several seconds, he nods and I sit down.

Lila quickly rises and turns out her pockets, which are also empty. Finally (and begrudgingly), we're dismissed. Bin-ro zips out into the hall first, a blur of silver and echoing beeps. Canter hangs back to say a quick and awkward extra goodbye to his father, then joins Lila and me at the door.

When we're a good distance away, Canter whispers to me, "What did you do?" awe lacing his voice.

Instead of answering, I turn to Lila. "What did *you* do?" I'm sure I'm gaping at her like she's the most amazing (and the most terrifying) girl in the galaxy.

"Did you know that human skin is composed of three main layers?" she answers breezily, smoothing back her curls. "The epidermis has five layers all on its own."

My stomach swirls, but Canter only furrows his brow. "So? What does that have to do with what happened in there and where the *you-know-what*s are?"

"The *you-know-what*s are currently hidden in Myra's stratum corneum."

"Her what?" Canter asks, looking even more confused.

I swallow. "She hid them in my skin."

Canter's eyes bulge as I stretch out my hand toward him. "That's galactic," he whispers.

"Not galactic," I say, running my left fingers over my right palm. I can just make out the tiny bumps. "But as long as you can get them out, I can handle it."

"I can. Don't worry," Lila says, patting me on the shoulder as we continue to the hangar. "You were a model patient."

"You're going to be an incredible Mender," I reply as we pass through the door, then pause to take in the waiting shuttle. Bin-ro circles us, beeping excitedly. "I can't wait for you to have real patients to use your skills on, though."

"Me too," Lila says as we climb the steps to the shuttle door.

"I want to watch her take them out," Canter says loudly behind me. "That'll be interstellar."

"For you," I snap, turning back to glare at him. "Next time, why don't you volun—"

I freeze, taking in rows and rows of seats, mostly filled with older S.L.A.M. students, and then one face that does not belong to a classmate but couldn't be more familiar.

CHAPTER FIFTEEN

"BERNARD!" I CRY. "WHAT ARE YOU DOING HERE?"

He shifts in his seat, smoothing out his gray coveralls, though there's not a wrinkle to be seen. "I was assigned to accompany the exchange program participants," he explains stiffly, his eyes locked on the window.

"Really? That's interstellar!" I say, plopping down beside him. "Aren't you excited to see more of the galaxy?"

"I *have* seen more, remember?" he replies, still not looking at me.

"Oh, right. The Old World." I glance out the window. The lights from the S.L.A.M. hangar dull most of the stars, but I can make out the edge of the Old World hovering hundreds of thousands of miles away. "But you've never been to Venus, have you?"

"It wasn't habitable when my original was on the Old World," he says, grimacing as Canter and Lila fill in the rest of the row. Bin-ro scoots under Canter's seat, whistling away.

"Tekkies only came up with the atmospheric clearing technology half a century ago," Lila adds. "And they created the oceans and waterways not long after."

"I can't believe you got picked to come to V.A.M.A. with us," I say, practically bouncing in my seat. "What are the odds?"

"Pretty good when you've got connections," Canter says smugly.

My mouth falls open. "*You* got him approved? And you didn't tell us?"

Canter holds up his hands defensively. "I didn't know if it would work. I had to ask my dad as a favor, and you know how that goes. . . . But, shockingly, he agreed. Plus, I thought it would be a fun surprise."

"Well, it isn't fun for me," Bernard grumbles. "And I don't appreciate you meddling with my work assignments. Even if you are the school director's son."

"What? I didn't—I didn't mean . . . But . . . but aren't you happy?"

"Can't you see how happy I am?" Bernard snaps.

"Crashing comets, I'm sorry, Bernie. Bernard." Canter

runs his hands through his hair. "I thought it'd be a fun surprise for you, too."

"I can't believe Director Weathers agreed to let you come." An uneasy feeling twists in my stomach. "Doesn't V.A.M.A. have their own Reps?"

"He said it was part of the exchange." Bernard's foot taps an odd beat. "An opportunity to learn new skills."

"We should have asked," Lila says, leaning forward to meet Bernard's eyes. "We shouldn't have made assumptions. We really are sorry."

He doesn't say anything for a few moments. Finally, he sighs and relaxes back into his seat. "I suppose a change of scenery won't be the worst thing . . . but I don't like boats, and I heard this school floats. It had better not be like a boat. My original used to get terribly seasick."

I giggle. "Lila's Mending skills will take care of any motion sickness. Besides, I'm sure technology has come a long way since Old World boats."

Many hours later, the engines shudder and purr beneath our seats as we make our final approach to Venus. "In a few moments," the shuttle captain's voice booms over the intercom, "you kids will get your first glimpse of Venus. If you're lucky, we may catch some of the boats crossing the waterways. This is the only planet in our solar system to use this type of transport."

I can feel Bernard burning a black hole in the side of my head, but I pretend to be fascinated by the seat in front of me.

"For those interested," the captain continues, "the windows on the right provide the best views."

Everyone scrambles to peer out, except for Bernard. He stays planted in his seat as if a magnetic charge is holding him there. Luckily, Canter, Lila, and I get the best window. We sound a collective *Ooooh* as we peer out.

Thick clouds cloak most of the planet like a misty sweater, wrapping around and around in thick puffy layers, but in the center, where the atmospheric clearing technology must be working its magic, a giant strip glows like molten gold. Flecks of deep blue glitter up at us like sapphires. *The waterways of Venus.* I wonder which one is the Sea of da Vinci, where we're going.

As we get closer, the scrape of gold grows bigger and bigger. Landmasses emerge, and I can see the sharp edges of mountains, sandy deserts, and even lava-spewing volcanos between vast stretches of navy, indigo, and turquoise.

As we approach one of the largest bodies of water, I can make out tiny dots—these must be floating vessels—as well as larger structures. *Massive* ones. Like floating cities or man-made islands.

The engines shudder again, and for the first time I see V.A.M.A. through the window. "Crashing comets."

It couldn't be more different than S.L.A.M. Our school's sleek, vertical design is considered an architectural marvel. V.A.M.A. looks more like a collection of bubbles floating on a vast body of water.

"That must be the main building," Lila says, pointing at a massive, rounded building in the middle. The exterior glistens in the sunlight, softer than the glaring, colorless light of the Moon. "I wonder if there's a structural advantage to the shape or if they just thought they were being clever."

"Either way, I like it," Canter says, his gaze never leaving the window.

We swoop closer to the main bubble. A long platform stretches before it like a giant silver carpet. Each glittering building just barely touches the rest, making it appear even more like a cluster of fizzy soapsuds, bobbing and swaying as azure waves crash against the sides.

"I can't believe we get to go to school here. Bernard, come check this out," I call, beckoning him over.

He shrugs. "I'll see it soon enough."

"What are we going to do about him?" I ask the others as I slump against the shuttle wall. "I've tried everything. He's still not Bernie."

Canter's expression turns serious. "If we can stop whatever's blocking Rep magic, maybe it'll help."

I nod. "This isn't just a fun field trip," I remind my friends. "We've got a lot to do while we're here."

"Let's just enjoy today," Lila says, still gazing out in wonder at the school floating on the turquoise water. "Tomorrow, we can get to work."

CHAPTER SIXTEEN

AS THE SHUTTLE LANDS, THE CABIN'S BUZZING WITH energy. Even I am bouncing in my seat waiting for the door to open. Finally, with a slight hum, the main entryway slides up and warm, misty air billows into the stale atmosphere of the space.

"This is going to be amazing," Lila says, her voice filled with awe.

Canter's silent as he scrambles to the door so he can be the first one out.

"Typical," I mutter to Lila, and she laughs. Soon, we join the line pushing to deplane.

It looks like half the school has turned out to greet us. They must not wear uniforms at V.A.M.A.; a collage of colors assaults my eyes as I scan the crowd. One student's wearing a sweatshirt and mismatched pants, both of which appear to be splattered with paint. Another is in what looks like a leotard decked out with layers and layers of multi-colored fringe like a swooshing string rainbow. Other students carry strange contraptions and machines, a few of which I recognize as musical instruments. The others could be, too, but they aren't like any instruments I've ever seen.

Yet they all have one thing in common. Every single face wears a wide, warm grin.

The kids step to the side to create a path, and a stocky man with golden, shoulder-length hair beams as he comes toward us. "Greetings, S.L.A.M. scholars," he booms. "And more importantly, welcome to our new friends!"

"Five, six, seven, eight!" someone else bellows as the first teacher disappears into the crowd. Another man, tall, with dark brown skin and black, curly hair, steps in front of the instrument-laden students, then raises and waves some sort of stick in the air.

I snort. "Is that a magic wand?"

"And can't these Venus kids count?" Canter whispers in my ear. "Who teaches Number Whispering here?"

I'm shaking with laughter, but Lila shoots us a sideways glance. "Music and dance use numbers for rhythm, not for counting. And that stick's called a baton. It's to keep everyone on the same tempo."

"Oh," I say, feeling a little silly. "Where'd you learn that?"

"My dad plays the saxophone," she says proudly.

There's a blast so loud I stumble backward, and I fight the urge to cover my ears. The racket quickly morphs from a sonic boom into an intricate tune that floats through the air in waves. Notes so deep and low they rattle my rib cage mix with high ones that tickle my ears. It's hard not to be carried away. Percussions join the ensemble, beating out a pulse that echoes my own, leaving me wondering if the music is in the air, inside me, or both.

I don't recognize the song, but it somehow feels familiar. Maybe it's all my years of Number Whispering theory, but after a couple of minutes, I sense a mathematical pattern. Distracted from the notes themselves, I start calculating the melody. I couldn't possibly name the contraptions the music is coming from, but now that I recognize the number influence, I can easily isolate the different tones from all the various instruments.

"They're using math to make this music," I whisper to Lila.

"Huh?" she replies, her eyes never leaving the performers. Canter seems just as transfixed.

"It's all calculated!" I exclaim, surprised by my own enthusiasm. Much to my parents' dismay, numbers have never thrilled me. But then again, I've never heard math applied this way. Maybe I would have been more interested in Number Whispering if I had. "They're using mathematical formulas to time the different notes. I can actually *hear* the equations!"

"Crashing comets, Myra!" Canter says, tearing his eyes away from the band to shoot me an irritated look. "Are you really talking about number theory right now? Just listen!"

Glowering, I turn back to the performance, but I couldn't stop calculating the mathematical relationships among notes even if I wanted to. Instead, I shift my focus to the musicians. *I knew it!* Looking closely, I can just make out misty numbers floating above them. I trace their path back to the man holding the baton. He's conducting the numbers into the air, directing them toward the various sections of kids grouped by instrument. As I watch, it all snaps into place. The floating numbers correspond to the patterns of notes being played, and the space between them. The resulting tune has a precision I've never noticed, despite all the times I've heard music on the Moon. Maybe it's because I've never seen a concert in person like this, only through vid-streams, and truth be told, I haven't even seen many of those.

The music shifts to a softer melody and a new group of students catches my eye. Clad in leotards, fringe, and ruffles, the troupe marches toward us in time with the hazy notes.

Another teacher, this one dressed in a black bodysuit, shouts the same odd count, "Five, six, seven, eight!" and the new group bursts into action. Leaps, twirls, kicks, and turns accent every note of music, which has picked up momentum again. The dancers stretch and twist in ways I didn't think possible. One jumps so high, she soars over our heads, landing behind us next to the ship.

"Leaping lizards!" someone cries beside me, and I turn to see Bernard just as dazzled as the rest of us. I hadn't even noticed him deplaning. Before I can say anything to him, the dancer spins by us like a human tornado.

"How are they doing that?" I ask Lila. Another dancer propels herself into the air, her body twisting in a way that seems beyond human.

"I think it's some sort of Mender magic," she says in a hushed voice, her gaze still glued to the dancers. "I can feel it in the air. They're using their powers to stretch their bodies to their absolute limits."

"Wow." It's all I can come up with. Lila nods, distracted. Between the Mender magic dancing and the Number Whispering–fueled music, I can't imagine how anything could top this performance, but then two more student groups exit the smaller bubble buildings on either side of the main one, and all I can do is hold my breath and wait.

And I'm not disappointed. One group, some of V.A.M.A.'s Tekkies, I'm guessing, construct a platform seemingly out of thin air. The dancers and musicians mount the stairs to stand on top of the newly assembled structure, their dancing and playing never faltering. My classmates' faces lift to follow them.

The last group crouches along the base, clutching something in their hands.

"Crashing comets!" Canter cries. Balls of electricity glow from between their fingers, and when they raise them over their heads, spotlights of every color bounce off the surrounding buildings, washing over the dancers and musicians. The light pulses with the music, and as the beat speeds up, the dancers move faster and faster, leaping and twirling around the musicians, building toward a grand finale.

I rock on my toes, eager to see what they could possibly have planned. With a blast like a bomb, the Elector students throw the balls of electricity into the air, where they join together into one giant beam of light as the dancers leap and the musicians hit one final resounding note. It's as if time has stopped, everyone and everything frozen in place, and then the beam fractures into a thousand tiny fireworks, floating down and then erupting around us like confetti made of lightning.

"Welcome to the Venusian Academy of Magical Arts," the stout blond teacher booms as the students take a bow.

Canter, Lila, and even Bernard turn toward me, their eyes shining.

I swallow, the sounds still ringing in my ears. "I don't think we're at S.L.A.M. anymore."

CHAPTER SEVENTEEN

Fourth Month, 2449

THE NEXT MORNING, LILA AND I HOVER OUTSIDE OUR Chemic Theory classroom. Or at least what I think is our classroom.

"Is this right?" I ask.

"I think so." Lila swivels her head, slowly panning the space like a confused weather vane. Instead of the usual rows of workstations, this place looks more like a Rec hall. A large counter lines the perimeter, with a few small tables strategically placed throughout the room. Putty loungers, stools, small cushy sofas, and even a hammock are scattered around the space. Not a rigid chair in sight.

"How will we get any work done? This can't be right."

"Excuse me," Lila says, turning to a boy lounging in a hammock. "Is this the Chemic II classroom?"

The boy tilts his head back to look at us upside down, squinting at our white-and-purple jumpsuits. I didn't realize until just now that we're the only ones here in any sort of uniform. "Yup, this is it," he finally says. "You two must be the transplants from the Moon."

Lila smiles. "We're the transfer students from S.L.A.M."

Still upside down, the boy grins back at us. "How do you like V.A.M.A. so far? It's out of this orbit, right?"

"It's definitely different," Lila says.

"Very different." I watch as a group of kids pours a solution directly onto the countertop. They whoop and cheer as it bubbles and burns a hole right through it. "Where's the teacher?"

"Over there," the boy says, his hammock lurching as he bounds out of it, landing easily on his feet. He points across the room. "That's Mr. Kote."

I follow the boy's outstretched finger to the blond-haired man who announced the welcome performance yesterday. He's standing beside a boy with dark skin and black, closely cropped hair. The boy nods glumly in response to whatever Mr. Kote's telling him, fidgeting in his seat, like he'd rather be anywhere but here. I know the feeling.

"Are all your classrooms like this?" Lila asks, her dark eyes still sweeping the room.

"Like what?"

"So . . . laid-back?"

Hammock boy frowns. "This is one of our stricter ones, actually. Chemic solutions can be dangerous if you don't know what you're doing." He narrows his eyes. "Are either of you Chemic track?"

"I'm a Mender," Lila says. "My name's Lila," she adds quickly. "And this is Myra. She's a Chemic."

I nod absently, still processing his comment about this being one of their *stricter* classes.

"I'm Jones," the boy says, sweeping long auburn hair out of his eyes. "And I'm a Mender, too. Are you in Mender Enhancements and Alternate Applications next period?" When Lila nods, he says, "Shooting stars! That's a great class. I'm in it, too. We can go together. If you think this class is strange, wait until you get a look at the setup there."

As the pair slips into Mender-speak, I tune them out and return to studying Mr. Kote, who's moved to the center of the room. The lesson must be starting.

"All right, folks," he says, clapping his hands. "Time for freestyle demonstrations. Chemic tracks, over here," he says, gesturing to his right. "All other tracks, on the other side to observe."

I must look panicked, because he immediately homes in on me. "Ah, hold on just a second. I need to make some introductions. We have some students joining us today from our Lunar-based sister school. Myra Hodger, our Chemic transfer, please introduce yourself."

I give a meek wave and an even weaker smile, swallowing down my nerves.

Mr. Kote smiles at me warmly. "After reading the supersonic essay you wrote, I'm honored to make your tangible acquaintance, Myra."

"Uh, thanks," I mumble, blushing. I move to rub at the Chemic Inscription on my arm, a nervous habit I picked up in Mr. DeGraf's class, but stop myself.

Mr. Kote turns back to the class. "And I believe we have our Mender track transfer here, as well. Lila Crumpler, would you say hello?"

"Hi, everyone," she replies brightly, positively beaming next to her new friend, Jones. "I'm excited to be here."

"We're excited to have you," Mr. Kote says, his eyes twinkling, and then he shifts his focus back to me. "I understand this might be *very* different from what you're used to at S.L.A.M. At V.A.M.A., we want our students to be enthusiastic about learning, so please know that these presentations are completely voluntary, and you can just observe if you want."

The tightness in my chest begins to fade, but he isn't finished.

"Of course, if you'd like to show off your magical stuff, by all means, jump right in."

Forcing what I hope is a nervous smile onto my face, I

quickly shake my head. "I think I'd rather watch for now, if that's all right."

"Of course!" he merrily booms. "Okay, my Chemic kids. Let's show our new friends what we can do."

The class does not disappoint. The first Chemic student steps up to the front of the room—a tall girl with blond hair that's cut to a point at her chin. She spreads her arms wide and liquids and powders stream from canisters, vials, and jars all around the room, swirling midair in as many hues as there used to be in my moongarden. I push the pang of sadness away, forcing myself to focus on her performance.

The colors blend until, with a flick of her fingers, the girl sends some of them splattering against the wall. Again and again, she uses her magic to siphon off a bit of this color, and a splash of that, until an image begins to form. I squint at the glistening streaks of cobalt blue, turquoise, and navy, accented by silvery orbs flecked with bronze, and realize it's V.A.M.A.

She did that with Chemic magic?

The room erupts in applause, and the girl bows before plopping back onto a sofa.

One after another, Chemic kids take their turns. Many create Chemic-magic-fueled paintings, like the first girl's. Others turn their mixtures into solid forms, building sculptures that morph before our eyes. One boy creates a series of bubbles, one inside another, each glowing a different shade of pink; then with a snap he dissolves the whole display into a sparkling violet rain.

By the time everyone has had a turn who wants one, class is half over.

"Very well done," Mr. Kote says, pulling his shoulder-length hair into a low ponytail. "I especially appreciated Emma's sculpting experiment, as it leads perfectly into today's lesson on creating adaptable structures."

Finally, the class shifts into a lesson format that feels more familiar. Mr. Kote talks through theory principles as students around me take notes. I try to concentrate but find myself distracted by the glowing, flashing, and even melting masterpieces scattered around the room.

They're impressive, sure, but I can't help wondering at their usefulness. What Mr. Kote's lecturing about *now* seems practical, but what about the bubble kid's work? Or the painting of V.A.M.A.? What good is all that to the galaxy?

Unfortunately, I seem to be the only one bothered by this. Beside me, Lila keeps peeking over at the student projects, shaking her head in wonder.

In fact, the only other kid who seems unimpressed is the boy Mr. Kote was speaking to at the beginning of class. He's slumped back in a putty lounger a few rows over. He didn't participate in the demonstrations, either, but maybe he's not Chemic track. Still, I don't see him taking notes.

The bell finally rings, and Lila barely even says goodbye before she's out the door, chatting animatedly with Jones. I check my schedule on the pendant V.A.M.A. provided, then head to my Elector theory class alone.

When I get there, Canter's just leaving some advanced seminar on Elector manipulation.

"Why are you here so late?" I ask. "Was the class really strange?"

"Crashing comets, yes!" he answers, and I let out a sigh of relief. "It was beyond weird."

"Mine, too! Did all the kids have to—"

"It was amazing! You should see the way the kids here can use their Elector powers! I never even thought some of it was possible. If I had, maybe I . . ." He pauses, running his hands through his hair. "Anyway, I've got to go. I have a Tekkie class next, and I can't wait to see what we do. Maybe they'll show us how they built the stage yesterday." He zips by me into the hall. "Later, Myra!"

I don't bother answering. He's already gone.

CHAPTER EIGHTEEN

LATER THAT EVENING, AFTER A LONG DAY OF completely bizarre classes, I search for Lila and Canter in the dining hall.

"I thought I knew every application of magic," I say with a sigh as I plop onto the bench-style seat beside them. "But these classes. I mean . . ."

"I know!" Lila exclaims, barely noticing the greasy imitation food on her plate. "Isn't it amazing?" She chews and spears another bite. "Oh, and Myra. Sorry I left in such a rush earlier. Jones was telling me about an elective Menders course he's in and, *shooting stars,* it sounds amazing. Did you make it to the rest of your classes okay?"

"Yeah, I found them all right, but—"

"I saw her coming out of my first Elector class," Canter interrupts, shoveling his own dinner into his mouth.

"The sea air must be good for your appetite, eh, Weathers?" Kyle Melfin strolls by, carrying his own dinner tray. I'd actually forgotten he was here, too. "Want to try some of mine?" he asks, smirking as he holds out his tray. "My dad says the burgers are way better than the pasta."

"Pass," Canter replies coldly. "It all tastes the same. Different name, same MFI junk."

"Maybe it's not the sea air helping your appetite after all," Kyle says, his eyes narrowing. "It's just relief at not having to embarrass yourself at S.L.A.M. hoverball games."

"You embarrass yourself on and off the court, Kyle," I snap. Canter hoots beside me.

Kyle rolls his eyes, then walks away without another word.

Lila shakes her head, watching his retreating back. "That was almost nice for Kyle. Do you think he wanted to sit with us?"

"No way," Canter says. "And even if he did, I'd rather eat with a Moon goblin."

"Same." I watch Kyle find a seat at another table near some kids from Chemic class. "If Kyle's being less than horrible, it's only because he's up to something."

"I hope he tries to join the Rec hoverball team," Canter growls, still glaring at Kyle's table. "I'd love to get him on the court and see how *embarrassing* it is when I knock him out of the air and—"

"What were you saying about classes, Canter?" Lila says.

"Huh? Oh, yeah." Enthusiasm quickly replaces his anger. "Remember that day last year when my dad announced the new menu, and me and my hoverball buddies, uh, livened up the assembly a bit?"

I smirk. "*Livened up* or short-circuited the whole thing?"

"Same difference," Canter says, shrugging. "We'd found instructions for how to make those pulses on the open network. But here, they actually *teach* students to do that. We spent the whole class practicing changing levels of static energy, and how that affects the color of the electric discharge. . . ."

Canter goes on and on about how great his classes are for the rest of the dinner block. After multiple attempts to redirect the conversation, I finally lean across the table and clamp my hand over his mouth.

"Wfut's fa maffer?"

"I get that this school is super strange, and maybe that's also interstellar in its own way, but in the name of Pluto, can we *please* talk about what we're *really* doing here?"

"Myra's right," Lila says as I free Canter. "We should check if there are any new meeting posts on the cooking sites."

"Okay, fine," Canter grumbles, pulling his computer out of his bag.

"Hey, Lila!" a new voice calls from behind me. I spin around to see Jones and another girl standing there smiling.

"Hi!" Lila answers brightly. "Jones, this is one of my best friends from S.L.A.M., Canter. He's an Elector track. And you met Myra in Chemic class this morning."

Jones nods hello, grinning at us as he gestures toward the petite brunette girl at his side. "This is Bette. She's in the other Mender unit, so we haven't had a class with her yet, but I was telling her your idea about using controlled hyperextension to create new poses, and she thinks it will *really* help the artistic lines of the movement."

I have no idea what he just said, but I quickly decide I don't like it.

"I'm in charge of the choreography for our next school showcase," Bette adds a little shyly. "Would you be interested in participating? I'd love to hear more about your ideas. Plus, we lost a few performers to S.L.A.M., and it'd be nice to add a little Lunar flavor to our ensemble. I think it could be just what we need to liven things up."

"Really?" Lila's eyes sparkle like two of Canter's Elector pulses. "Sure! When do you want to get together?"

"Are you free now?" Bette asks eagerly. "We have rehearsal tonight."

"If it's anything like yesterday's performance, I'm dying to see more!" Lila exclaims.

"Crashing comets, that was nothing," Jones says, already turning to lead them toward the door. "Wait until you see the full ensemble. Hold on." He stops, turning back to our table, and anticipation bubbles in my chest. He couldn't possibly want *my* help with their performance. I don't know anything about dancing, and I don't know what he could expect some newbie Chemic to do in their show or—

"Do you play hoverball?" he asks Canter, and I clench my fists under the table.

Canter nods, puffing out his chest. "My team was the JV hoverball champions two years ago. We had a good run last season, but we had some injuries. . . ."

Jones waves his hand, as if erasing the non-champion season from the universe. "A bunch of us play, and we usually try to pull together a quick pickup game after practice. Want to come? I'm sure we could use some extra Elector skills in the performance, too."

"That'd be interstellar!" Canter stands, and he's halfway to the door before he even glances back. "Oh, Myra. Do you want to come?"

"We could always use more performers!" Bette says enthusiastically.

"I'm not a Mender," I snap back, then force my temper

under control. "Thanks, anyway. I wouldn't be much help, though."

"There're all sorts of other roles," Bette continues. "Set design, music, artistic showcases . . ."

"Not really my thing," I say, shaking my head. "We don't have any of that stuff on the Moon."

"Oh," Bette replies, her cheeks flushing slightly. Her face falls like she feels bad for me.

Irritation rips through my skin again. "Weren't we going to, er, start on that research project?" I ask Canter and Lila. Neither will look me in the eye.

"Research project?" Jones frowns. "For which teacher?"

"It's for our old school," I reply.

"That's not due for ages, though," Lila says slowly, still avoiding my gaze.

"Yeah, we can start it tomorrow," Canter adds, shuffling from foot to foot. "Okay, Myra?"

"Sure," I reply, because what else is there to say?

Canter grins, and I can see that Lila's suddenly much more relaxed. "Why don't you come with us? It'll be fun!"

"You can be our test audience if you don't want to participate in perform," Jones offers. "No forced demonstrations, like Mr. Kote said."

"Thanks, but I'm going to get started on that project." I see my friends' enthusiasm falter, but they still turn to go.

I sink back into my seat, surrounded by half-eaten dinners and abandoned trays. With a sigh, I'm leaning across the table to clean up the mess when a familiar voice makes me jump.

"I can take those," Bernard says.

"Hi!" I leap up, helping him to clear the trash and stack the dinnerware in a neat pile. "How's it going? Are you helping out the kitchen staff?"

"No, I'm starting a collection of dirty dinner trays," he replies dryly, scooping the mess off the table.

"Wait! Do you want to hang out after the dinner rush? We could explore the school and—"

"Nope," he says, disappearing into the crowd, leaving me alone at the table. Again.

CHAPTER NINETEEN

THE NEXT WEEK STREAKS BY LIKE WE'RE ON JUPITER time, and with each passing day, I see Canter and Lila less and less. They're both busy with the upcoming V.A.M.A. performance. On top of that, Canter's joined the recreational hoverball team and Lila's joined a club on hair and makeup for the stage, so they're both with their new friends from the breakfast block until just before curfew.

I use my classes to distract myself. Or I try to, anyway. V.A.M.A. classes are completely different from S.L.A.M.'s. So different, it's hard to believe they're even in the same Creer fields. A weird sense of déjà vu crashes over me as I peek through the window into my Number Whispering class, taking in the kids perched on desks and tables, and their teacher, Mr. Finch (the one who conducted the music at our welcome reception), chatting animatedly with them.

Bin-ro chirps at me, and I'm about to back away when Mr. Finch looks up and catches my eye. "Myra!" he calls, waving to me. "Come on in. I was looking forward to getting your input on today's lesson."

Crashing comets, I should have moved faster. I cautiously step inside, Bin-ro on my heels. No one seems to mind him zipping around. In this place, he's definitely the least strange thing in the school halls.

Mr. Finch grins. "We're just getting started on cascading multiplication tables."

My stomach drops like I'm on a hover coaster. *Of course we are.* "I know that theory."

"I'm not surprised."

I pause, waiting for him to give the class a speech about my renowned Number Whisperer parents, when he says, "Your explanation of complementing theory on yesterday's homework shows you have a stellar command of the formulas."

My eyebrows shoot up. "Oh. Thanks."

"After reading your paper, it struck me that you might have a hidden talent you haven't had a chance to discover at S.L.A.M."

Hidden talents are something I'm fairly familiar with, but I doubt my real magical gift is something Mr. Finch would recognize as an asset. Bin-ro must be thinking the same thing. He lets out a low whistle.

"It might be easier if I show you," Mr. Finch says, reaching toward his temple and drawing out a number. He gives it a flick, and it tumbles across the room as if rolling over invisible hills. As it spins, more numbers—complementing equations—spin off from it.

Does he seriously think I've never seen a practical demonstration of cascading multiplication tables before?

"Now, I'm sure you've seen practical demonstrations of cascading multiplication tables plenty of times before," he says merrily, and I cough in surprise, "but I noticed you spent a lot of time discussing the rise and fall of equations as they progress—and you're absolutely right to note that. What I'm guessing you've never had an opportunity to explore is how that rhythm corresponds to music."

I'm not sure how to respond, so I don't say anything.

"Did you ever take any music classes at S.L.A.M., or anywhere else on the Moon?"

I shake my head. "Our Rec hall sometimes had vidstreams of concerts, though."

"Ah," he says, rubbing his dark goatee. "I'm sure most were broadcast from here. Venus *is* known as the musical center of the galaxy."

"They might have been. . . . I'm not sure. But I never took lessons, or anything."

His eyes sparkle as he leans toward me. "Would you like to?"

"Uh . . ." I want to say no, but I actually like Mr. Finch, and I don't want to hurt his feelings.

"I'm sure you're racking your brain for a way to politely tell me no right now."

Bin-ro chirps, and it sounds like a giggle.

"Uh," I say again.

"I think you might find you take to it quicker than you expect." He walks to a cabinet behind his desk.

"It's just not something I've ever really thought about trying before."

"Isn't that the point of the exchange program, though?" Mr. Finch is crouched in front of the cabinet now, clearly looking for something, but he pauses to shoot me a wink over his shoulder. "A new environment means trying new things—ones you might never have considered or that you aren't entirely comfortable with. But as my longtime students will tell you, a little discomfort often leads to big discoveries."

"Discoveries about what?" I hear myself asking.

He shrugs, his back still to me. "The universe. Ourselves. Sometimes both." He stands, holding some giant metal monstrosity. The curved golden tubes making up half of it are so ridiculously long, it looks like a Tekkie stretched it out as a joke.

"What's that?" I ask, taking a step back.

He chuckles. "A trombone. And it won't hurt you. Here. Take a closer look."

Since it would be rude to refuse, I reach out and gingerly pluck the instrument from his hands with my fingertips.

Mr. Finch laughs. "It isn't going to bite. I promise!"

I grasp the instrument more firmly, turning it side to side to inspect it. "People actually play music on this thing?"

"They actually do. And lots of others. I've got a whole array in here." He pulls out an expensive-looking case from the cabinet, opening it to reveal something far more elegant than what I'm holding. Bin-ro whistles low and long. The instrument looks like it's been carved from wood, which is impossible. Objects haven't been made from actual trees since we left the Old World. I'm probably one of the only people in the Settlements today who's even seen a real one.

"What is that?" I can't help but ask, transfixed by the instrument's sleek, gentle curves. The delicate-looking cords strung up the front of it look like a cascade of silvery water, frozen in time.

"This is a violin," he says. He picks up a long, thin stick that appears to be made from the same woodlike material. Inscriptions cover the back of his hand in an elaborate pattern, numbers stretched to resemble music notes. Or musical notes warped into numbers. Against his dark skin they shimmer like they're cast in silvery ink, almost glowing in the classroom lights. "I play lots of instruments, but this one has always been my favorite. It was handed down to me from my great-great-great-grandfather."

My eyes bulge. "So is that made of—"

"Real wood. Yes," he says, patting it tenderly. "From the Old World."

"Wow," I whisper, and the for the first time, I desperately want to hear some music.

I don't even have to ask. A hauntingly beautiful melody fills the room. The other kids stop their chatter to listen as Mr. Finch's fingertips flutter over the strings, pressing them, holding them, wobbling them, and at the same time, he slides the slim wooden piece over the instrument. It's like a dance. Bin-ro rolls and swoops between the workstations in time with the notes, performing his own robot waltz. The other students lean over to pat his metal hull as he spins lazily by.

I don't know how long Mr. Finch plays—time seems to stand still as notes float in the air—but whenever he finishes, it's too soon.

"That was amazing." And I really mean it. A few kids even break into applause before turning back to their projects.

Mr. Finch inclines his head in a humble sort of bow. "Were you able to hear the numbers?"

I hadn't been thinking of math while he was playing, but

I consider the notes. "I did, actually. Not at the time, but I can hear them now."

"See. I knew you'd have the knack." He holds out the violin to me, brown eyes sparkling. "Want to give it a try?"

My mouth goes dry. "Me? Crashing comets, no! What if I break it?"

"Are you planning on using my violin as a hoverball?"

"No . . ."

"Then you'll be fine. Here."

He takes back the trombone and practically shoves the violin into my hand. I can't help but marvel at the smoothness of the wood, and the dainty but surprisingly strong strings lining it. I trail my fingers over them gently and they tickle my fingertips. With another nod of encouragement from Mr. Finch, I grasp the neck of the violin in one hand and tuck the rounded end under my chin like he did.

"Try gently plucking the strings with your free hand," he says. "Experiment with the different sounds they make."

Watching Mr. Finch's face for a signal that I'm about to break his treasure, I gingerly strum one finger against each string, listening as they vibrate at my touch, humming distinctly different notes. As I pluck, Mr. Finch names the notes: G, D, A, and E.

"Hear the differences in tone?" he asks, and I nod. "Great! Here's the bow." He hands me the long, thin stick. Bin-ro gives a startled *beep,* then disappears under a desk.

"Thanks for the support," I mutter, and Mr. Finch laughs. "Just rub the hair gently over the strings. Don't worry about holding them at the same time. That's next-level stuff."

"Okay," I say, easing the bow down over the strings and then pulling it back. A loud screech warbles from the instrument and I gasp. "I'm sorry, Mr. Finch! I don't know—"

"You didn't break it, Myra," he says with a chuckle. "That's perfectly normal the first time someone plays violin. Even the tenth time, if I'm being honest."

Sweat still beads the back of my neck as I hand it back to him.

"Give it another try," he urges.

"I think that's all my nerves can take for today, but thanks. That was interstellar. Really. I don't know how you made music come out of that thing. It's definitely magic."

"Can't argue with you there," he says, smiling as he takes the violin back and places it inside the cabinet. "You struck me as more of a brass instrument kind of girl, anyway."

"Brass?"

"This guy." He nods at the trombone and passes it back to me. "Give it a try." He must notice my confused expression. "There're no strings and no bow. You just buzz air into here," he explains, pointing at the mouthpiece. "Stretching and retracting the slide changes the notes."

I give it a try, and a non-screeching note actually comes

out! "What was that?" I ask, shocked at the deep, rich sound.

"That, my dear Miss Hodger, is music." Mr. Finch spends a few minutes showing me the basics of the instrument—how stretching the long, curved pole out as far as my arm can extend changes the notes. Before I know it, I can play a basic melody.

"Shooting stars, this is cool," I whisper, feeling a little light-headed.

"Take it with you. Use it to practice your number theory."

My eyebrows shoot up. "Really? I still don't get how it will help."

"Just start composing melodies, and you'll see" is all Mr. Finch says in reply. "Consider it your homework in place of that paper due tomorrow."

Well, I can't argue with that. I thank him and take the trombone back to my seat, securing it carefully inside the black, bulky case he gives me. Bin-ro beeps, annoyed, as I set it down beside him, now much more interested in today's lesson.

After class, I drop Bin-ro back off at Canter's room, then head back to my dorm, feeling awkward carrying the giant trombone through the hall. But the embarrassment fades quickly. At V.A.M.A., every kid is carrying something strange, dressed in something strange, or acting strange.

Sometimes all three at once. Weird here isn't weird at all.

After huffing and puffing down several hallways, I pause, resting the case on the ground. It's nearly as tall as me.

"What's that thing?" a voice asks from behind me. "A new friend?"

I whirl around and find myself face-to-face with Kyle Melfin. I sigh and swipe a hand across my sweaty forehead, not in the mood.

"Can't say I blame you. That thing's got to be a better conversationalist than that space cadet Weathers."

"Go kick Moon rocks, Melfin."

"What's Canter been up to lately, anyway? I haven't seen him around much."

"That makes two of us," I mutter, then instantly regret it.

Kyle raises his eyebrows. "Ditched you already, eh?"

I can't muster the energy to lie, so I just roll my eyes. Kyle nods like I agreed with him, though. Maybe I did.

"I don't get why everyone thinks this place is so great." He scans the hall, taking in the usual magic-fueled chaos. Paint gases swirl through the air over a crowd of kids, dripping colors on the ground like confetti. A pair of Reps trail after the group, scrubbing away the splotches. "Even you're joining the club now." He nods toward the trombone case. "Just seems like a waste of time to me."

"Then why are you even here?"

He sighs and leans back against the wall. "My dad made me apply."

"Why would he care? It's not like you need the experience for your university applications. I'm sure he already has a cushy office waiting for you."

Kyle smirks. "I'm pretty much already working for him."

"What's that supposed to mean? Like on your school breaks?"

He scoffs. "I don't work in the factory like some Rep, if that's what you mean."

"As if you could manage half the work a Rep does."

"The things I do are way more important than that."

"Like what? Do you go to the kitchen and help stir the slime we're all forced to eat now?"

Kyle's eyes flare like embers. "Our strategies are proprietary. But you can bet a Jupiter Jackpot that MFI is going places, and big moves require big tactics."

"What sort of big moves? Getting kicked off the Governing Council?"

He shrugs. "As long as the Council works for you, doesn't matter if you're *on* the Council. It's better this way, actually. Whoever leaked that story did my dad a favor. Now he's free to focus on the company . . . and figure out how to pay back whoever he owes for getting him kicked out."

I may be imagining it, but Kyle's eyes seem to narrow as they meet mine.

Trying not to look like I'm rushing away, I heft the trombone case and continue down the hall without another word.

"Tell Canter I said hi!" Kyle calls after me.

I don't bother turning around.

CHAPTER TWENTY

CANTER AND LILA HAVE PRACTICES EVERY NIGHT FOR the next week. Sometimes, Jones or Bette whisks them away as if by magic. Sometimes I don't see my friends at all. I tried telling Canter about my run-in with Kyle, but he barely sat still long enough to listen, and didn't seem to care that Kyle thinks it was Director Weathers who leaked the broken food codes news last year. I almost blurted out what Ms. Goble told my mother about Jake Melfin and what happened to Fiona to see if Canter even reacted, but clamped my mouth shut at the last second. It didn't seem like the right time or the right reason to share that piece of news. I still wonder if I should have told him, though.

We've been on Venus for two weeks and aren't any closer to finding out more about Melfin or how to contact the group of free Reps. We haven't found a place for a new garden, either.

I slide open my dresser drawer, fumbling around until I find a wad of green socks. Carefully unrolling them, I peer into a toe at our stockpile of seeds. I pluck one out, holding the smooth umber shape on my palm. I haven't tried using my magic since we undid our S.L.A.M. kitchen garden. To be honest, I needed time to recover after watching Lila remove the seeds from my skin.

I shudder, pushing the memory from my mind as I gently form a fist and let my eyes flutter shut. I imagine tasting a freshly grown blueberry plucked straight from the bush, and my mouth waters as I remember the taste, how the skin pops before the insides flood my taste buds with tartness.

I remember Bernie's smile the first time he ate a blueberry in our garden. How it reminded him of the garden he grew with Fiona.

Heat sears my palm, and my eyes fly open. When I uncurl my fingers, I expect to see a bud, or at least a sprout. Some sign of life. Instead, the seed is blackened. Burnt. Dead. Fear runs through me as I quickly tuck it back into the sock and shove the wad in my drawer.

I pace the room, eager for a distraction. Usually, I'd spend my time practicing the trombone. I've gotten decently good—well, not hopeless—but I can't force myself to pick up the instrument tonight.

"I'm going for a walk," I tell Bin-ro. "Want to come?"

He chirps, and we set off down the hall.

It's not a random wandering, though. I have a purpose, if not a destination.

Bin-ro and I move from hall to hall and building to building. I've learned that each bubble has a name, or more accurately, a category. The central, largest one is called Spectacle. It's where all the assemblies and performances take place, which means Canter and Lila spend just about all their time there.

The five smaller orb-shaped buildings are Plot, Character, Rhythm, Language, and Theme. Plot's bubble building contains the cafeteria and the hoverball court. The dormitories are (fittingly) located in Character. Classes take place in Rhythm, Language, and Theme, though I don't have anything in the last one.

We check all the buildings, one by one, but have no luck. Finally, after a lot of wandering, we find him in Rhythm at the very back of the floating island.

"Bernard!" I call, and Bin-ro whistles a greeting. "We've been searching for you all over."

"Haven't been all over," he says, not looking up from the wall of mirrors he's polishing. "I've just been here."

"Well, I'm glad we found you!" I say, plopping onto the gleaming floor and gazing at myself in the mirrors. "What is this place?"

"Mender dancing room," Bernard replies, drying a sparkling corner. "They use the mirrors to watch their movements and make corrections."

I wrinkle my nose. "Sounds like a lot of work."

He shrugs. "They seem to enjoy it."

Before Bernard can start on the last panel of mirrors, Bin-ro scoots by him, a spout emerging from his metal hull. A mist drifts out, coating the surface in a fizzy foam, and then another arm extends, and with a soft *wurrrr* Bin-ro blows air onto the mirror, drying it to a gleaming finish.

"I don't know how anyone can enjoy this place," I blurt out. "Nothing's organized. Nothing makes sense. Everyone just does whatever they want. Uses their magic however they feel like." I drop my chin onto my hands. "I don't like it."

"Different takes getting used to sometimes," Bernard says slowly, leaning against a non-mirrored wall as he watches Bin-ro work. "It can be jarring at first, but even if it's not your thing, sometimes a jolt to the system can show you what might be."

He sounds so much like my old friend. "Lila and Canter have been completely sucked into V.A.M.A."

Bernard shrugs. "If they're your friends, you must have things in common."

"I thought so."

"Isn't it possible that whatever they're into now, you might find interesting, too?"

"No."

"Why not?" Bin-ro finishes with the last wall of mirrors, then rolls over to join us. Bernard leans over and pats his hull affectionately.

"Because I don't like what they're doing. I don't want to be in a performance. Or learn about these weird ways to use magic. We came here to—"

Bernard's eyes narrow. "To what?"

"To . . . work on our Creers and learn about Venus."

"Isn't that exactly what they're doing?"

I slap my hand on the sleek floor. "But it's not the way I want!"

Bernard rolls his eyes. "Do you always make everything about yourself?"

"No! Well, maybe sometimes." I cross my arms. "But doesn't everyone?"

"All I'm saying is, maybe they don't have to do things the way you do."

"Well, they should."

"For all you know, they're thinking the same about you."

"They seem pretty happy."

"So maybe you should be a good friend and be happy for them," Bernard suggests. "If it's a real friendship, they'll come back around. They're probably just swept up in all the newness."

I hadn't thought of it that way before. And Bernard's right. They do seem happy. Happier than I've seen them in months. Thinking back, I can't remember the last time Lila was stressed about school or the last bizarre plan Canter's come up with to get in touch with his mom.

"I guess I haven't been a great friend to them."

"Even if this place isn't really your thing," Bernard says, "maybe it's worth giving it a chance. Sounds like it would mean a lot to your friends."

"I guess I could try a little harder. And what about you?"

"What about me?"

"Are you going to give it a chance, too? You don't seem very happy here, either."

Bernard's expression darkens, and I immediately regret saying anything, especially since it's the most he's spoken to me in ages. I open my mouth to change the subject, but he answers before I can.

"I've given this place a chance. Before I got to S.L.A.M. I'm not interested in giving it another."

I cock my head to the side. "What do you mean? On the shuttle over, you said you'd never been to Venus."

"No." He shakes his head. "I said Venus was uninhabitable when my original was on the Old World. Which is true. This is . . . where *I* came from." He glares at the wall. "Where all Reps come from, actually."

A sinking feeling sweeps through me. "This is where the labs that—"

"The facility's on the other side of Venus. On the River of Monet. It's called Advanced Repetition Cloning Services, or something like that. There were signs with the acronym all over the place."

"I'm sorry, Bernard. I didn't know."

"Most people don't. Even other Reps."

"What do you mean?"

"None of the others seem to have any idea that the facility we came from is here. They don't remember anything before showing up for their first assignment."

I frown. "Then how do you know?"

"I'm . . . young for a Rep," he explains. "Like I told you before, most don't start working until they're at least in their twenties. I think the administrators at A.R.C.S. must do something so that memories of the facility fade once they leave. Mine didn't." He shrugs. "They must not have had time before I was sent to S.L.A.M."

Do the rogue Reps know where the facility is? If not, maybe that piece of information can help them. "But why? How did you end up at S.L.A.M. so quickly?"

He shrugs. "A lot of what happens to Reps is a mystery."

"I'm sorry we got you pulled into the exchange program," I finally say.

He turns to collect his cleaning supplies. "You didn't know. And it wasn't you, anyway."

"I'm still sorry," I say, meeting his eyes. "And Canter would be, too. If he knew."

"Canter?"

"Because he asked his dad to assign you to the exchange program."

"Oh. Right."

"Do you want to come explore the school with me and Bin-ro?"

Not surprisingly, Bernard declines. "I've got work to do." The way he says it, I know nothing in the galaxy will change his mind.

After a while, Bin-ro and I find ourselves at Language and the entrance to V.A.M.A.'s modulab. I haven't been here before. "Why do they even have a modulab?" I ask as we slip inside. "The teachers hardly even use a lesson text." Not that I'm complaining. Even in my Chemic classes, I've barely had any homework, and Mr. Kote hasn't given a single test.

As if proving my point, the room's deserted. I sigh. "This would be perfect to do our research. That is if Canter and Lila remembered why we're actually here."

Guilt trickles through me. If my friends are finally happy, I shouldn't interfere. That was part of why I wanted to get them away from S.L.A.M. And I can still try to make progress.

Bin-ro scoots to the far corner. I notice that the V.A.M.A. modulab is set up differently than the one at S.L.A.M. Back home, you can pop off whatever size and shape screen you want from the wall and use it wherever you like. Here, screens are mounted all over the room—on walls, on the floor. Some even hang from the ceiling.

Bin-ro stops next to one embedded in the fuzzy carpet next to a stack of large, fluffy pillows. I pull down one of the cushions and flop on top of it. I'd never admit it to anyone (except maybe Bin-ro), but it's a pretty comfortable setup.

After tapping the screen to power it on, I navigate to the open network. "I'm officially taking over the mission," I say, sounding more determined than I feel. "That way, Canter and Lila can enjoy their new activities."

And their new friends.

No. This is a new start. With a deep breath, I push the last thought down so hard it almost disappears—almost— and get to work.

CHAPTER TWENTY-ONE

THE WHOLE NEXT WEEK, I THROW MYSELF INTO researching every lead I can find. I start with the recipe sites and their strange comments. I scroll through what must be hundreds of posts but don't find any with coded messages apart from the ones Canter and I already stumbled upon, and nothing new seems to have been added recently.

In addition to my search, I've also taken on a secret hobby. Or not *so* secret. The fact that I'm enjoying it is definitely classified for now. After breakfast, once Canter and Lila clear off for class with their herd of new friends, I head for Mr. Finch's room. But first, I swing by the dorms to pick up the trombone.

"Hiya, Myra." Mr. Finch beams as I struggle inside with the bulky instrument. "Have you been practicing that piece I showed you yesterday?"

"Yes," I grunt, placing the trombone carefully on a workstation before shrugging off my bag. The instrument wobbles on the edge, starting to tilt, but before it can crash to the floor, a dark-skinned boy next to me jumps up and saves it. "Thanks," I say, taking the brass contraption from him and positioning it over my shoulder as I turn back to my teacher. "I'm having trouble hitting the note at the end, though."

"Let's hear it," Mr. Finch says, settling on the corner of his desk.

I lift the instrument to my mouth and begin to play, hardly even noticing that other kids are listening.

I get through the song pretty well. The tune's definitely recognizable, up until the end, where the last few notes sputter.

Mr. Finch nods as I finish. "I see what you mean. But Myra, the rest sounds absolutely interstellar! You've really been working hard."

I grin. "The mathematical rhythm in the beginning is really clear. I don't get what it's doing at the end, though. It doesn't make sense."

Mr. Finch taps his lip. "Ah, I see the problem. This can happen, especially when you try to tie the melody to a pattern of equations. Sometimes, the music isn't just a progression of notes and rhythms. It's a balance of melodies." He must see my confusion, because he chuckles. "Let me try to explain it a different way . . . or, better yet!" He glances around the room. "Zach! You hear our problem. Any advice?"

The boy next to me, the one who saved my trombone, leans back in his chair and tilts his head back so the black braids cascading over his shoulders fall away from his face. "That ending, it doesn't really fit with the rest, right?"

I nod. "It feels like it goes off track."

"Well, that's because it does. It's supposed to. The ending's more dramatic. Like a big finale. It still matches the math, though." He thinks for a second, then snaps his fingers. "I've got it! You know how when you're little, you practice your multiplication tables?"

I nod. I could recite them in my sleep by the time I was four.

"Okay, so it's like trying to balance them with division. Three times four equals twelve, but twelve divided by three is four, right?"

"Yes . . ."

"The notes are like that. Opposite, but still linked."

"They balance out the rest," I say slowly. "Different, but balanced." I look up at my teacher. "Can I try it again?"

"Please do!" And this time, I hit every note perfectly.

Zach high-fives me when I finish.

"Well done, Myra!" Mr. Finch beams. "We'll make a musician out of you yet!"

The next few nights, as soon as Canter and Lila leave for rehearsal, I practice my trombone. Now that I've figured out the trick to some of the melodies with Mr. Finch and Zach, the next couple of songs come more easily. I never practice in front of my friends, though. I'm waiting for the perfect opportunity to show them. And luckily for me, it comes sooner than I expect.

Lila is bustling around our room one morning, getting ready to head out. "I can't make breakfast today," she calls over her shoulder as she pulls on a sweater. "We don't have practice Friday, since a bunch of kids are taking a trip to a performance on one of the other waterways, and there won't be enough of us left to do a proper run-through. We're making up for it with an extra rehearsal now."

"Oh," I say, packing my own bag for the day. "So Canter will be gone, too?" Which means I'll be eating alone this morning *and* tonight. I close my eyes and push the dreary thought away.

"Yeah," Lila says, a shadow flitting over her face before her sunny smile returns. "Why don't we do something special on Friday? Just the three of us?"

Immediately, my spirits soar like a rocket. "That'd be great!"

"Let's see, what should we do?" Lila taps her cheek. "Oh, I know! Declan told me that kids sometimes hang out on the dock in front of Spectacle. We could take our food out there and have a picnic. The sunset's supposed to be the best in the galaxy."

"Sounds great!" I say, and I mean it. Plus, it'll be the ideal moment to debut my new talent and show I'm trying new things, too.

"Perfect! I'll tell Canter."

The rest of the week, I practice my trombone every chance I get. Mr. Finch is thrilled with my progress. I have to admit, I am, too. More and more kids have started paying attention when I perform in class. During Friday's lesson, the room erupts in applause when I finish.

I know my face is burning redder than a ripe tomato, but I don't even mind. I glance down at my pendant, counting down the hours until Canter and Lila hang out.

That evening, ten minutes before we'd planned to meet at the dock, I head over to Spectacle. I don't want Lila to see me carrying my trombone and ruin the surprise. Canter's bringing the food, so I figure if I get there before them, I'll have time to set up my instrument and music. I pass Kyle in the hallway, ignoring his snide remarks about falling under V.A.M.A.'s spell.

The dock really is a pretty spot. I'd been so distracted at the welcome reception, I hadn't noticed. From here, you can look out and see nothing but water. It definitely beats the view of endless moondust we have back home. I pick up my trombone to practice a few notes, all the while keeping a careful eye on the door to make sure Canter and Lila don't sneak up on me.

The songs sound perfect. With a satisfied grin, I carefully put the instrument down and grab my pendant. They're late. Probably Canter's fault. He must have forgotten the food, and then bumped into Lila. I'm sure they went back to the cafeteria together. They'll be here any second.

Another few minutes pass. I check my messenger. Maybe one of their classes ran late?

A message from Lila flashes in my in-box.

Hey, M. So SO sorry. Practice is back on. The field trip got canceled. We'll do our sunset dinner another day, OK?

I read the message again. And then again. My hand hurts; I'm clutching my messenger so hard, the sides are biting into my skin. A drop of water splatters on the trombone, and I wipe it off, then swipe my hand across my eyes. After sending back a thumbs-up symbol, I hit the off button, grab my trombone and music, and drag both back to my room.

CHAPTER TWENTY-TWO

MR. FINCH IS BAFFLED WHEN I RETURN THE TROMBONE first thing on Monday. I don't have time to tinker around with silly, pointless music. Not if I'm going to figure out how to contact the rebel Reps, keep tabs on Jake Melfin and MFI, *and* find a home for a new garden so I can fix whatever's wrong with my magic. It's going to be a lot of work. But I'm used to doing things on my own.

Maybe it's better this way.

Since V.A.M.A.'s a lot more laid-back about everything, I decide to skip for the day. I have my own assignments. My fingers swirl around our stockpile of seeds tucked away in my pocket. Part of me feels better—and less alone— having them with me.

Besides, with all of Lila's and Canter's new friends hang- ing out in our dorm room, it doesn't seem safe leaving the seeds there anymore. Not that they'd show anyone . . . but they've been so distracted lately. An accidental slip might not be out of the galaxy of possibility.

Even though the bell for the first period rang ages ago, quite a few students are still milling around the halls. It makes it easy to blend in.

Over the next few minutes, the crowd thins, and thankfully, I spot no teachers. One final glance around to make sure the coast is clear, and then I pull a seed from my pocket, gently laying it on my palm. Creased ridges frame its ivory teardrop exterior. It glows up at me as if a tiny flame burns within it.

I imagine all the possibility hiding inside the tiny shell, and as I do, the seed shines brighter, a speck of starlight, on my palm. The plant's life is just paused, waiting to begin.

Or end.

Flowers turned to ash. A rake lying abandoned on the dusty ground. An empty room filled with ghosts.

It's like dousing the ember. The light's gone. The seed's almost gray now. I carefully pluck it from my hand, the case more brittle than it was a moment ago, and tuck it back in my pocket.

I need a new home for them, I tell myself. I'll never be able to fix my Botan magic without a place to practice. I need a real garden.

I spend the whole day exploring, and find a lot of

possibilities—abandoned classrooms, dusty supply closets, hidden nooks. I bump into Bernard outside a stairwell, but he just mutters something about a forgotten assignment, turns, and doubles back the other way before I can even say hello.

The fourth or fifth bell of the day—I lost track hours ago—hums overhead, and I duck into a bathroom as the hall floods with students. Pausing by the mirror, I pull my dark hair into a ponytail and polish my glasses while I wait for the halls to clear. In the reflection, something moves behind me. I spin around.

It's a woman in a Rep uniform, bent over a sink on the other side of the room. I open my mouth to say hello, but she speaks first.

"Weren't you working this shift yesterday?" she asks, her back to me. "Why are you on bathroom rotation?"

My mouth falls open. "Wh—"

"They're short-staffed again," another voice answers from inside one of the stalls, and I duck out of sight. "If they keep sending workers to the MFI factory, they aren't going to have anyone left here."

"Where are all the MFI Reps going?" the first woman asks. "Or are they just expanding their staff?"

"They're emergency substitutes," the woman in the stall replies. "That's what I heard, anyway."

"Well, I hope they send me soon. I'd rather package

up their products than clean what's left after the kids are through with them."

The hallway outside the bathroom is quiet, and I tiptoe out. *What's happening to MFI's workers?* Could they be joining the rogue Reps? But how would they find them?

With more questions, and no answers, I continue my survey of the school, moving building to building. My gaze sweeps a darkened room in Theme. Certain it's empty, I step inside.

"Not a good choice," a voice says quietly behind me.

I whirl around to find the glum-faced boy from my Chemic class standing in the shadows.

"Neither is skulking around scaring the new kid," I snap, backing into the room.

"I wasn't skulking, and you're not that new. You've been here for weeks."

"If you weren't hiding, what were you doing?" I demand, hands perched on my hips.

"Same as you."

I raise my eyebrows. "And what's that?"

"Skipping class."

Okay, maybe he does know me a little. "Even if I was, how's it a bad idea if you're doing the same thing?"

"I didn't say cutting class was a bad idea." The boy leans against a wall. "I meant using these rooms."

"Why? They're all deserted, right?"

"Wrong. They'll be packed within the hour."

"For what? There's nothing in here."

He doesn't answer. Instead, he takes a few steps farther inside, then slaps his hand against the wall. I squint. Apart from a slight discoloration, it looks no different than the rest of the surface . . . and then the room erupts with light.

"What's happening!" I shriek, shielding my eyes. "Turn it off!"

"Just give it a minute."

I'm about to insist he take me to the Mending wing when I peek between my fingers. A sandstorm blasts out of the wall, through the center of the room. The swirling golden grains look so real, I expect a mouthful of grit. In the next instant, a turquoise wave crashes toward me, silver-white foam bubbling along the edges. I duck before I can stop myself, but just like the sand, the wave is simply a trick of the lights—some sort of advanced hologram.

The boy watches me closely as I drift to the center of the room. All I see is gray. Pearly white dust clouds mask my feet with every step. This scene couldn't be more familiar—a simulated Lunar landscape.

"Next!" I call, and the boy laughs as he taps the wall again.

The dust changes from ashy gray to crimson, a projection of Martian terrain? Massive craters edged in umbers and golds rise around me, while a bloodred haze floats up wherever my feet touch. The boy hits another button and I gasp as the room changes again. Without realizing it, I dig my hands into my pockets and clutch at the trove of seeds.

I'm back in my garden. Emerald vines weave over my head, dripping leaves and blossoms like a rainbow-colored veil. I pass beneath them, and even though I know they're not real, I can't resist lifting my hand to brush them. My fingers slide right through, but the flowers still sway as if nudged by my touch. Magenta roses, periwinkle lilacs, and patches of canary-yellow daisies tangle on either side of me. I can practically smell their sweet fragrance hanging in the air.

The boy must confuse my astonishment with fear. "It's not dangerous. It's just a projection," he says quickly. "It's my favorite, actually," he murmurs, walking through the hologram garden to meet me in the center of the room.

"I can't believe it's allowed," I softly reply as I turn to look into the boy's dark brown eyes. "We can barely even talk about flowers where I'm from."

"We had to get special permission from the Venusian Governing Council for a performance." He reaches toward a branch drooping from a weeping willow. "We were supposed to delete it straight after."

"But you didn't."

He shrugs. "As far as the teachers know, it's gone. I found

a way to save the projection before they could wipe the file. It only activates at my touch now." He flutters his fingers through the cascading leaves.

"And you're showing me because . . . ?"

He shrugs. "I don't know, actually. It just seemed like I could trust you." He turns back to face me, and I notice glints of gold shimmering in his eyes. "I guess I probably shouldn't have. For all I know, you'll go straight to the school director."

"I'm not really the tattling type."

He makes a show of swiping a hand across his forehead. "Phew. That could have gotten awkward." Studying me studying him, he adds, "I'm not like the other kids here. I'm not like anyone, really." The last part is quiet enough, I wonder if he meant it for me or for himself.

"I could tell. I'm not like most people, either."

"Most people are boring." He watches me for a moment. "What about the kids you came here with? Are they like you, or are they dull as a dwarf star?"

"My best friends, Canter and Lila, are interstellar. And Bernard is, too. The only dud is Kyle."

"Kyle Melfin?"

"Yes," I say, my eyes narrowing. "Have you met him?"

"No. He's just in my Advanced Chemic Instrumentation and Magication class. Which is as boring as it sounds."

"Nothing seems boring here. Not like where I'm from, anyway. Everything there is so . . . strict."

"Boring is still boring, even if you add a bit of song and dance," he says darkly. "Maybe the take on magic here has a few new angles, but deviate too far, and you're an immediate outcast."

"What sort of magic do you do?" I ask.

"I'm a Chemic," he replies stiffly. It's the same way I answer when people ask me, and my heart skips a beat.

"So, you use your magic to make pictures and sculptures and all that visual kind of art?"

"I said I'm not like the rest of them, remember?"

"Then what *do* you do?" I press.

The darkness evaporates from his eyes, and a mischievous glint replaces it. "I haven't decided if I trust you *that* much yet." He glances at the garden around us. "I'd better turn this off. Like I said, this building will be filled with students soon."

"Then this is the last place I want to be."

"Me too." He presses his hand against the wall and plunges us back into darkness. He's about to slip into the hall again when he pauses in the doorway. That glint is still there when he glances back at me, burning like a sun flare. "Come on. I'll show you the good hiding spots."

The old Myra would have followed him in a second.

What would she have to lose? But New Myra should be more cautious. I don't even know this kid's name, and getting into trouble will mean a one-way ticket back to the Moon. I should really talk to Canter and Lila. Maybe bring them with me and ask him to show us all these hiding spots.

I'm sure they're too busy.

I shouldn't go.

Somehow, I still follow him out the door.

CHAPTER TWENTY-THREE

"IF WE'RE CUTTING CLASS TOGETHER, AND YOU'RE going to show me your best hiding spots, don't you think we should know each other's names?" I ask as we pass through Theme's halls.

"I don't see how a word someone assigned you at birth matters in the grand scheme of things, but I guess if you want."

I snort. "Someone as in your parents?"

He shrugs. "Yeah, them."

"Okay . . . well, the word I usually use to refer to myself is *Myra*."

"People tend to use the words *Noah Morris* when they're talking to and about me." He looks thoughtful for a moment. "Usually more *about* me than *to* me."

This kid is like my Venusian twin. "Um, nice to meet you, Noah."

He doesn't answer. When we reach an all-glass door, he presses it open and salty, humid air blasts my face. A walkway of the same clear glass connecting the buildings winds around the perimeter, and my stomach drops as we step onto it.

"It's so strange being on a planet where you can actually go outside," I say, squinting in the bright sunlight. "Back on the Moon, everything's in gravity enclosures with carefully controlled artificial atmosphere."

"I think I'd like that better," Noah says, leaning over a railing to scan the sea below. "It's so bright here. I feel like I'm constantly under a spotlight."

"I bet most kids at V.A.M.A. love being in the spotlight." I peer down beside him and watch the navy-blue water splashing against the side of the building.

"You're absolutely right," he says, turning to face the school. "So where are your best friends?"

"In class having an interstellar time with all their new friends." I take a breath and try to erase the bitterness from my voice. "They got swept up in the next V.A.M.A performance."

"Corrupted by the dark side. My condolences." He walks to where Theme and Language meet, plants his hands on either side of the seam, and hoists himself up so he's sitting on the crease between them.

"What are you doing?"

"It's perfectly safe. Don't worry," he says, then turns and crawls farther back between the buildings. "I've done this hundreds of times."

Before I can yell at him to get down, he drops behind the walls and disappears.

"Noah!" I stand on tiptoe, trying to see over edge, holding my breath as I wait for the inevitable splash.

His head pops up, and he scowls at me. "Do you want to see my favorite hiding spot or not?"

"If it involves falling into the Sea of da Vinci, then *not*."

"There's a walkway on this side, too." He hoists himself up so he's once again sitting on the seam. "It's just over this gap."

"There's no way on the Moon I'm doing that," I say crossing my arms.

"We're not on the Moon."

I'm about to snap that it's just an expression when I hear a soft thud and Noah disappears again. My stomach drops to my toes as I lean as far as I can over the railing, but I don't see a trace of him. "Noah?"

"I'm right here," he calls back cheerfully. "In my perfect hiding spot. Thoroughly undetectable by teachers. Lying here thinking how I'll never get caught aimlessly wandering the halls during class."

I sigh and lean back against the rail, listening to the waves crash below me.

"All right, never mind. I get it. I guess you are like the others."

I know he's just trying to bait me. Still, I find myself pressing up against the outside of the bubble building. Only then do I notice the handholds carved into the wall. Looking down, I find small ledges jutting out at the perfect height for my feet.

I stay still for a moment, calculating the risks against the potential rewards. All the while, I can feel the building moving beneath me. Inside, the bubbles' shifting and bobbing in the water are imperceptible. Out here, my hands are increasingly slippery from sweat or sea mist—maybe both.

"Blast it," I whisper, taking a deep breath before scurrying up the building and swinging my legs over the side. Several feet below me, a narrow deck runs along the inside edges of the two buildings, and a triangle of open sea stretches to Spectacle.

Noah's standing with his back to me, looking out at the water.

When I hop down beside him, he jumps, backpedaling away from the railing, his expression shifting from surprise to elation. "Wow, you really did it! Guess you're not like the others after all."

I push my glasses up from where they slipped down my sweaty nose and take in my surroundings. The space isn't much bigger than the living room in my apartment back home. "What's this for?"

"I think it used to be some sort of maintenance access, but no one uses it anymore. I doubt anyone even remembers it's here." He glances around at the secluded nook and smiles. "I call it the secret cove."

I sit in front of the railing, watching the navy water sloshing against the walls. "It really is a perfect hiding spot." I look up at him. "Do you come here a lot?"

"Every chance I can," he says, settling beside me. "They're super lax about attendance, as you probably noticed, but you can't skip all the time. I make an appearance every now and then. Give the teachers a song and dance about homework . . ."

"And they buy it?"

He squints at me. "There's nothing *to* buy. I literally do a song or a dance about what I studied. Sometimes both."

I shake my head. "This school is so strange."

"What do you actually do on the Moon?" he asks. "Just study theory and demonstrate practical magic exactly how the textbook says?"

"Yes," I reply with a laugh. "If I tried to play a song

instead of doing math equations, Ms. Goble would put me in detention for a month. And probably send me to the Mender wing."

"I'm jealous." The glum look I saw Noah wearing in our Chemic class has returned.

"Why? It's so boring."

"That's why I like it. It's simple. Everything here is too complicated. Sure, you have to know your Creer inside and out. The proper way, like how you study. But once you've gotten the basic principles, you have to put this whole artistic spin on it." He turns and looks at me with tired eyes. "Do you have any idea how exhausting it is to be creative *all the time*? And in ways you don't even like? I'd give anything to recite theory and perform magical experiments step by step, straight out of a lesson plan."

"But didn't you say you had your own magical angle?"

He sighs. "If I could do that all day, I wouldn't mind the whole *creative spin* thing so much, but around here, no one likes my kind of magic. Plus, nowadays, it's pretty much impossible anyway."

"Why?"

He narrows his eyes. "Remember I said I wasn't sure I trusted you that much?"

I narrow mine right back at him. "Remember when I followed a kid I barely know over an *ocean* risking almost certain death to get to a supposed hiding spot I couldn't even see?"

"Sea."

I glare at him. "Why are you mimicking me?"

Noah bursts out laughing. "You said over the *ocean*. It's not an ocean. It's a sea, see?"

"Oh, for comet's sake," I mutter. "And don't change the subject. I think I've more than proven I'm trustworthy. Tell me what your magic is, why people don't like it, and why it's impossible."

"Fine. Don't go all supernova," he grumbles. "Did the Lunar Network have any buzz about a food shortage last year?"

My stomach rotates like a satellite. "Yes," I say slowly.

"*Yes,* you saw, or *yes,* the Moon had a food shortage issue?"

"Yes and yes," I say, forcing myself to breathe normally. "Yes to both."

"The shortage hit here, too, as you can probably tell from the nasty food they're serving in the cafeteria."

"What does that have to do with your magic?"

"Everything." He hesitates. "I'm a Chemic, officially. But really, I use my magic to . . ."

"To what?" I all but yell. "Sorry."

He waves away my apology, then presses his chin onto

his hand, staring out at the horizon. "I make food," he says quietly.

"Like, like . . . you *grow* food?"

"Shooting stars, no!" he says with a laugh. "I said I'm weird, not delusional. I know only food production Chemics can *grow* food. Even our upper-year Chemics hardly study that. The processes are way too rigid. I bet not a single Venusian works in the food labs, though with the current situation, maybe a little creativity would do some good. Anyway, what I mean is, I like to *cook* food. My passion is the culinary arts."

"Oh," I say, wilting with disappointment, then realize Noah's *big secret* probably warrants more of a reaction. "I've never heard of Chemics cooking before. But it sounds like that should be right up V.A.M.A.'s alley."

"Not this," he says sadly. "They really don't count it as art, but the faculty let me plug along with it so long as I participate in other *creative outlets*. But with the food shortage, my ingredients have mostly dried up, and so has my ma—"

He stops himself, looking terrified.

I gently put a hand on his shoulder. "And your magic has, too?"

He nods, pushing his legs back so he's leaning against the wall. "Mr. Kote keeps trying to help me translate my culinary passions into other artistic media. He sends me links to new *recipes* he finds, but they aren't really cooking instructions." Noah sighs. "They're more like exhibitions of people making edible sculptures. He thinks it might *inspire* me. Get me to transition my Chemic magic into some more acceptable art form."

"Did you like anything about it?"

He shrugs. "It gave me some ideas for new garnishes. He's a pretty nice guy, for a teacher. But it's no use."

"Is that what he was talking to you about on my first day of class? It looked like you were having a pretty serious conversation."

Noah nods, studying me. "Sorry, I know this probably makes next to no sense to you."

"It makes more sense than you think," I accidentally say out loud.

Noah eyes me curiously. "Why?"

I bite my tongue, then adjust my glasses. "Only one secret trade per day."

"Okay, that's fair," he answers with a chuckle, that mischievous glint back in his eyes. "Meet you here tomorrow?"

CHAPTER TWENTY-FOUR

A FEW DAYS LATER, I PACK MY BAG FOR THE DAY. NOT with books, but with my messenger and an extra sweatshirt. I made an appearance in all my classes yesterday, so today I'm free to orbit.

"What time did you get back last night?" I ask Lila as she emerges from the bathroom. "I didn't even hear you come in."

"It was a little after curfew," she says, digging around in her dresser. "We had to do a test run with a new lighting sequence, so we had special permission to stay late."

"How are you getting any studying done for your Mender classes with so many rehearsals?" I ask, careful to keep my tone light and upbeat.

"It's bizarre, but I haven't had a single Mender test since we got here. My Mender teacher says in our Creer, practical magic is more important than reciting theory." She beams. "My grades have never been higher. They're so good that when we're back at S.L.A.M. next year, I could actually get a question wrong on an exam and not completely panic."

"Wow, that's really interstellar," I say, and mean it. Even a slightly less stressed Lila will be a vast improvement over last term.

"Want to walk to class together after breakfast?" Lila asks. "We've got Kote's Chemic class first period."

"Can't," I say, closing my bag and slinging it over my shoulder. "I'm not going today."

Lila frowns as she grabs her own bag and follows me out the door. "You've been missing a lot lately. Canter says he never sees you going to or from classes."

I fight back a grin, and an unexpected swell of surprise that they even noticed. "The teachers don't seem to care."

"Still," Lila says, chewing her lip. "It's going to affect your grades at some point."

"What is?" Canter asks, falling in step beside us. His hair is slicked up in a new style, his blond locks pointing straight at the ceiling as if he's been electrified.

"Myra's back to skipping class all the time, like last year," Lila says, shooting me a stern glance.

I shrug. "I'm doing my own thing. Just like you guys."

"But *we* go to class," Canter counters.

"Look, everything's fine," I reply. "We're not at S.L.A.M. Like I said, the teachers here don't care."

"But what are you doing when you're not in lessons?" Lila asks, looking far from convinced.

I toss my hair over my shoulder. "Oh, nothing all that exciting. Just hanging out with Noah."

Canter's eyes narrow. "Noah? Who's Noah?"

Excitement bubbles in my chest—*Is he jealous?*—but I squash it down. "This kid in my Chemic class. He's been showing me around. He knows all the best hiding spots."

"That's galactic!" Canter says with a grin. "Maybe you can find a good spot for the you-know-what," he adds in a whisper. Instinctively, I stick my hands in my pockets.

"You haven't told your new friend about, er, anything, right?" Lila asks.

"Of course not," I say quickly. Not that it hasn't been tempting. "We've got plenty of other stuff to talk about."

"That's great, Myra!" Lila's face lights up with a smile. "I'm so glad you met him. That's the whole point of the transfer program, right? To make new friends from other Settlements."

"No," I say, stopping in the middle of the hall, heat rising in my face and neck. "The point was supposed to be finding the Reps."

Canter flinches. Lila's smile falls like a meteor. "I know.

I just meant—We *will*, Myra, I swear. We're going to find them."

"We're just getting settled," Canter adds, then adds a wink. "Working on fitting in. Otherwise, people will suspect our motives."

"Right," I say, turning into another corridor.

"Wait!" Lila calls. "What about breakfast?"

"I'm meeting Noah," I reply, not looking back.

"Oh, okay. Have fun!"

"Keep an eye out for you-know-what!" Canter adds.

I wave over my shoulder before disappearing around the corner.

Three women in Rep uniforms carry a sculpture suspended on a small platform. The colors of the form shift and glow with some inner Chemic magic. Or maybe Elector. It's hard to tell if the piece is lit from within or the material's actually glowing. I carefully maneuver around them. I don't want to startle them and have them lose their grip.

Usually, Noah and I meet at the secret cove, but today he promised to show me his magic while the other kids are at breakfast. He swore it would be galaxies better than anything the cafeteria was offering up. I don't doubt that.

A few minutes later, I'm knocking on his door. He answers, dressed in a button-down shirt and pants so crisp, they look like they're straight out of a compression chamber. I glance down at my own baggy sweatshirt and faded leggings. "I didn't know this was a formal thing. I would have dressed up."

Noah laughs and beckons me inside. The door whizzes shut behind me. "I like to look professional when I'm doing my culinary thing." His cheeks color slightly. "It makes me feel like I'm in a real restaurant."

"Okay, you're seriously hyping this up now," I say, taking a step back. "I thought you were going to swish some Chemic compounds around and make bread or something."

He grins. "That's more or less it, but I hope it'll be more impressive than just a hunk of bread."

"Anything is better than that junk they're serving in the cafeteria," I say, sweeping by him and flopping onto a neatly made bed. "Don't you have roommates?"

"I got a single this year," he replies, turning away to poke around some jars and bins on the desk. "There aren't many available, but I volunteered to do extra work around the school last term. And it's a good thing, too. I'm, um, technically not supposed to have this stuff."

I peek around him at the assortment of powders, liquids, and packages arranged in neat rows. "I was wondering how you scored all those ingredients when the whole galaxy is scrambling."

"I started stockpiling a long time ago so I could practice my magic in private." He selects three jars and a vial of crimson liquid and empties them into a bowl. "It really wasn't a big deal back then. And I guess I should have turned them in when everything went cosmic, but . . ."

"It wouldn't have done much good, anyway," I finish. "How much food could all this possibly produce?"

"Not enough." He chooses another vial of what looks like emerald sand and raises it to his eye. "I'm almost out of most of them, anyway."

Noah keeps pulling ingredients and I power on his bookpod while I wait. A Chemic textbook materializes in the air, and I swipe through the pages until I find a chapter on food production. The photos accompanying the text remind me of the ugly beginnings of my Chemic-grown plant in Mr. DeGraf's class, just shadows of the real thing—gray, wilted, feeble. The unit details how Chemic magic reduces the plants to compound form, either dried or liquefied, then reconstitutes them into the various food items that were sold at stores for cooking.

"I've never seen a Chemic make actual food before," I say eagerly, powering off the bookpod.

"Not many people have. Even in normal times, they didn't want just anyone messing around with it. Not to mention it's really difficult. Teachers usually save that sort of work for older students."

"Pretty amazing you picked it up then," I say, and his cheeks go pink. "What are you, some sort of Chemic hotshot?"

He scoffs. "Not likely. Just food-obsessed. Okay, you ready for some culinary arts, M?"

"Sounds better than the other arts I've heard so much about lately."

Noah picks up the bowl and gives it a swirl, and then another. He keeps rotating the contents, swishing them around like a whirlpool of sand. After a minute, he crosses the room and shoves the bowl into my hands.

"What—"

"You'll have a better view this way," he says, his eyes twinkling. "Just hold it still."

I'm motionless, though what's inside the bowl is anything but. Noah screws up his face, concentrating, and the ingredients spin faster, rising out of the bowl, rotating in midair. He flicks his fingers and the crimson liquid in one of the vials on his desk bubbles up. When it connects with the dry ingredients, they fizz and crackle, shifting from red to violet to sunshine yellow. After a moment, the mixture merges, settling into a lumpy, fluffy form. He guides the mixture back into the bowl, takes it from my hands, and sets it aside.

Next, he scatters blue powder across the top of his desk, then dips his hand into a container holding something clear and gelatinous, scooping out a handful. He works the goo into the powder, molding and shaping it with his fingers until he's formed the concoction into a couple of round patties. He wipes his hands on a towel before picking up a small container, then shakes white flakes over the cobalt-blue mounds, and they glow like flat, round bulbs. I blink and the blue's vanished; the patties are now a creamy beige.

Noah is really in the zone now. He barely looks at me as he conducts the rest of the ingredients. Multicolored sand whirls overheard. Liquids fly through the air like sideways rain, combining, and then mixing with the sand or hovering until called for, pulsing like floating prisms.

Soon, the room is filled with mouthwatering aromas. It's been so long since I had normal food (apart from the freshly grown fruits and vegetables from my garden), I've forgotten what real cooking smells like. My stomach rumbles as Noah cooks his newly created ingredients, dropping them onto a small griddle on the corner of his desk.

Finally, he assembles everything on two plates. Scrambled eggs with diced tomatoes and a sprinkling of cheese and parsley. Toasted bread heaped with some sort of nutty chocolate paste. A hash of potatoes, ham, and onions, flecked with spices.

My plate's cleared faster than you can say *interstellar*. Noah's fruits and vegetables don't taste nearly as good as the ones from the moongarden, but even so, it's the best meal I've had in years. Maybe ever.

"You should try it all together," Noah suggests.

I snag a bit of everything onto my fork and pop it into my mouth. "How in the galaxy does V.A.M.A. not count this as art?" I mumble through my last bite.

Noah's been watching me inhale my food with a look of apprehension on his face, as if he's worried I've been faking my enthusiasm. "You like it?"

"Like?" I swallow and look down at my empty plate. *Would Noah judge me if I licked the crumbs?* "That was incredible! I mean, the food we've had lately has been horrible, so it's not a fair comparison, but I've never had anything even close to this."

Noah's whole face lights up.

"The flavors and the textures and the *smell*. It all just *works*, you know? Everything goes together, like the notes of a song."

"Thanks, M." Noah's smile is so big, it almost reaches his ears. "I try to find ingredients that complement one another. Flavors that might not seem to go together, but they build into something even better. The idea's to make the meal an experience, like you're on a trip and each bite is a new destination."

I flop back on the bed, holding my full stomach. "I'll take two tickets back to wherever I just visited, please."

Noah laughs. "Unfortunately, that may not be possible. That was my last compound for eggs, and I'm almost out of the ham powder, too."

I sit back up. "You cannot tease me with such an amazing meal and then send me off to the cafeteria for tasteless jelly squares."

"Believe me, I wish I didn't have to." He sifts through his jars and canisters. "I might have enough left for more bread and that chocolate spread. If you want to invite your Lunar friends over sometime, I'm happy to show you all a bit of Venusian culinary hospitality."

"No way," I quickly respond. "I'm not sharing any of this, especially if your ingredients are almost gone. I wonder, though." I lean back on my elbows. "Not all food was plant-based. We've got animals. Why can't we use real chickens for eggs and animals for protein?"

Noah rubs at his hair. "We could, but the Settlements don't really have the space from a production standpoint. Not like back on the Old World. Plus, mass farming contributed to the climate collapse." He shrugs. "We've been using plant-based meat substitutes even before we left the Old World. The only way to get food production back on track is with plants."

I'm quiet, considering what he's said.

Noah chuckles. "Too bad Venus doesn't have gardens."

Neither did the Moon. But maybe it's time to fix that.

CHAPTER TWENTY-FIVE

AFTER OUR SECRET BREAKFAST, I FORCE NOAH TO show me all his other hiding spots, determined to find one that could work for a new garden. Of course, I can't tell him that.

"I don't know why we're bothering, M," he grumbles. "I already showed you my best spot. Speaking of, let's go hang at the cove."

"It's good to have options," I say, peering into a bathroom. Inside, it's dark, but not pitch-black. There must be a window letting in natural light. And obviously it has access to water. "Why don't you hang out here again? Seems totally deserted. And you don't have to worry about bad weather, like at the cove."

"Think about why a bathroom might be out of service."

I frown as I step inside. That's when the smell hits me. "Oh," I say, pulling my sweatshirt up over my nose. "Never mind."

"Told you," he mutters, hurrying past. "When I first found it, the stench wasn't so bad. But it's gotten worse, and now . . ."

"It smells like a solar-powered sewage plant?"

"Exactly. Now, can we *please* go to the cove?"

"Oh, fine." None of the other options were interstellar, but there were a few I could maybe circle back to later. I adjust the hem of my sweatshirt, discreetly nudging the seeds in my pocket. *I'll find a home for you soon. I promise.*

Noah and I emerge into the sunlight. At the cove, he stretches out on the ground as usual, folding his hands behind his head, while I sink down to lean against the railing. The water's darker than usual, churning a navy so deep it's almost black. I reach through a gap in the bars and wet my fingertips.

"Storm's brewing," Noah comments, watching me.

I look up. There's not a single cloud in the pale orange sky. "How can you tell?"

"You can always see a storm in the sea before the sky. It's like the water knows what's coming."

As if the weather heard him, a breeze picks up, whipping strands into my face. "Should we go?" I ask, trying to tuck my hair behind my ear. I don't really want to leave. I've never seen a storm in person before. But the water below my feet is looking angrier and angrier.

Noah shrugs. "It might pass us by. We'll know when it's time to leave. If you don't want to get soaked, though, we should head inside now."

I gape at him. "You mean it's going to *rain?*"

"Why?" he asks with a smirk. "Are you going to melt?"

"Even if I were, I wouldn't leave. I've never seen rain before."

He laughs. "It's not that interstellar. It's just water. We've got tons of it here."

"Not falling from the sky!" I tilt my head up to watch the storm roll in.

The wind's blowing stronger now, and crimson clouds sweep quickly across the sky. I'm not going to miss my first rainstorm. I'm determined to wait it out. That is until the ground starts rocking like a seesaw.

"Uh, is the building supposed to be moving?" I ask, pulling myself to my feet.

"V.A.M.A.'s technically more of a boat than a building, so yes. If it didn't move with the waves, it'd capsize."

"Capsize?"

"Sink."

"Oh." I grip the rail tighter and glance up at the sky again. It's turned the color of amber. Still no rain, though. "Then this is normal?"

"Just another day on the Morning Star," he says with a glint in his eye as he rises and joins me.

"The what?"

"It's a nickname for Venus," he explains with a shrug. "I don't know why."

The walkway gives another lurch and I stumble, smashing my hip into the metal. I gasp and dig my hand into my sweatshirt pocket. Noah must think I've hurt myself, but I couldn't care less about an injury. It's that the metal pole hit exactly where the seeds are hidden.

Please let them be okay. I gather some in my hand, doing my best to inspect them with my fingers. *I'm sorry. You'll be okay, I swear.*

"Are you all right?" Noah asks as he stares at the hand still clutched in my pocket. "You hit that railing pretty hard."

"It'll just be a bruise. No big deal."

"Should we go inside? It's getting pretty rough."

"Let's stay another few minutes. I really want to see rain."

We wait and watch as the sky turns from amber to mahogany. Clouds swirl overheard, and the wind's gusting so hard now, I don't even bother trying to keep my hair out of my face.

"It's sort of beautiful!" I yell over the roar. The whole building's rocking; I can see the neighboring bubbles bobbing on either side.

"Let's go!" he shouts back. "We can come back out when the storm passes."

I reluctantly nod, but as we turn to leave, water splatters in front of my feet. At first, I think it must be spray from the sea, but then more drips onto my shoe, onto my shoulder, onto my head.

"It's rain!" I shriek, turning my face upward to watch the droplets. They run down my cheeks, as if I'm weeping the sky's tears. I thrust my hand out to catch more, but as I do, the sound of ripping echoes in my ears louder than the rumble of the storm. I look down and see my pocket sagging at the seam. Seeds cascade from the tear, scattering across the deck.

"What was that?" Noah demands, squinting as the seeds, caught by the wind, fly into the water. "What was in your pocket?"

"*No!*" I half yell, half sob, though it's barely audible over the pounding of the rain. I hurtle to the railing, watching as the seeds—*all my precious seeds*—bob away. I reach out, willing my magic to call them back, but they swirl in the waves, and then begin to sink. "*NO!*"

Disbelief, then icy despair wash through me. "Oh no. *No. Please. No.*"

"What happened?" Noah shouts, leaning over to see why I'm so upset.

I sink to my knees, resting my head against the metal.

Noah stoops beside me, then plucks something off the ground. He holds the tiny dark fleck between his thumb and index finger, squinting at it so closely, his eyelashes brush against it, and I can feel my stomach sink. "M, is this what I think it is?"

I look at him but can't answer. *My seeds. All the seeds. Gone. Forever.*

"Is this—were those—seeds?" Noah asks. The wind's died down now, so he doesn't need to yell for me to hear him. The rain's still falling in sheets, though.

I can't see through my glasses, so I yank them off and wipe them halfheartedly on my soaked, ripped sweatshirt. My throat is so tight the words won't come out. *It doesn't matter what they are. What they were. Now they're nothing.*

Noah's eyes go wide. "And now they're—" He frantically looks out over the water, the surface already much calmer than it was minutes before. "Do you have more?"

I shake my head, and Noah sinks beside me, looking almost as sad as I feel. "You had seeds," he whispers. "Real seeds." When I don't respond, he asks, "Were they for growing flowers? Or were there . . . were there seeds for food, too?"

"They were for everything," I whisper. *What am I going to do?*

Noah holds the solitary seed out to me on his palm. "There's still this one," he says hopefully.

I pluck it up, raising it to my eyes, then shake my head and drop it back into his palm. "It's not enough."

"Can you get more? Where did you get those ones from?" he asks, his brow furrowed. "You had seeds! For growing *food*. Do you know what we could do with those? We could feed the galaxy! They could save everything!"

"There are no more," I say dully. "And that was the plan." My eyes well with tears. "And I just ruined it. Over *rain*."

Noah's quiet. He sits staring at the tiny seed like it's the most precious commodity in the universe. And maybe it is. Especially now. "Tell me," he finally says, his gaze sad but determined.

I wipe my eyes with the back of my hand. "Tell you what?"

"The whole plan."

I don't know why—maybe it's the loss of the seeds, and with them, my magic, my hopes, and my whole future, or maybe it's that I haven't had a real conversation with Canter and Lila for so long—but for whatever reason, I do. The words start pouring out of me as easily as I spilled the seeds, and don't stop until I've shared everything: the moongarden, my Botan magic, Bernie, the elusive group of free Reps, the run-ins with Jake Melfin, and how my anonymous tip exposed the food cloning crisis to the public. I leave out the parts about Fiona and Canter's Botan magic, though. That's not my story to tell.

After I finish, Noah's silent for a long time.

"Say something," I finally blurt out.

"I don't know what *to* say." He stands and peers out over the railing. "So you were the one who exposed Jake Melfin's cover-up?"

I cringe. *Maybe I should have left that part out, too.*

But Noah looks impressed. "Because of you, he got kicked off the Lunar Governing Council."

I raise my eyebrows. "I'm surprised you heard about that." I wouldn't think the Lunar Council would be of much interest to a kid on Venus.

He shrugs and looks away. "MFI supplies the food for everyone. It was big news here. I remember hearing about the Council thing, too."

I shrug. "Well, he got to keep his company."

Noah shakes his head, his focus fixed on the horizon. "I can't believe it. I've never heard of plant magic."

"You weren't supposed to," I reply bitterly. "But it's real."

"I know," he says quietly. "I don't know how to explain it, but I can feel it in my bones." He turns and hands me the last seed. I clench it in my fist. "I wish I could have seen them," he says, his voice quiet. "More than anything."

My chest hurts, as though it's been dented like a moon crater. I study my last seed, and love blossoms within me, replacing the ache. At least for a little while. "Watch this, then."

I twirl my fingers over the bluish-black seed on my palm

and it glows, first a pearly white, then silver, then as gold as the sunlight now sparkling on the sea. Noah gasps as an emerald stem sprouts up and a tangle of roots trail through my fingers. Leaves curl out, one at a time, and finally, a peony the color of a Venusian sunset bursts out of the top of the shoot.

I hold the flower out to Noah, and he slowly extends his hand, gingerly brushing the layers and layers of delicate, ruffled petals with his fingertips.

"Not food," I say, patting the bloom and watching sadly as my magic wobbles. The flower shrivels and the plant shrinks back in on itself until it's once again a small seed. "But still pretty cool."

"I'll say." Noah leans against the railing, still in a daze. "And there're more of them. Loads more. Right in front of us!"

"And who-knows-how-many feet down," I say, sighing as I look down at the waves.

He stares out toward the horizon. "I don't know why, but all I want to do is just reach out and touch them. I mean, they're right there." He turns to me. "Can you use your magic to pull them back up?"

I hold out my hand toward the sea, as if reaching for a friend to help them back onto the walkway. For a wild moment, I consider diving in before the seeds can drift too far. I even lift a foot onto the railing.

"What are you doing?" Noah demands, panic lacing his voice. "It's too deep. You can't go in there."

"That's about the only thing I can do!" I scream, then kick at the metal pole. "Maybe it's better they stay down there where they can't hurt anyone anymore."

"You mean can't hurt *you* anymore?" Noah asks quietly.

"What are you talking about? Finding the garden was the best thing that ever happened to me."

"Do you always feel that way, though?"

I open my mouth to snap *Of course,* but the words shrivel and die on my tongue. Shame rushes through me, and I sink to the ground. "No," I whisper. "If I'd never found the moongarden, Bernie might still be alive. The plants might still be alive. Because I found them—because I *interfered*—they're both gone."

"Do you think if they had a choice, they'd wish that, too, though?" Noah asks. "They'd prefer you never found the garden?"

"I can't exactly ask a plant," I reply, my voice harsher than I intend. But I know that's not completely true. I force myself to relive those last terrible moments in the garden as Director Weathers's mixture burned the garden to the ground. All except one flower—one perfect daffodil that survived just long enough to say goodbye.

"What about Bernie?" prods Noah. "He could have refused to help. But he didn't."

"He wanted to be there," I say slowly, remembering my earliest conversations with him. "He wanted to help the garden to continue on."

"It sounds like he wanted to give the plants a chance. He wanted to try."

"*If you try, you never know what sort of magic could happen,*" I blurt out. Bernie's words.

Noah nods. "Exactly. I bet he'd want you to keep going."

"He'd want the garden to keep going, too," I whisper, stooping down and reaching my hand out. The water sloshes against the side of the building, spraying my hands and arms and face. For a moment, I'm back in my garden, the leaves and stalks and vines tickling my cheeks, brushing against my arms, snagging in my hair. Bernie chuckles as he explains horticulture to me, leaning on his rake, scanning our progress with pride. Singing with the sunflower bloom.

If I'd never found the secret lab, I wouldn't have those memories. I wouldn't even know what a garden looks like, or what Bernie's laugh sounds like, or what having magic glow and bubble inside me feels like. I wouldn't have Canter for a friend, and maybe not Lila, either.

I smile as I see the whole, sprawling garden in my mind's eye, rising in spite of everything out of the chalky moondust. If a garden could grow there, couldn't it grow anywhere?

For the first time in a long while, I want it to. Without any trace of regret.

The sea boils below me, bubbling and swirling. Before I can push myself up, something surges from the water. At first, I think it's a tentacle from a sea monster.

I go to pull Noah back, then freeze, my eyes wide.

There's a tree growing out of the sea.

CHAPTER TWENTY-SIX

THOUGH DRIPPING SEAWATER, THE PALE BRANCHES
and jade-colored leaves are unmistakable.

"What . . . is that?" Noah asks.

"It's a plant," I explain. "A tree."

"But that's impossible."

"It's not." A joy I haven't felt in what feels like a hundred
light-years burns through me. Then, without even thinking, I reach my hand toward it. The tree shoots up another
two feet.

"How can it grow, though?" he asks, his brow furrowed.
"All the way from the seafloor, through the water, to the
surface? That's impossible."

"A moongarden is supposed to be impossible, too," I
remind him. "The magic filled in what nature couldn't,
I guess."

"What about the rest of them?" Noah asks. "The other seeds."

Hope flickers inside me like an ember, and I roll up my sleeves. Lila hasn't been drawing fake Chemic Inscriptions over my Botan ones lately. She's been too busy, and I haven't been able to bring myself to remind her. Noah's gaze crawls over the exposed skin on my arms, both of which are now covered with Botan Inscriptions. One of my earlier ones, an oak tree, looks exactly the same as the one stretching up in front of us. I stare at the water, calling up my magic. My hands and arms tingle like they fell asleep, and a tickling sensation trails over my skin, burning hot. The water bubbles like it's boiling, the turquoise churning to a foamy white, and I can just make out something beneath the surface. A lot of somethings.

Noah gasps as stalks and stems and bushes and branches sprout up out of the waves along the perimeter of the cove. Vines crawl over the railing, winding around it like a trellis, spilling across the deck. Flowers burst from the vines, and on some of the other plants pushing up from the water, peonies and sunflowers and lilacs, all turning their prism of petals toward the sun.

I recognize other plants, too. Ears of corn, stalks of wheat and barley, fruit trees, and bushes overflowing with berries.

I can't help laughing.

Noah whips around to look at me. "What's so funny?"

"I was just wondering how we're going to harvest the foods that grow underground, like potatoes and carrots."

"If you can do this," Noah says, shaking his head, "I'm pretty sure you can do anything."

I reach out and pat a blueberry bush like it's an old friend. "This area isn't visible from anywhere else at V.A.M.A., right?" I ask, plucking a couple of berries and popping one in my mouth before handing the other to Noah.

"Nope." When he bites down, his face sparkles like a star. "I've checked. The only place you can see this cove is here. None of the walls bordering it have windows, and the glare from the buildings along with the shadows they cast make this area look like a dark hole to any ships overhead."

"Perfect." I turn and meet his eyes. "You can't tell anyone about this place. You know that, right?"

"Of course I know that," he says, taking in the seagarden. "Who would believe me, anyway?"

Noah and I agree to meet at the cove during every class we skip. We also decide to scale back on cutting. Even if V.A.M.A.'s faculty seems lenient, we don't want to push it and risk someone searching for us.

As the days pass, I teach Noah all I know about gardening. Using tools scavenged from supply closets, I show him when and how to prune. We begin harvesting crops already ripe and ready for picking. Noah brings his cooking equipment from his room and sets it up in the cove. The dishes he can create with our freshly grown fruits and vegetables are out of this orbit.

Under our care, the plants are thriving, maybe even more than they did in the moongarden. It must be all the sunlight and water.

I'm not sure if it's the size of this garden or the peace I've found with what happened to my old one—maybe a little bit of both—but my magic seems fully recovered. And the seagarden isn't the only thing that's growing. New Inscriptions sprout all over my skin, covering my arms, creeping over my shoulders and completely obscuring the lone Chemic Inscription from last term. Vines crisscross my collarbone like a bronze necklace, dotted with sharp crimson thorns and pale ivory flowers.

Canter and Lila don't notice. Which might be for the best. I haven't told them about the seagarden yet. Or Noah learning our secret.

Part of me knows I should. But would they even care? They don't seem interested in much lately if it's not about their silly performance.

It's been a week since the seagarden burst to life. Lila's not usually back from rehearsal until after I'm asleep, but tonight she's early. Something about waiting for the Tekkies to finish the next phase of set design.

While I get ready to go to sleep, she seems intent on

catching up. She sits cross-legged on her bed, still in her school clothes, as I pull on my pajamas and clean my glasses.

"Hey, Myra," she says suddenly, making me stumble. She'd been in the middle of another monologue about the performance, and I'd tuned out.

I spray another cloud of cleaning mist on the lenses and look up. A smile tugs at my lips as I remember how the rain splattered my glasses. "Yeah?" I ask hesitantly, glancing over at her.

"I'm really sorry."

I quickly polish my glasses, then pop them back on my face so I can see her clearly. "For what?"

"Canter and I were talking earlier. We know we've been totally absorbed by these rehearsals. I hope you don't feel like we've been ignoring you or that we don't want to hang out."

"I . . ." The truth is, I have felt that way. Exactly that way. "It's fine."

"It's not," Lila says firmly, shaking her head. "I guess we convinced ourselves that since you were making new friends, too—"

"Friend," I correct before I can stop myself. "Noah."

"Right." She shifts, looking guilty. "Well, what I wanted to say—what *we* wanted you to know—is that we miss you."

A strange feeling swirls up, like the cool air from the sea

cleansing me from the inside out. "I miss you both, too," I admit.

Lila beams. "Once the performance is over in a couple of weeks, things will be back to normal."

I grin over at her.

"And I think you'll really like Jones and Bette once you get to know them. Oh, and there's Emma. And Declan. The whole crew is really great. I can't wait for you to meet them all."

My face falls. "You're still going to hang out with them after the performance?"

"Well, yeah. Probably." Lila brushes some loose curls from her face. "Just like I'm sure you'll still hang out with Noah, right?"

"What about the investigating we're supposed to be doing?" I ask, a little sharper than I intend.

"We'll have loads of time for that," Lila says, a slight edge to her voice.

"Unless another performance comes along," I grumble. "And knowing this school, I'm sure it will."

"Myra, that's not fair." She furrows her brow. "You know, the performance is actually a great cover. We have loads of time between scenes, and none of the teachers question us roaming around the school during rehearsal season, even late at night. If you joined *in*, we could sneak off to the modulab all the time."

"The teachers here don't care where you go," I say, yanking my glasses back off and tossing them onto my nightstand. "I should know. I wander around all the time. *Alone.*"

"You're not alone!" Lila says, losing her patience. "You're with your new friend. It doesn't make *us* any less friends just because we have new ones. Friendship isn't a Chemic solution that can be diluted with each new added ingredient."

"I never said it was," I growl from under the blankets.

"You didn't have to."

When I don't reply, I hear Lila huff and then rise to get ready for bed. She flips out the lights without even saying good night.

CHAPTER TWENTY-SEVEN

Fifth Month, 2449

THE NEXT MORNING, I SLIP OUT BEFORE LILA WAKES UP. Outside Canter's room, I tap softly on the door. Not that I needed to be quiet. Canter could sleep through a sonic blast. A few seconds later, his roommate appears in the entry and Bin-ro scoots out, zipping around my feet as the sleepy and confused boy shakes his head and shuts the door. Bin-ro and I head to the cove to meet Noah. We agreed that today would be a go-to-class day, especially since another storm's forecast for later this morning, but that doesn't mean we need to suffer through another revolting breakfast.

Noah's already waiting. "What's cooking?" I ask eagerly, the scents of butter and cinnamon and fresh-cut strawberries floating on the air.

"Cinnamon strawberry waffles with chickpea-milk

whipped cream." He presents me a plate with a flourish and a modest bow.

I hold it under my nose and take a big sniff. The aroma makes my eyes and mouth water. Noah barely has time to hand me a fork before I dig in, and my plate is clear so fast, it might be magic.

"You can breathe between bites, you know," he says with a chuckle as he carefully cuts and then chews his own waffle.

"Impoffible," I mumble through a mouthful of strawberries. I swallow, then flash him a sheepish smile. "Show me which plants you used." As I scrape up the last morsels, Noah points out a minty-colored plant with hanging pods that look like cocoons; tall, feathery stalks of barley; and the mounds of strawberry bushes. "Amazing," I say more clearly, watching Noah slowly chew another bite. "How come you eat so slowly? Analyzing your work?"

"Actually, yes," he admits, blushing. "I'm testing out textures and flavors, seeing what modifications I might want to make next time."

"That's easy," I say. "None. It's perfect."

"You know, M, you're good for my cooking confidence."

"We need to figure out what we're going to do with all this," I say, sweeping my arm to take in our surroundings. "I can't be the only one who gets to appreciate your culinary art creations."

"Can't we just go with what you planned for the moon-garden?"

"That didn't turn out so well."

"Well, you never got to execute your plan, though, right?" Noah leans back, letting the sun wash over his face. "If you'd gotten to broadcast the garden to the galaxy, it could have changed so much."

"Maybe." I chew my lip. After everything that happened with the moongarden, I'm hesitant to try again. "Even if we did manage to broadcast that the plants are safe, it wouldn't be enough. The whole galaxy is using MFI's imitation food now. Let's just say we did convince the public that the garden is safe. It'd take ages to grow a garden that could feed all the Settlements. It took us the whole school year to get the moongarden going."

Noah glances over at me. "Us?"

Shooting stars, Myra! "Uh, me and Bernie."

A whistle blares at my feet and I giggle. "And Bin-ro, of course."

"Can't forget about this little guy." Noah pats Bin-ro's hull. "But you got this garden growing in seconds."

"And look how fast we're depleting it, and it's just the two of us. I don't know if I could do it all over again on command. It kind of takes a special moment, a strong feeling, to fuel that kind of magic."

"What do you mean?"

"I don't really know," I admit. "My magic seems to be charged by how I'm feeling. Like a Mender, but not exactly. That's the other problem." I run my hands through my hair, tugging at the ends. "I don't have other Botans to learn from. I've been figuring it out on my own."

"Sounds like you need to find more Botans, then. So you can harness more of your magic."

"And grow a lot more food."

"What if . . ." Noah trails off, fiddling with his shirt buttons. "Never mind."

"No, what were you going to say?"

"You'll hate it. It's a bad idea, seriously."

"Bad is better than nothing. Spill it."

"What if you tried to partner with MFI?" he says slowly. "Contact Mr. Melfin. This could save his company. If he vouched for the food—told the galaxy it was safe—it could clear the way for you to publicly use your Botan magic."

"You're right," I say, and his eyes widen. "I do hate it."

"Okay, but besides that, what do you think?"

I think that's exactly the plan proposed to Fiona and look how that turned out. "Jake Melfin wouldn't go for it in a hundred million light-years. He's got too much invested in his fake food," I say carefully. "Plus, he won't want just anyone growing their own supplies. What would happen to his bottom line?"

Noah's shoulders slump. "That's true."

"We'll think of something else," I say, nudging him. "Keep the ideas coming." I fold my hands behind my head and lean back next to him. "If only I *could* get in contact with other Botans."

"If they're out there, why haven't they done anything yet?" Noah wonders aloud.

"Maybe they don't have any seeds. No seeds mean no magic. Some of them might not even know they *have* magic, making them just about impossible to find. Like the free Reps."

"Have you and your friends done more searches?"

I stare up at the hazy goldenrod sky. "Nope."

"I'd help."

"You would?"

"Sure," he says, grinning. "I'm invested now, too."

"We'd have to go inside," I remind him. "Away from the sky and the sea. To a place with walls and a ceiling and computers."

"True . . . That *would* be rough. But still worth it."

"Speaking of going inside," I say, sitting up, "we'd better get to class."

CHAPTER TWENTY-EIGHT

LATER THAT AFTERNOON, I'M ON MY WAY TO ELECTOR Studies II when Canter turns the corner with a group of kids I don't recognize. A tall, dark-haired boy slaps Canter's shoulder and lets out a guffaw.

Canter the Comedian. I try to look away before he spots me, but he catches my eye. "Hey," I mutter, breezing past him.

"Myra!" he calls, his face lighting up as he pivots, linking his arm with mine and spinning me in the opposite direction. "I was hoping I'd bump into you."

"Well, consider us *bumped,*" I murmur, trying to twist my arm free. "I'm going to be late for class."

"No, you're not." With his free hand, he waves to the other kids as he pulls me down the hall. "I'll catch up with you later."

"No, you won't," I snap, finally tugging my arm free. "You can catch up now. I've got to get to class. I haven't been all week."

"I already talked to Ms. Neil and told her I wanted to show you an Elector project I'm working on for the performance. She said that was fine."

"Well, it's not fine with me." I try to dodge past Canter, but he blocks my path. Stupid hoverball skills. "Maybe you should've asked *me* before breaking me out of class. What if I was looking forward to the lesson?"

"Since when have you ever wanted to go to class?"

"Things are different here, right? Maybe I love school now. Maybe it's my favorite experience this side of the sun. Like you would know."

Canter looks wounded but not surprised. "That's why I wanted to talk to you. Let's go for a walk."

"I don't want to see your stupid Elector props." I fold my arms across my chest and will my feet to meld with the ground. *If he wants me to go anywhere, he'll have to drag me.*

"That's the story I told Ms. Neil. I seriously just want to take a walk."

"Why?" My eyes narrow. "Were you and Lila talking about me?"

"Yes. Well, no. Not in a bad way!" Canter throws up his hands. "Will you please just come? You've got an excused absence and everything."

"Great. I've got a bunch of things I could be doing," I say, spinning on my heels and heading in the opposite direction.

"That's fine," Canter calls, jogging to pass me and then stopping in my path. "I'll go tell Ms. Neil you weren't interested."

I sear him with a glare, weighing if he's bluffing.

"C'mon, please? We haven't hung out in forever. Which *I know* is mostly my fault."

I raise my eyebrows. "Mostly?"

"You've been busy, too. With your new friend, Nate."

"Noah."

"Right. Okay, if you'd rather go hang out with him, that's fine. I'll explain to Ms. Neil . . ." Canter slowly ambles past me, whistling one of Bin-ro's favorite tunes. He's halfway down the hall before I sigh loudly.

"Okay, fine. But just until the end of the period. I've got plans after."

"Great!" Canter links arms again. "What do you want to do? Where have you been hiding away, anyway?" He drops his voice. "Have you been looking for a new spot for the garden?"

I bite my lip, twist my arm out of his grasp, and give him a good-natured shove.

"What's with the face?"

"What do you mean?" I ask. "This is the face I always have."

"No, that's the face you make when you have something to say but don't want to say it."

Guilt bubbles in my stomach. I've been keeping lots of secrets from Canter lately. I don't know what to say, so I don't say anything at all.

"What's up?" Canter asks. "Did you find a spot already?"

"Uh, yeah."

"Seriously? Where? Have you gotten anything to grow?"

I rub my throat where my new Botan Inscriptions are barely hidden beneath my collar. "A few things." I toy with lying to him. Telling him it's nothing. Not worth even looking at. Instead, I blurt out, "I'll show you."

Neither of us says much as I lead Canter through the winding halls to the walkway. He doesn't even make a sound when I disappear between Language and Theme. But when he jumps down beside me and takes in the garden bursting out of the water, he gasps.

"Leaping Moon gargoyles! Are you kidding?" His face is a mixture of shock, glee, and—there it is—anger. "You did all this alone? And you didn't say a word to us about it? What the meteor, Myra?"

My hands are fists at my sides. "How many spots have you staked out? When's the last time you so much as thought about the seeds or about—" I stop midsentence. Tears prick my eyes, but I refuse to let them fall.

"About what?" Canter demands, some of the anger evaporating from his voice. When I don't answer, he sighs and reaches out to touch a cluster of periwinkle blueberries hanging over the rail. He plucks one and pops it into his mouth. His eyes flutter shut as he chews. "This is incredible," he finally says. "How'd you get them to grow out of the water?"

"It was sort of an accident," I reply, my throat still tight. "The seeds spilled when Noah and I were out here waiting for rain."

Canter's mouth falls open. "You *told* someone about this place? Some kid you hardly know?"

Anger zaps away any lingering guilt. "One, it was an *accident*. I didn't mean for him to see. And once he did, it was too late. Two, I know Noah as well as you know your new friends. Probably more. There's only *one* of him."

Canter runs his hands through his hair. "I can't believe someone else knows about this. And about your magic?" When I nod, he winces, then asks more quietly, "Are you sure we can trust him?"

"Positive."

Canter's quiet for a while. "I still can't believe you didn't tell us."

I kind of can't believe it, either. Now that Canter is

here, it seems absurd that I wouldn't share this. I shrug and slump down to the ground. "I guess it was my way of getting back at you."

He sinks beside me. "Myra, I'm really sorry Lila and I haven't been around. I know you're not into the artsy vibe here . . ."

I consider telling Canter about my grand plans to surprise Lila and him with my music, and how it felt when they didn't show, but decide against it. Why make him feel bad again just when we're finally making up?

"I guess that's not your fault." I shoot him a sideways glance. "Even though I really enjoy blaming you for things."

He flashes me a grin. "Oh, I know."

"It's my favorite pastime."

"Still," he continues, his voice serious again. "It wasn't interstellar of us to ditch you."

I rest my head against the cool metal. "I liked the way things were," I say quietly. "Just the three of us."

"Hey, even though we've got new friends, that doesn't mean you're not still our *best* friend." He nudges me with his elbow and I smile before shoving him back.

"I'm sorry I didn't tell you about the garden and Noah and everything. Can you tell Lila for me?" I ask hopefully.

"Not in this galaxy. That's all you."

I groan. "She's going to be really mad, isn't she?"

"Supernova."

"As long as she doesn't use Mender magic to injure me like last year, I guess I'll survive."

"I wouldn't count on her being that merciful. And you'd better tell her quick, or she's going to wonder where we're both disappearing to all the time."

I sit up. "You mean . . . ?"

"Did you really think I wasn't going to help you now that I know about the garden?"

I grin, but a strange feeling slithers through my stomach. *I wonder how Noah will feel having Canter and Lila here?* I push it away. Besides, Lila and Canter, especially, have as much right to these plants as I do.

"We can try to find out more about the Rep settlement, too," Canter adds.

I sigh, relieved. "Sounds interstellar."

"Let's start tonight."

"Don't you have rehearsal?"

Canter shrugs. "I'll skip it."

Cautiously, I ask, "Isn't your performance coming up, though?" When he nods, I say, "I'll start the search. You and Lila can help when your practices are over."

"Are you sure?"

"Definitely. Noah said he'd help me, anyway."

Canter frowns. "You told him about that, too, huh?"

I look away, more guilt flooding through me. "It all kind of went hand in hand."

Canter lapses into another long silence. "Let's go to the Number Whispering wing." His voice is far brighter than I'd expected.

"Why?"

His eyes glimmer slyly. "That's where Lila is right now. And I'm sure she'll have *lots* to say about all this."

CHAPTER TWENTY-NINE

LILA WAS LESS THAN PLEASED. *WAY* LESS. AFTER CANTER got her excused from class, he marched us straight back to the cove. I'm actually surprised no one came running to see what all the screeching and yelling was about.

She's calmed down now. Mostly. Enough to agree to help—and to not murder me in my sleep. I'm sure I'll still have trouble dozing off, though.

At the bell, we go our separate ways on much better terms since arriving at V.A.M.A.

After classes, Noah and I meet in the modulab. As usual, it's deserted. "Doesn't anyone study in this place?" I ask, surveying the empty putty loungers and workstations.

"Our studying is more hands-on," he answers as he heads to the back corner. "Oh, hi."

Apparently, the modulab *isn't* entirely empty.

"Hello," Bernard says stiffly, rising up from where he'd been cleaning behind a row of workstations. "I was just finishing."

"Why don't you stay?" I suggest. "This is Bernard," I tell Noah. His surprise melts into recognition.

"*The* Bernard?" he asks. "Wow. It's great to meet you. I heard your original was a gardener! That's out of this galaxy!"

Noah had thought it was strange at first, when I told him my friend Bernard was a Rep, not a student, but he came around faster than most others probably would. Being on the fringes has a way of making some people more accepting.

Bernard's expression darkens. "It's so far out of this galaxy, it's not even worth mentioning," he says, gathering his supplies and heading out the door.

"Bernard, wait!" I call, following him into the hall.

"I'm no help with research projects," he says, trying to step around me. "No magic, remember?"

"That's why we're here," I hiss, and he goes still.

"What do you mean?"

"Haven't you ever wondered why Reps don't have magic?"

His silence spurs me on.

"It turns out, there's something that blocks Reps' magic. Some sort of chip or device. Since Reps are made on Venus, we thought maybe there was more information about it here."

"You're meddling in things that have nothing to do with you," Bernard growls.

"It does have to do with me," I reply, heat flushing my face and neck. "Bernie was my friend, and if I can help—"

"You can't help! Don't you understand? You can't just swoop in and save the day like some superhero."

"I'm not trying to save anyone," I counter, though I'm not sure it's true. "I'm just trying to help."

"No one asked you to." Bernard's blue eyes narrow. "Did your precious friend Bernie ask for your help?"

"Well, no, but—"

"Then leave it alone." He brushes past me.

"So why don't *you* help us, then?" I fire back.

"Don't want to. Too busy. Nothing I can do. Take your pick."

"There's a settlement of free Reps on Venus," I say quietly. "Did you know about it?"

He freezes halfway to the door. "That can't be true."

"Why not? That's why we applied to the exchange program. To find them."

"If it does exist," Bernard says slowly, "a couple of kids aren't going to be able to find it. They'd keep too well hidden."

"Maybe a *few* kids could find them, then. Stay and help us," I add more gently.

Bernard doesn't reply. He doesn't take another step away, either.

"It's not fair that you're locked into whatever contract your original signed back on the Old World. That wasn't your fault, and—"

"You think I think I *deserve* this?" he asks, turning to face me. "My original was one of the first in the program. Hardly any other Repetitions date all the way back to the Old World. In his *infinite* wisdom, he signed on for *infinite* Repetitions. I know I'm stuck. And I know it's not fair. And I know there's nothing I can do about it."

"But the free settlement—"

"It doesn't exist," he says firmly.

"What if we find proof?"

"Just leave it alone," he says, his voice stony. "And leave me alone, too."

Once he's out of sight, I head back into the modulab with a sigh.

"You tried, M. He's not interested."

"Well, I'll just have to *make* him interested," I reply, plopping down in front of a computer screen.

"I don't know if—"

"Are you helping or not?"

Noah doesn't answer, but he does take the seat next to me and taps the screen to life.

I start by showing him the recipe posts with their cryptic comments. Noah agrees that the posts must have something to do with coordinating a meeting. Frustratingly, there still aren't any new ones.

"Do you know these sites?" I ask as Noah scrolls through older Venusian recipe posts.

"I've read some of them before for cooking tips," he replies, rubbing his chin. "Have you tried the Morning Star recipe database?"

"No," I say, bending over the hologram keyboard. "I only searched the ones with *Venusian* as a keyword."

"A lot of people use *Morning Star* instead," Noah explains, squinting at the screen as the results populate. "See. Morning Star Sweet Bread, Morning Star Pasta Bake, Morning Star Soufflé."

"Are any recent?" I ask, peering closer.

"There!" Noah says, tapping an entry. "This one's from a month ago. And look at the comment by that user, Perennial-Purpose4630."

Don't forget to add a pinch of sugar, and bake at 320 degrees for twelve minutes and thirty seconds.

"We figured out that the temperature and baking instructions are the meeting date and time," I explain, "but we still don't know what *pinch of sugar* means." Noah and I try other variations in the search parameters, but nothing else pops up.

"Let's see if we can find anything about MFI," Noah suggests. He types the name into the search bar and rows and rows of results fill the screen.

"This is all recent"—I skim through the headlines and ledes—"and none of it seems relevant. Lots of coverage of the initial food cloning issues, but not a lot since, except a new processing plant opening soon on another Venus waterway, Banksy Bay."

"They're expanding?" Noah asks, eyebrows raised.

"It looks like a new shipping facility. MFI plans to shuttle their products around the solar system 'faster than a shooting star.' Interstellar. Because the only problem with their slimy food is it doesn't arrive fast enough."

Noah chuckles. "Apparently, the new facility is replacing the Lunar one."

"Planning a trip back home?" someone asks. We look up. Mr. Kote grins, leaning against the doorframe. "Did we scare you away already?"

"N-no," I stammer. "Just doing some reading."

"I'm only teasing," he says, stepping into the room. "I

was just curious what my two Chemic protégés are up to in the modulab when I'm certain I didn't assign any research projects."

"We were interested in MFI," I say carefully. "They, er, seem to hire a lot of Chemics, so we were looking into it. For the future."

Mr. Kote's gaze flickers to Noah, and I realize too late what he's thinking. "I'm not sure their need will . . . match your passions."

Noah flushes.

"Oh, not for Noah! For me. I'm fascinated by the way they've streamlined their production and wanted to learn more about it. Do you know anyone who works there?"

"Not many of my students have gone on to work at MFI, to be honest," Mr. Kote says, rubbing his chin. "Not a great match for us creative types. But MFI used to be headquartered here on Venus, and as a lifelong resident, I know a bit about them. Anything in particular you're interested in?"

"Oh, nothing specific," I murmur. "I didn't know their headquarters used to be here. Where is it now?"

"Mercury. They moved there about twenty, twenty-five years ago."

I raise my eyebrows. "I didn't think there was anything on Mercury but the prison."

"There isn't much else. A few other businesses. I was surprised when I heard about the move. The Melfins were always very proud, well-known Venusians. The family had been here since the first Settlement was formed. Everyone was shocked when the old CEO sent his son to the Moon for school, but at the time, it was the premier Creer academy in the solar system, so I suppose it made sense. A few years later, they shocked everyone again, announcing the MFI headquarters was relocating to Mercury." He shrugs. "Maybe they found it easier, transportation-wise. Lots of space traffic going back and forth to Venus. Not as much going to Mercury."

Mr. Kote studies me for a moment. "I'm not surprised you're interested in food production, Miss Hodger."

My stomach drops like a meteor. "Really?"

He nods. "With your family background in Number Whispering, it makes sense you'd gravitate toward a more technical application of your Chemic powers. We'll see," he adds with a wink as he turns to go. "Maybe a little more time at V.A.M.A. and you'll discover secret talents."

"I think I have enough of those, thanks," I whisper once Mr. Kote is out of earshot. Noah laughs as we turn back to our screens.

We search for other food production companies, but apart from a few start-ups that closed almost as soon as they popped up, we don't find any others in the past thirty years.

"I don't think we're going to uncover much more about MFI on the open network," Noah says after a while.

I sigh and agree, filing away Mr. Kote's new information to think about later. "Seems like our best bet is to figure out the Rep meeting place. Let's go back to that last post and do a search for PerennialPurpose4630."

A comment from a new username catches my attention.

Can't cook it that long. My oven is broken. I'll try your next recipe though.

—NaturalHacker3130

We search the new handle, cross-checking any new usernames in the comments, and find more recipes with more instructions dating back several months. Only the temperatures and cooking times change; the *pinch of sugar* is always there.

I sit back and fiddle with my glasses, just like my dad does when he's trying to work out an equation. "We've got to figure this out."

"Hang on," Noah says suddenly, typing in another search. "This one's different." He narrows his eyes. "I think they may have had to change their meeting spot. And look." He points at the time stamp. "This was posted last week. The meeting had to be recent."

Don't try the pinch of sugar. It's too sweet. A dash of salt works much better. Keep the temp and the time, though.

"*Pinch of sugar . . . Dash of salt.*" I turn and look at Noah. "What could it mean?"

"Maybe they're initials? *PS* and *DS?*" After a moment, he says, "Let's try searching that username. I haven't seen it before."

I lean forward to click and freeze. Noah may not recognize the username, but I do.

CHAPTER THIRTY

"WHAT'S WRONG, MYRA?" NOAH ASKS. "YOU LOOK like you saw a ghost."

"I think I have."

CharmHandler0305 blazes on the screen in front of me. "I know this poster. It's my old best friend, Hannah."

Noah frowns. "Are you sure?"

"When we were younger, before I left for S.L.A.M., we had a whole crew of friends. We called ourselves CHARM. And Hannah always said she was the Charm Handler, because she planned all our get-togethers."

"That could be a coincidence. . . ."

"Her sister's birthday is the fifth day of third month."

"Okay, I'll reclassify my assessment as highly likely."

"And she lives on Venus. It's got to be her."

"But why would she be involved in all this?" Noah asks. "Especially if she's just a kid."

"We're kids, too," I remind him. "And I think—I'm pretty sure—her sister is a Botan."

Noah's eyes widen like saucers. "Is her sister on Venus, too?"

I shake my head, my stomach dropping to my toes. "No, she—I think she's on Mercury."

"Have you seen your friend since you've been at V.A.M.A.? Can you ask her about it?"

"I didn't think we were supposed to leave campus without permission."

Noah smirks. "We aren't. But that's never stopped me before."

I sigh. "I'm not sure it matters, anyway. She's not talking to me. Actually, she basically hates me. Long story." I shoot him a sideways glance. "But maybe I can use this new info to change that."

Later that night, I'm perched on the edge of my bed, watching Lila twist her long, curly hair into neat braids. I've seen her do this dozens of times before, but with her hands. Not with magic.

"Cassie taught me," she says as her hair weaves itself together. "You should see the stuff she does with her

Mender magic. She can even change the color of her hair, her eyes . . . I never realized my magic could be used that way."

"It's pretty amazing," I reply. "And also a little creepy. You're not going to change your eye color, right?"

Lila laughs. "No way."

"Good. I like them the way they are."

Lila beams. "Me too. Still, it's nice doing my hair without feeling like my arms are going to fall off."

A *tappity-tap-tap* sounds at the door, and Lila leans over to hit the button on the wall panel. Canter saunters in, already in his pajamas.

"Loud-enough fabric?" I say, pretending to shield my eyes. "What'd you do? Have a Chemic splash paint compounds all over your pants?"

"I did, actually," he replies, flopping onto Lila's bed. The electric-toned fabric is even brighter against the dark comforter. "Larson is a genius with colors."

"You look like a human firework." Canter grins like I mean it as a compliment.

"How'd it go with Noah?" Lila asks, settling on my bed next to me. "Any luck?"

"Actually, yes." I fill them in on everything, including the *very* familiar-sounding username.

"Could you use the handle as leverage?" Canter suggests. "It might force her to meet us."

I don't think blackmailing Hannah into seeing me is going to help mend our relationship.

But maybe helping the free Reps is bigger than our friendship.

"I *could* try that," I say slowly.

Lila, always perceptive, can see the idea makes me uncomfortable. "It's not ideal, but it's the best lead we've got."

"I know. It could backfire, though. She might shut down. Block my messages. Or worse."

"She's not going to want this getting out," insists Canter. "If Hannah's tangled up in what we think she is, it'll probably make her want to meet with you more to convince you to keep quiet."

Lila flashes me a small smile. "It's worth a shot, anyway."

I hate to admit it, but they're right. With a sigh, I pull out my messenger and start drafting a note to Charm-Handler0305.

The next morning, I wake up and immediately check my inbox.

"She answered!"

Lila bolts upright, fully awake. "What did she say?"

I read the message, frown, and read it again.

"Myra!" Lila swings her legs over the side of the bed and hurtles to my side. "Let me see!" She leans in, her brow furrowing. "Is that it? What's it mean?"

Mine. 12:30.

"Are there mines on Venus?" Lila asks. "I thought the only active mines were on Mercury."

"When Hannah and I lived in the same building, we used to message each other after school about whose apartment we'd meet at. *Yours* or *mine.* I guess she wants me to go to her place at twelve thirty today."

"You mean *we.*"

"But we don't know her address. I couldn't find her family in the Venus directory. I looked."

"Then ask her."

And I do. I quickly type out a message and hit send. A response pings almost immediately.

You're so clever. You figure it out.

Lila scowls. "She seems nice. . . ."

"She's pretty mad at me," I remind Lila. "And I kind of deserve it."

"Well, how are we going to figure out her address before lunch?"

I shrug. "Maybe Canter will think of something."

It takes several minutes for us to get Canter awake enough to listen. When he finally rolls out of bed, his hair sticks up and sleep lines are pressed into his cheek.

Yawning, he asks Lila, "Can you help with this?" and then gestures at his head and face.

She beams, then obliges. A snap of her fingers has his hair swooped neatly and his creased, red skin even and smooth.

"Thanks," he says sleepily. But once we explain about the exchange with Hannah, we have his full attention.

"Let me see her recipe site post," he insists, eyes bright. After a few minutes of typing, swiping, and cursing, Canter looks up and grins. "Got her!"

"Where? How?" I grab the device from his hand. A map of Venus fills the screen with a dot in the middle—Stardust Estates.

"I traced her location from her original post using some Tekkie tricks I picked up over the summer," he says proudly.

I shift the map a little. "It's not too far from here."

"But how do we get there?" Lila asks. "All there is between us and that building is water."

"I'll ask Noah. He'll know."

"I'll go with you," Lila offers, and my stomach drops.

"No, it's okay," I say, fidgeting. "He doesn't know I looped you guys in on the garden yet."

Canter frowns. "Uh, it's not like it wasn't our thing originally. He can't exactly be mad."

"I know," I say, still uneasy. "But it is his hiding spot, and he's been helping me. . . ."

"If you'd feel better telling him alone, that's fine," Lila replies gently, elbowing Canter in the ribs. "We understand."

Canter doesn't look like he does, but another sharp nudge from Lila and he keeps his mouth shut.

I leave Canter to finish getting ready, and Lila to make sure he doesn't take twelve light-years, and head out to track down Noah.

It doesn't take long. He's at the cove tending to the garden, just like I expected.

"I heard back from Hannah," I announce as soon as I drop down beside him.

He stops pruning a new apple tree and whirls around to face me. "What'd she say?"

"She said she'd meet. Though in fewer words. She's definitely still angry. Canter tracked her location to the Stardust Estates."

Noah grimaces. "That's not a great area. And did you say *Canter*?"

I nod. "He knows about the garden and everything. Lila, too." I shift from foot to foot. "I probably should've let you know sooner. I only told them a couple of days ago . . . but I was worried you'd be upset."

Noah raises his eyebrows. "How could I be upset? The garden was originally your secret."

"I know. . . ." Noah's voice is calm, and he's saying all

the right things, but somehow, I can't shake the feeling that he's angry. Or disappointed.

"It's no big deal, Myra. Really." He studies me for another moment. "I get it if you don't want me to come with you to meet Hannah, but if you want backup, or a guide . . ."

"Of course I want you to come!" I grin. "You're in it now, too."

He smiles back, though it doesn't quite reach his eyes. "When are we leaving?"

"Hannah said to meet her at twelve thirty, but we don't know how we're going to get there."

"Easy. We call an aquaxi."

"A what?"

"It's a water transport," he explains. "Students aren't really allowed, but teachers use them all the time, so it wouldn't be really weird for one to show up at the school. Plus, I know some tricks so our absence won't be noticed." He stares across the sea. "To get to the Stardust Estates for twelve thirty, we should leave by noon. I'll make the arrangements."

"Great!"

He's still staring thoughtfully out over the water. "I wonder why she lives there."

I frown. "What's wrong with it?"

"It's, I don't know, really run-down. Not somewhere people with Creers tend to settle."

"Her parents don't have Creers anymore," I say quietly. "I think they got taken away after her sister was sent to Mercury."

The color drains from Noah's face. "How?"

I quickly tell him what my mother told me about Hannah's family and the rumors my dad investigated.

"I didn't realize members of the Governing Councils had that much power."

I focus on our garden, tucked in this cove far from prying eyes.

"Maybe they shouldn't."

CHAPTER THIRTY-ONE

A FEW HOURS LATER, NOAH AND I WAIT ON THE walkway behind Rhythm. There's a commotion farther down the corridor and we freeze, but the voices are familiar ones and the panic melts away.

"It's them," I explain as Canter and Lila round a corner, Bin-ro rolling behind them. I smirk. "Took you long enough."

Noah frowns at me. "There's plenty of time before the aquaxi arrives."

"Don't ever take Myra too seriously," Canter says, grinning.

"Oh."

After a few more seconds of awkward silence, I debate how to break the tension between my old friends and my new one. Thankfully, I don't have to. Like the hoverball hotshot he is, Team Old Friend strikes first.

"I'm Canter."

"Noah."

The boys exchange a stiff handshake, hardly looking at each other.

"And I'm Lila," my roommate adds, smiling brightly, though if I'm being honest, it looks a little forced. "Thanks for calling the transport. We didn't have any idea how we'd get to Hannah's development."

"I'm happy to be your travel coordinator," Noah replies, but he doesn't look happy. Not at all.

Canter goes pale. "Wait, what about the driver? Won't they wonder—"

"It's automated," Noah cuts in. "You just plug your destination into the computer and its GPS guides the transport wherever you want to go." He winks. "Don't worry, I'm not about to accidentally out us to anyone. At least not today."

Canter stares at Noah, but I know him well enough to recognize irritation sparking in his blue eyes.

I force a weak laugh. *Noah's probably just nervous to meet my best friends.*

"What should we be looking for?" I ask, trying to ease the tension.

"Bubbles." Noah resumes squinting at the water. "A whole row of them, like . . . *there!*" He points at a spot where white foam streaks through the navy blue like a scar. A moment later, a small ship surfaces, right below the walkway.

Its hull is a gleaming ivory, and with its rounded shape, the ship looks like an oversized egg. A hatch pops open, revealing two rows of three seats inside. We carefully maneuver ourselves over the railing and drop inside the transport. I take a space in the back. Lila plops next to me, and Canter next to her with Bin-ro on his lap, leaving Noah alone in the first row. *Why didn't I let Canter and Lila get in first?*

I wince as Noah sits, glancing over his shoulder at the rest of us. After a second, I nudge Lila, then tilt my head toward the empty seats in front of her. She nods and pushes Canter's foot with her toe. When he scowls at her, she looks pointedly at the empty spots. Canter sighs but scoots out and into the front row.

"I don't need a travel buddy," Noah says curtly. "You can sit with your friends if you want."

"Nah, I'm good," Canter replies. "Better view up here." He deposits Bin-ro at his feet. "And there's more room for this guy."

"Besides, who wants to feel like the chauffeur," Lila adds with a laugh. One Noah doesn't return. She shoots me a worried look.

"He *is* my official V.A.M.A. tour guide, though," I add.

I wish he'd lighten up and be the funny, good-natured friend he usually is with me. "You'd better point out all the good stuff."

Noah smiles, and this time, it actually seems genuine. "You got it, M."

"M?" Canter asks.

"Yeah, hotshot," I say, rolling my eyes. "M. As in, the first letter of my name."

"Ohhh." He spins in his seat to face Lila. "Did you get that, L?"

She pushes him back around with a laugh. "Leave them alone, Canter."

He frowns at her. "It's C. Like the sea, see?" He gives Noah a good-natured nudge. "Mine's the best one, clearly."

Bin-ro whistles his agreement.

"It's definitely on-brand," Noah says with a sigh. "Everyone ready?"

We all buckle up. Canter glances at me as he snaps in his belt. I can practically hear him asking me *What's up with this guy?*

The aquaxi gives a hum, then shudders, catapulting into motion. Foam bubbles around the massive windshield as we dive deep underwater. The transport's lights flick on, illuminating giant boulders dotting the seafloor below us. Fish stream around and over them.

"Wow, look at all the different kinds!" Lila exclaims,

pointing as a school of puffy pink fish the size of hoverballs swim by. A different species, long and thin, their scales striped silver and turquoise, streaks below us, weaving in and out of the holes in the rock. A row of tentacles curl from their spines, reflecting neon in the light emitted from our vehicle. Drifting along a few feet from the aquaxi window, a large, pale fish seems to be keeping pace and peering in at us with wide crimson eyes. I shudder and turn back to the others.

"They were brought here when they built the sea," Noah explains. "The marine life helps keep the water clean."

"What do they eat?" Canter asks.

"Artificial food, like us." Noah points to one of the boulders, this one a slightly darker gray than the rest. "See that? It's a synthesized food source. Bits flake off and float through the water, and the fish gobble it down. Inside is a filtration system that cleans the water and keeps the oxygen and carbon dioxide balanced."

"That's interstellar." Lila leans closer to the window. "We don't have a lot of animals on the Moon. Only pets, and those are pretty rare. I've never seen anything like this."

"MFI makes it," Noah explains. "They supply more than human food to the Venusian Settlements. We might see one of their supply transports today. They're much bigger than this ship, so they use a sea-lane over there." He points to an area on the other side of a massive boulder with an opening so large, it's really more of a cave. "The MFI transports usually stop at V.A.M.A. after the lunch block to bring supplies for a few days at a time."

"How do you know all that?" Canter asks.

Noah shrugs. "I used to help unload the shipments."

"Really?" I ask. "When did you stop?"

"Last year. The school doesn't really need help now, with the new food products."

We all grimace, but no one says anything, all focused on the scene passing the ship.

Strange forms emerge from the darkness, illuminated by the transport's lights. Fuchsia trees with long, feathery leaves flutter in the water on one side. Violet bushes dot the other. As the ship shoots past, tall, umber-colored grasses wave and bob, tangling with shiny, slimy-looking stalks.

I gasp. "Are those *plants*?"

Noah laughs and shakes his head. "No such luck. They're fake. But they give the fish and other sea life places to hide and nest."

"Yeah, obviously, M," Canter adds. "Venus has a whole underwater forest. Didn't you know?"

I flick the back of his head. "You thought they were real, too. I saw your eyes bug out like twin moons."

"Only because I was shocked at how *fake* they looked."

"Yeah, well—"

"We're almost there," Noah interrupts, pointing ahead.

A giant rock wall appears in the distance. The aquaxi slows. As we get closer, I realize the boulders aren't really boulders at all, but manufactured blocks joined to form a massive square base. It must be the floating foundation of the apartment complex.

The water around us grows brighter as we move toward the surface. The golden daylight is so dazzling after the sea's murkiness, I find myself shielding my eyes when we pop up next to the foundation. I blink, allowing my watering eyes to adjust, then stare up at the building rising above us.

While V.A.M.A.'s curves glisten and sparkle like actual bubbles, this building looks like a crude brick carved out of concrete and dropped here without a thought.

Peering closer, I'm even more convinced that's true. The structure itself seems to be collapsing into the sea. Whole chunks have crumbled away, while large patches of grayish-white paste coat whole sections of the exterior. "What is that?" I wonder aloud, pointing at a particularly large blotch.

"Salt deposits build up if you don't scrub the surface every so often," Noah explains. "Eventually, they'll eat away the building."

"Then why don't they clean it?" Lila asks.

He shrugs.

Canter glances around the deserted dock. "So where are we meeting this girl?"

I glance down at my pendant. "You saw the message. It's almost twelve thirty. Let's walk around. Hopefully she finds us."

"If not, we made this whole trip for nothing," Canter grumbles.

I cross my arms. "If Hannah doesn't show up, I'll go door to door until I find her."

Turns out, we don't need to. When we tumble out of the transport, Noah pausing to set the aquaxi's computer to wait, I notice a figure hovering at the far end of the dock, half hidden in the shadow of an overhang. Sleek black hair glistens in the bright sunlight as she pops her head out. I recognize her stance when she crouches, hands on hips. It's exactly how she used to peek from her hiding spots when we were little. My stomach swoops like a wayward rocket.

Lila rests a hand on my shoulder. "Is that her?"

I can only nod.

"It'll be okay," she says. "We'll talk to her together."

"Yeah, don't worry, Myra," Canter says, giving my other shoulder a soft shove. "If she starts anything, I'll knock her into the sea."

I burst out laughing. "I'm pretty sure she won't tell us anything if you do that."

He shrugs. "No one messes with my friend."

"Maybe don't tell her that's your Plan B," Noah suggests as we cross the dock.

Hannah meets my eyes; then she flips her hair and dis-appears around the corner.

"Uh, did she just try to lose us?" Canter asks.

"I think she wants us to follow her," I say, hurrying forward.

The back of the building is in even worse shape than the front. Chunks of stone are missing, and long cracks stretch up the sides like giant splinters.

But there's no Hannah. We spread out, exploring every nook and corner, but it's like she's disappeared. I slip into a recess ringed by a railing like our cove. The fence here is discolored from the sun, and some of the bolts are loose, so it isn't very sturdy. I grasp the shaky metal, peering down into the drop, surprised to see a thin walkway winding along the back of the dock. It's empty, too.

As I stare out over the glistening sea, waves crashing against the side of the dingy building, anxiety and antici-pation mix in my stomach.

Then someone's at my shoulder.

Before I can turn, I hear a voice that makes me shiver.

"Come to ruin my life again?"

CHAPTER THIRTY-TWO

I TURN MY HEAD AND FIND MYSELF NOSE-TO-NOSE with Hannah. A million memories crash over me, and I can almost see them reflected in her eyes. Happy memories. And dark ones. She seems to falter, blinking away silly exchanges and good-natured mischief, inside jokes and late-night conversations.

I intend to say something profound. Something clever. I came up with a half dozen options on the boat ride over here.

"Hi, Hannah" is what comes out instead. I want to put some space between us but fidget with my glasses, my feet firmly planted on the damp, gray ground.

Hannah smiles. "You always play with your glasses when you're nervous." But then her eyes narrow. "Look, I don't know what game you think you're playing, but you need to stay out of this."

"Hey," Canter barks, coming up beside me. "It's not Myra's fault you picked a completely obvious username."

"No one apart from Myra and a few others would ever in a million light-years be poking around a random cooking site and recognize that name," Hannah fires back. "I'm not surprised you're in her new little Lunar crew, or that you think you can insert yourself wherever you feel like with no consequences. Canter Weathers, right? Son of S.L.A.M.'s director?"

"How do you know who I am?"

Her nostrils flare. "I was supposed to go to S.L.A.M., except my *dear friend* made that impossible. Before she jettisoned my future, I did my research."

Canter looks torn between flattered and insulted. He settles for indignation, puffing out his chest. "What's your point?"

"My *point* is I see Myra's still orbiting anyone she thinks can advance her Number Whispering Creer, even if it means moonwalking over anyone who gets in her way."

Bin-ro hurries over, blows a loud raspberry, and promptly rolls over Hannah's foot.

She yelps, glaring down at the little robot. Bin-ro moves

back and forth, clearly threatening to do it again. Hannah retreats a few steps.

"I'm not a Number Whisperer," I say quietly.

Hannah raises her eyebrows. "Then what are you? Besides a terrible person." Bin-ro whistles sharply. "Can you call off your attack-bot?"

"Myra's an amazing person," Lila interjects, hurrying over. Noah's not far behind her. "And an even better friend."

"Oh, more of your fan club?" Hannah glares into Lila's dark eyes. "I think I'm in a far better position to judge Myra's character."

"Just because someone makes a mistake doesn't mean they're a terrible person or a horrible friend," Lila replies, hands on her hips. "It means they're human."

"She ruined my life. And my parents' lives. And my sister . . . my sister is . . . gone." Hannah swallows, her lips pressed tight together. "All because she was jealous. And insecure. And—"

"And all the things kids are every day." Lila glances over at me. "And adults, too. Myra knows what she did was wrong. She regrets it. She told you so last year."

"Yeah, her message was so touching I instantly forgave her for destroying my family and ruining my chances at a Creer. . . . Jupiter Jackpot! Everything's fixed! Do you want to have a sleepover to celebrate? We could laser-color our nails, then patch up the holes in the ceiling that leak toxic rainwater into my miserable apartment every time a storm whips through."

Canter rubs his chin. "Not that I don't like a good bit of sarcasm, but do you think you could spin it back a notch? *You* agreed to meet with us. It's not like we ambushed you."

"You may as well have," Hannah snaps. "She didn't give me much choice."

"Hannah, I really am sorry," I say. "Everything spun out so quickly. After our fight, I went home. My mom was there and I just blurted everything out. I thought the story about the seeds was just that—a story. If I'd known . . ." I slide my glasses up and down my nose. "I would never have done any of that on purpose."

Hannah's silent, her gaze icier than the core of Neptune. "Why are you here, Myra?"

"I want to meet with the free Reps."

Hannah crinkles her nose, a habit I recognize. She's nervous. "I have no idea what you're talking about."

"You're lying," a voice says behind me. Noah steps closer. He'd been so quiet, for a minute I'd forgotten he was there. "We saw the posts. We know about the code for the next meeting. We need to know where."

"Going to turn them in, too?"

"Look," Canter says, stepping between us. "If you're going to hate someone, hate the Governing Councils. They're the ones who make the rules and enforce them.

Myra didn't arrest your sister. Or send you here. You're angry at her because it's easier than blaming the people who are really responsible."

For a moment, Hannah's silent. When she speaks again, her voice is quieter, her eyes softer. "Explain to me why you want to meet with the Reps, and I'll think about it."

I tell her everything. About the garden. And Bernie. And Jake Melfin and his company's corruption. When I mention MFI, Hannah stiffens.

"I know all about that. My parents work in one of their factories." She shakes her head. "How did you get the garden to grow?"

I hesitate. I've conveniently left out the bit about being a Botan. Telling Noah was one thing. He's my friend, and he wants the garden to succeed almost as much as I do. But telling Hannah . . .

I can't expect her to trust me without risking something to prove she can.

I don't say a word as I pull up my sleeve.

CHAPTER THIRTY-THREE

HANNAH'S EYES CRAWL OVER MY SKIN, DRINKING IN the intricate lines that form trees and flowers and plant anatomy.

"Meredith had seeds for a plant like that," she finally says, pointing at an Inscription of a cluster of leaves from a pothos vine. She closes her eyes, but that doesn't stop a tear from escaping down her cheek. When she looks up again, her gaze is hard. "Did you know you had Botan magic when you told your mom about Meredith's seeds?"

"Of course not! Our fight started because I was worried I didn't have any magic. I'd never even *heard* of plant magic. . . ."

"Oh, sure."

"Listen, Hannah," I snap. "I've told you how sorry I am about Meredith. And I mean it, I do. But apologizing every nanosecond isn't going to change the past or bring her back or get you off this floating space dump or make the Governing Council admit you to S.L.A.M. If you help us, maybe no one else will get sent away for having plant magic, or a garden, or a drawerful of seeds. Maybe we can stop some other family from being stripped of their Creers. Maybe we can help the Reps, who never get a chance at a Creer at all."

Hannah watches me silently.

"I'm going to try my best to do all of it. But I need your help. I need to know about the settlement."

"What do you want with them?" Hannah finally asks.

"I have information that might help them." I hesitate. "The Rep facility is here on Venus. If I can help them find it, maybe they can flip the switch and unblock their magic."

Hannah doesn't look convinced. "Where on Venus?"

"The River of Monet."

"What part? That river's hundreds of miles long."

"Uh . . ." Bernard never said. "I don't know the precise location, but I know someone who does."

"Oh, they'll love that," Hannah says, rolling her eyes. "Nothing thrills them more than shaky, secondhand information."

"How did you connect with the free Reps?" Lila asks.

"My teacher works with them," Hannah says slowly,

weighing each word. "They move around a lot, so they're difficult to trace. They have to be."

"Are your parents involved, too?" asks Canter.

"No. I think they're afraid of what could happen if we were caught. I'm not sure it could get much more awful, though."

"So it's true?" I say cautiously. "The Council blocked your parents' magic? How?"

"They injected something to suppress it."

"And . . . yours?" I'm not sure I want the answer.

"My Tekkie powers are untrained, so they didn't bother with me," she replies, her voice bitter. "Without any Creer training, the result's basically the same. I have a little magic still. It flares up sometimes." A light sparks in her eyes. "My teacher recognized my Tekkie powers immediately, even though my school is non-Creer. She told me about the group, since they're barred from using magic, too."

Lila shifts her weight uneasily. "And she took you to meet them?"

"Eventually." A small smile flashes across Hannah's face. "It took some convincing."

"So then, not everyone in the group is a Rep?" I ask.

"No. But they all share the same goal."

"Flipping the switch," Canter says. "Getting their Creers back."

She nods, looking out at the sun glinting on the sea. "Magic is magic. It shouldn't matter who has it or what type it is. How can you say some people can use their abilities and others can't? It's like taking a piece of them away." She turns back to face us. "It's wrong. And I'm going to stop it."

We're all quiet as her words ring in our ears. Finally, I say, "I want to help."

"We all do," Lila says, reaching out to put a hand on Hannah's arm. Surprisingly, my former best friend doesn't shrug it off.

Hannah lets out a deep breath. "I'll talk to my contact. If she says you can meet them, I'll send you a message."

It's the best we can hope for. "Deal," I say.

A loud hum vibrates overhead. Hannah grabs my elbow and hauls me under the overhang. The others hurry to squeeze up against the crumbling stone.

"What is that?" Canter asks, shielding his eyes as he peers into the orange sky.

"Not what, who." Hannah is grim as a ship descends, on course to land in the front of the building. "That's Jake Melfin."

CHAPTER THIRTY-FOUR

I SHUDDER. "YOU TOLD HIM WE WERE COMING?"

"Of course not," Hannah snaps. "Do you think I have his direct line? Or if I did, that I'd tell *him* anything, except maybe to jump headfirst into the sea? He comes here from time to time. And it's your bad luck that he's decided to make the trip today."

Lila frowns. "But why would he come here?"

"It's a long story." Hannah peeks around the building. "And we're a little short on time, unless you're itching to say hi."

"What do we do?" Canter demands. "He'll recognize me for sure."

Hannah scans the area. After a few moments, she grabs my arm and hauls me closer to the building. "I know where you can hide."

At first, I think Hannah's about to lead us inside, but as we near the back door, she makes a sharp turn. A stairway leads to what must be the basement. It's blocked halfway down by a gate. I shake the rails, but it holds firm.

"It's a maintenance access point," Hannah explains. "We don't have time to hack the gate. The only other way in is from inside the building . . . or some maneuvering."

"*Maneuvering?*" Noah asks with a frown.

"Remember when we snuck into our old school's teachers' lounge looking for snacks?"

I nod. "We squeezed onto a ledge and shimmied around the building until we found an open window." Without hesitating, I swing one leg over the railing and wedge myself into the gap, carefully lowering myself down before dropping onto the stairs below. "This is actually way easier than back then. If we fall, we end up where we want faster."

"And we don't have to worry about dropping like meteors past one of the classroom windows."

Lila sets Bin-ro behind the post securing the railing— it's wide enough that it hides him perfectly—then quickly follows me down, twisting through the tight space easily. Noah takes a little longer, grimacing as he drops beside me, while Canter grunts and moans as he tries to squeeze through, suddenly all elbows and awkward angles.

"Just push," I hiss. "And stop flailing around like you're caught in a hoverball net."

"It may as well be one," Canter snaps, trying to extract his foot from a gap it somehow got wedged into. After a lot more groaning and thrashing, he finally drops down beside us, red-faced and sweaty.

"You made that way more difficult than you needed to," I say before he can complain, then turn to Hannah. "Come on. Mr. Melfin must have landed by now."

"Stay there," she insists, scanning the area. "I'll come back when he's gone."

"Hannah, wh—"

"Shhh," she hisses. "He's here to see me. Just stay there and stay quiet."

Heavy footsteps sound overhead, followed by a booming voice, which echoes across the dock. "Miss Lee! Just who I was hoping to see."

"I can't say the same," she replies, her voice fading as she steers him away.

But Mr. Melfin doesn't follow her. Instead, he leans his weight against the railing above us. "Now, is that any way to talk to the only person on this planet trying to help you?"

I exchange a nervous glance with my friends. *Help her how?*

Hannah laughs, but there's no joy in it. "I don't know if *help* is the word I'd use. I've already told you. My answer is no. It's always been no. And it will always be no."

"Of course I'm trying to help," Mr. Melfin says, laying an arm across the metal rail. Familiar cuff links glisten in the Venusian sunlight. "Don't you and your parents want your Creers back? Don't you miss your magic? Tekkie, wasn't it?"

I inhale sharply. *So it's true. Melfin is taking people's Creers from them.*

Beside me, Noah's mouth falls open. The color drains from his face.

"I miss my sister more," Hannah growls. "I'd trade anything for her, including my magic. And including . . . what you want. If I had it to give."

I frown. *What could Jake Melfin possibly want from Hannah?*

"If you'd agree to bring her back," she continues, "I'd try to find what you're looking for. I'm sure I could figure it out."

He taps his fingers on the metal. "Unfortunately, that is out of my hands."

"Don't you have all sorts of connections? Couldn't you just arrange for her to be moved? No one even knows she's on Mercury."

Canter goes rigid, and I know he's listening for any clue about how to get his mother off the prison planet.

"She's outside my reach. There's nothing I can do."

"Then we don't have anything to talk about."

"Oh, I don't know about that. Just imagine it, Hannah. You and your family move into an apartment not at risk of being swallowed by the sea. Your parents' magic, *snap*, returned. You could enroll at the school of your choosing. Weren't you supposed to attend the Scientific Lunar Academy of Magic? You know, the director's an old friend of mine."

Canter clenches his jaw, and I nudge his arm, then motion for him to keep quiet.

"I could easily make arrangements for you to be reenrolled," Melfin continues smoothly. "All you need to do is tell me what I want to know."

I exchange a look with my friends. They appear as confused as I am.

"I've told you thousands of times," Hannah snaps. "I don't know where Meredith got the seeds. My parents told you the same."

"I don't feel your parents considered my last offer as carefully as they should have. They're blinded by their anger. Otherwise, they'd see what they stand to gain. What *you* stand to gain."

"You had my sister sent away," Hannah says, so quietly I barely hear her. "Of course we're angry."

"That was a Council decision, but I can still offer you your old life back."

"Our old lives included Meredith."

269

"As you well know, her life is gone. Yours isn't." Melfin pushes off the railing and heads back toward his transport. "Think about it."

His footsteps echo across the platform and then disappear. A minute later, his ship hums to life, and then that fades away, too, leaving behind only silence.

CHAPTER THIRTY-FIVE

LATER THAT DAY, I'M WATCHING CANTER WORKING IN the seagarden. As he prunes a sprawling rosebush, vines inch up out of the water, winding themselves around his arms and legs. "Hey, cut that out!" Canter scolds, gently shaking them off. "You're going to trip me."

"Maybe they want you to go for a swim," I suggest with a smirk. Behind my back, I flick a finger, and the vine curls up his back and into his hair.

"Pass," Canter says. A cluster of grapes bursts from the end of the plant, the amethyst-colored fruit flopping onto his forehead. "Thanks!" He plucks a handful and pops them into his mouth, then mumbles something around the half-chewed food.

I grimace. "Sorry, I don't speak grape."

He rolls his eyes and finishes chewing. "Anything yet from Hannah?"

"Nope," I say with a sigh, looking down at my darkened messenger screen. "Hopefully she sent her contact the message."

After Jake Melfin left Stardust Estates, Hannah wouldn't talk about anything we'd overheard. Before slamming the door of our transport, she promised to reach out to her contact and let us know about the next meeting. But it's been hours and she hasn't messaged.

"She said she would," Canter reminds me. "She's probably just waiting to hear."

"I wish they'd hurry up. Maybe that space slug Melfin went back to convince her again."

"Doubt it," Canter says. "But he is a space slug." He plucks another grape, chewing slowly. "If Melfin's trying to find out how Hannah's sister got seeds, he must be searching for the source."

"What's it to him? The Governing Councils deal with the plant offenders." I run my fingers over a cluster of fruit but don't pick any. "Unless he thinks catching the source will get him back on the Council."

Canter snaps his makeshift shears a little too hard. "Or maybe he just loves throwing seed offenders into cells."

"Why do you think he said getting Meredith off Mercury was out of his hands?" I ask quietly. Normally,

I wouldn't bring up the prison with Canter, but I can tell by the haunted look in his eyes it's already on his mind.

He shrugs. "Melfin made it sound like once you're there, you can never leave. That can't be true, unless you're—"

"They aren't dead, Canter," I say quickly. "If they were, you know he'd have said so."

"Seems like he has his hands in just about everything these days. All the food for the Settlements. He's even controlling people's Creers." Canter turns to me. "What if Melfin's been questioning my mother, like Hannah? Trying to figure out where she got her seeds. If she told him, do you think he'd get her off Mercury?"

"She got the seeds from Ms. Curie, remember? No way she'd turn in her friend."

"You're probably right. Ms. Goble told me once that my mom was the type of person you could share anything with. They told each other everything, and she never once betrayed a secret. She trusted her more than anyone."

Guilt floods through me. He still doesn't know that his dad was the one who outed Fiona to the Melfins. "Uh, Canter . . . there's something I—"

My messenger lights up, and I snatch it off the ground. "It's Hannah! She says to meet her back at her apartment. Tonight."

Canter's eyes are wide. "Does that mean we're in?"

"I think so," I say, tapping out a quick reply. "We should go let the others know."

"I'll tell Lila. You can find Noah if you want."

"What do you mean *If I want?* He's part of this, too, now."

"Meeting with the group is a whole other level," Canter says with a shrug. "It could be dangerous, and he might not be on board with that kind of risk. These Reps are in hiding, and I don't know what happens if they get caught. Or if we do."

He's not entirely wrong, but Noah will want to come. "Meet back here in an hour?"

Canter nods and disappears. Something twists in my stomach as I watch him go.

I check Noah's room first, but when he doesn't answer, I roam the school. I have no idea where he could be.

Soon it's close to the dinner block, and the halls are filling with students. I dodge colorful blobs, sparkling fog, and a barrage of musical instruments, and still no sign of Noah.

I turn down a hallway and walk straight into a violet haze. "Crashing comets!" I sputter, trying to clear the space around me, then realize it's not just the air that's purple— I am, too.

"Oh, sorry!" a short, brown-haired girl squeaks. "I

thought you saw my color screen. I'm practicing for one of the scene changes in next week's performance."

My hair, shirt, and pants are all coated in wet paint. "Do you always practice in the middle of the hallway?"

"Yeah, usually," she says, bobbing from foot to foot. "It'll wash right off," she calls after me.

"Branching out from your new hobby?" a voice ahead of me drawls. Kyle Melfin leans against the wall, watching me leave a trail of purple footprints.

"Not on purpose," I mutter, not slowing as I pass him.

"I thought memorizing notes was bad, but between the painting, sculpting, dancing, and whatever it is the Electors do, I can't decide which is the worst."

A thought occurs to me, and I pause midstride. "I thought you'd love Venus."

He cocks an eyebrow. "Why on the Moon would you ever think that?"

"Don't you have family roots here?" I ask. "And we're not on the Moon."

He blinks but quickly regains his composure. "Yeah, my dad lived here when he was young, and a whole bunch of generations before that, but my grandparents moved them to the Lunar Settlement when Dad was a kid. Doesn't mean I think the culture here is interstellar."

"Why'd they move?"

"Why do you care?"

I shrug. "Just curious why your dad would force you to join the exchange program when you clearly hate it."

"He wanted me to 'embrace my Venusian heritage.'" Kyle rolls his eyes. "He's all over me to learn to play the dull music he and my grandfather are obsessed with. They're always dragging me to some performance or other. Plus, he said he wants me to get to know other Settlements. He thinks it'll make it easier when I take over the company someday."

I frown. "Why music? What does—Noah!"

Farther down the hall, a dark-haired form freezes like I caught him in a tractor beam. He turns slowly, eyes bouncing between Kyle and me.

"He was just leaving," I say, cocking my head toward my S.L.A.M nemesis. "And I need to talk to you."

"I'll catch you later, Morris," Kyle calls over his shoulder as he strolls away.

Once he's out of earshot and I've made sure no one else in nearby, I launch into my updates about Hannah and the meeting.

"I'll order the transport," Noah says when I finish, pulling out his messenger. I watch him silently for a moment.

"How do you know Kyle Melfin, again?" I ask. "He called you by your last name."

Noah shrugs but doesn't look up. "We have class together."

"You hardly ever go to class."

Noah keeps tapping away. "Aquaxi's ordered. It'll be here in thirty minutes, but you guys should probably head over now. Sometimes, they're early, and they'll leave if you're not there."

"You're not coming?" My stomach lurches like someone turned off the artificial gravity.

Noah runs his hands over his face and hair. "This is a little more than I signed on for."

I gawk at him. "We grew an illegal garden together, Noah."

"Shh!" he says, grabbing my elbow and steering me deeper into the hall. "No. *You* grew the garden. I just cooked the ingredients."

My mouth falls open, but he continues before I can say anything. "Sorry, M. I didn't mean it like that. It's just I'm not as wrapped up in all this as the rest of you." He drops his voice even more. "I'm not a Botan."

"Neither is Lila."

"True." His brow furrows. "Just Lila?"

Crashing comets, Myra! "*And* Canter," I add quickly. "But I thought you cared about the garden. . . ."

"I never said I didn't. But what you're about to do, it's dangerous. Especially knowing what the Governing Council can do with your magic. And Mr. Melfin." He runs his hands through his hair again. "If anyone catches you with a group of free Reps . . . Listen, I'm not saying anything is going to happen, but if it does, don't you want someone here to watch over the garden?"

I hadn't thought of that. "I could rewind it back to seeds, like I did before."

"Then what would you do with them? Take them with you to the Reps? If you're caught, not only will you have been plotting with them, but you'll also have a pocketful of illegal seeds."

While what Noah is saying makes sense, I don't want to undo the garden, and if Noah was going to out me, he's had plenty of chances.

"You'll be back in a few hours." All of the tension is gone from Noah's voice as he glances down at his messenger. "But if you're going to get the others and make it in time for the aquaxi, you'd better go."

I give him another wary look, then rush down the hall.

"And M?" he calls. "I'm sorry."

CHAPTER THIRTY-SIX

I TAP OUT A QUICK MESSAGE TO CANTER AND ZIP back to my room to get de-purple-fied. Luckily, Lila's there. Her Mender magic cleans me up a lot faster than soap would have. She heads to the cove while I change, and I slip into the hall a few minutes later, racing down the corridor in the opposite direction.

When I burst into the cafeteria a few minutes later, I'm out of breath. I quickly scan the noisy room, then blaze a path to the back corner, where a young man in a Rep uniform is carefully stacking trays.

"Bernard!" I call, skidding to a halt in front of him. "I need to talk to you."

"You already are." He grunts, hoisting the trays into his arms before turning toward the kitchen.

"No, really. It's important."

"I'm busy," he growls, his eyes darting left and right.

"I'll help." Before he can protest, I've taken half the stack and am speeding toward the door. He has no choice but to follow me.

"You're not supposed to be doing that," he hisses.

"Why not? They looked heavy." Inside the kitchen, I drop the trays on a prep counter with a grunt. They immediately sink down to be cleaned. "That's what friends do."

"I don't know much about that," he says quietly as he sets his own stack down. "I haven't had a friend in a long, long time."

"Not true. I convinced you to be my friend, remember?"

"More like forced," he replies grumpily, though there's a spark of humor in his voice.

"Same difference. Friends help friends carry loads that are too heavy for one person."

Bernard sighs. "You're not talking about the trays, are you?"

"We're going to meet the free Reps," I whisper. "Come with us, and you can tell them exactly where the A.R.C.S. facility is."

Bernard's gaze turns hard again. "I told you. I'm not interested."

A crash causes us both to jump. I open the door and spot a group of Tekkies huddled around a teetering tower of trays. Nearby is a massive heap of more trays. Probably the remains of another tower. A pair of women in Rep uniforms cross the cafeteria and begin stacking the trays in in neat piles, even as the other tower sways. The kids cheer as a few more trays float up to the top, teetering but holding.

"You know you can use your magic to clean up messes, instead of making them," I snap. "Or making more work for other people."

The Tekkies turn and watch the women hunched over the heap of trays. After a moment, a blond girl flicks her wrist, and the collapsed tower quickly rearranges into tidy piles. A dark-haired boy in a paint-speckled hoodie nods at the still-intact tower and the trays swoop down, joining the other neat stacks. "Sorry," he mutters as the women collect the piles, placing them back on the counter.

I shoot the kids one last glare before returning my attention to Bernard, who's gaping at the scene. "Just come," I plead as I close the door. "We'll bring you straight back."

"I . . . I can't." His brow furrows as he turns away.

"You don't have to do this alone," I say. "And if you don't want me to help, I'm okay with that. Well, not really," I add quickly as he shoots me a dubious look over his shoulder. "But I'll pretend I am. Still, someone in the group might be able to help."

He doesn't turn around, but he does stop walking away.

"It's just a conversation." I start to say more, then catch myself. Sometimes, silence is louder than words.

"Why do you care?" he finally asks. "Why are you so determined I come? I could tell you exactly where the facility is, and you can tell the others."

"I care because you're my friend."

"I'm not Bernie, I'm—"

"You're Bernard. I get that now. And you remind me of Bernie, but you're also you. You tell me what you think—Bernie did, too—but it's different with you. Harsher, but maybe I need that. Sometimes."

He grins, but the smile quickly fades. "If I get caught, they could change my assignment," he explains, his voice small. "My contract requires that all my Repetitions are assigned to schools, but leaving is a breach of the agreement. They could move me anywhere they want."

"We won't get caught," I say with confidence, but a meteor shower bounces around my insides as I think about what could happen to Bernard if we are. It's too late to turn back now.

"What would they want with the facility anyway?" Bernard asks.

"The group might have a way to undo whatever's suppressing your magic. All Reps' magic."

He stiffens.

"What if they have the tools to do it, but they don't know where to go? You know where Reps come from, and they don't. You could help them. Your knowledge could be exactly what they need."

Bernard is quiet for a long time, and I switch between disappointment and relief. Out of all of us, he has the most to risk. Maybe it is better if he stays.

"All right," he finally says. "I'll come."

An hour later, our aquaxi cuts smoothly through the water toward the Stardust Estates. Hannah's waiting for us on the dock.

I wave as we climb out of the transport. She doesn't wave back.

"Should we keep the aquaxi here?" Lila asks as she steps onto the dock. "Are we taking it to the meeting?"

Hannah rolls her eyes. "Yes, I always take a highly traceable transport to secret, dangerous meetings."

"Well, how are we getting there, then?" Canter snaps as he climbs out.

"They'll come for us," Hannah says, her gaze fixed on the sky.

Bernard emerges from the aquaxi and Hannah does a double take.

"Who's this?" she hisses. "You brought someone new? Where's the other kid?"

"He didn't want to come. But he's not going to tell

anyone," I add quickly. "Noah's watching over the garden, just in case—"

"Just in case of what?" Bernard asks, frowning. "I thought you said we were going straight back."

"Just in case!" I repeat, shifting my weight. "I couldn't exactly bring it with me." I turn back to Hannah. "It's okay. Bernard's been involved since the beginning. Well, his original was. Bernie."

Realization dawns as Hannah takes in Bernard's gray coveralls. "He's a copy of your friend, the Re—"

"He's *Bernard*," I cut in.

"They aren't going to like this," Hannah says slowly.

"Why not? He belongs there more than any of us."

Hannah eyes Bernard. "You're going to tell them where the facility is?"

"I'm not sure what I'm going to do yet," he replies coolly.

"They are *really* not going to like this," Hannah repeats, turning back to me.

"Too bad." I don't have much to bargain with, and I know it, but I hope Hannah remembers how hard it is to change my mind once I dig in my heels.

"Fine," she says, sighing. "But you'll be the one explaining."

"What's that?" asks Canter, pointing at a speck of light streaking across the sky. It does a U-turn, swooping back toward us.

"That's our ride." Hannah turns and hurries toward her apartment building. "Come on."

I lean back inside the aquaxi, scoop out Bin-ro, and place him carefully on the dock beside me as the transport sinks into the water and disappears.

Hannah glances back over her shoulder and pauses. "You brought your foot-crunching pet again?"

Bin-ro blows a raspberry, and I swear Hannah almost laughs. "Don't ask me to babysit."

"I wouldn't dream of it. And he'll be helpful. You'll see. He always is."

She shrugs and continues toward the building. We follow her past where we hid from Mr. Melfin.

"Where's it going to land?" I ask. "Won't people around here notice?"

"It's not landing." Hannah keeps her eyes fixed on the speck as it grows brighter. I have no idea what it's doing, and Hannah doesn't offer any clues.

The light zips closer and then blinks out.

"What happened?" Canter demands. "Where'd it go?"

"It's still there," Hannah replies. "Listen!"

A hum fills the air, growing louder and louder, but so gradually, it probably wouldn't alert anyone not listening for it.

Bernard points out at the sea, just past the railing. "It's there." A small shuttle hovers over the water, its propulsion fueling choppy waves.

"How are we supposed to board?" Canter asks. "I don't feel like swimming."

Hannah turns and shoots him a glare. "Do you realize that every question you've asked could be answered if you just paid a nanobit of attention?"

I can't help but laugh. "I tell him that all the time."

"Clearly he doesn't pay attention to you, either." For a second, it feels like old times, but Hannah's reply reminds me a lot has changed: "Get ready."

"For wh—" Before Canter can finish, a thick cord lowers from the transport.

Hannah climbs up onto the railing, hauling the cord toward us. It's so long it coils on the ground. "Who's first?" she asks, taking in Bin-ro and me, an evil glint dancing in her eye.

Dangling from a thin rope out over the sea in the dark was not on my list of Things I Want to Do on My Trip to Venus, but I know it should be me. "Any ideas?" I murmur.

Bin-ro whistles and a hatch opens in his hull. A cord extends from his interior, and I use it to secure him around my chest and shoulders like a metal backpack.

With his encouraging beeps in my ear, I grip the cold metal, whisper a quick Worship Center prayer, and start to climb. My arms ache almost instantly, but then the rope retracts, pulling me up with it.

"Everyone grab on!" Hannah yells behind me.

"Shooting stars," I mutter, realizing that Hannah knew about the mechanized rope all along. I funnel my irritation into tightening my grip.

A few minutes later, we're all safe and dry inside the ship. I glance around at the crude interior. There aren't even seats. Or a pilot.

"It's automated," Hannah explains. "We'll be there soon. It's not far."

"Where are we going?" Canter asks.

She winks. "You'll see."

I detach Bin-ro from my back as we all settle on the floor to wait. When the shuttle begins its descent, I peer out the dingy window and spy a strange building rising from the water. The structure itself is flat, square, and unremarkable, but poles and wires extend from it like antlers. Lights flash on the tips of some of the devices. Others rotate like space junk orbiting a planet.

"It's a weather monitoring station," Hannah explains, seeing me study it. "The Moon doesn't need them, but Venus gets a lot of storms, as you've probably noticed."

I frown, remembering the code from the posts. "*Dash of salt*—I don't get it."

"*D-O-S*," Hannah spells slowly. "Add in an *R* and a *P*, and you have *D-R-O-P-S*. As in *drops of rain*. When we see that, we know it's the weather station."

"*R* and *P* . . . Like *Reps?*"

Hannah nods, and I recall the other meeting location code name. "*Pinch of sugar. P-O-S-R-P* . . . No, that's not right." I think for a moment. "*P-R-O-P-S. Props?*"

She nods. "That's the stage where all the vid-stream concerts are broadcast from. We were supposed to be there tonight, but they rescheduled a performance."

"What Creer runs this place?" I ask, nodding toward the building below us. "Electors?"

"Not all storms are electrical," Hannah answers, tossing her hair over her shoulder as the shuttle sets down on the roof among the poles, wires, and antennas. "The station isn't controlled by a Creer. The Governing Councils are technically responsible for it, but non-Creers oversee the operations."

I seem to remember hearing about some type of science involving the weather, but before I can recall the name, the hatch opens. I tell Bin-ro to stay put. He's less than pleased, but I feel more comfortable with him guarding the shuttle.

We hurry after Hannah, crossing the roof, where lights blink all around us. A figure stands in the shadows of an open doorway. They beckon us forward. But as we get closer, they step back inside.

For just an instant, I catch sight of dark hair and pale features, and gasp. I know who Hannah's contact is.

Ms. Curie.

CHAPTER THIRTY-SEVEN

CANTER FREEZES AND WE EXCHANGE A PANICKED look. "What is Ms. Curie doing here?" I whisper.

"How do you know her?" Hannah demands, her eyes widening.

"How do *you*?"

"She's my teacher."

"The one who introduced you to this group?"

"Yeah, but how—"

"Charmhandler," Ms. Curie says, nodding at Hannah. Her gaze is far less friendly as it settles on us. "I would imagine as S.L.A.M. students, you'd recall how much I value punctuality." She cocks her head toward the door.

Hannah's mouth falls open. "I didn't know you taught at S.L.A.M."

"M-Ms. Curie," Canter stammers. "Wh—"

She pulls him into a tight hug, and Canter looks even more shocked. She releases him just as quickly, leading us down the dim hallway. "I'm sorry. It's just I haven't seen you since . . . I'm sorry about everything that happened at the end of last year. I wish I'd done more."

"To stop us?" I ask, falling into step beside her. "Or to help?"

"That's an excellent question, Miss Hodger." She gives me a stiff smile but doesn't say anything more.

"But Ms. Curie—" Canter begins.

She holds up a thin, bony hand. "I go by Indra here."

"You're the one who sent me the message," I say.

"I established a connection with this group when I first arrived on Venus and offered my Elector skills to aid their mission. They've proved useful with communications. I discovered a way to bounce electrical signals off satellites—" She shakes her head. "When I heard from Ms. Goble, and by extension your mother, about how upset you were about losing your Rep friend, I thought you'd appreciate an introduction."

"How did you even know we were here?" Lila asks. "Did Ms. Goble tell you we'd been accepted into the exchange program?"

"I'm the one who suggested she set up the program in the first place."

I frown. "So Ms. Goble is involved with the group of rogue Reps, too?"

"Of course not. She was always much more of a rule follower than me. But she happened to tell me who'd been selected for the exchange program."

"But why didn't you just send a message as, er, you?" I ask as we wind through cluttered halls. "Or why didn't you ask to meet with us once you found out we were at V.A.M.A.?"

She tilts her head to the side. "I had to be sure you were serious about this endeavor. It's not one to be undertaken lightly. Simply being here is dangerous."

"But why are you even involved?" Canter asks.

"The same reasons as you, Mr. Weathers," she replies, her voice icy. "Helping where I can when I can't help where I want."

"We want to help here," I say, glancing uneasily down a dark stairway as voices float from somewhere beyond the wall.

Ms. Curie studies me closely. "It seems you do." She turns to Bernard, who's been silent until now, her eyes lingering on his gray uniform. "And who are you?"

"Bernard," I answer quickly. "He's with us."

"I can see that," she says. "You'll be wanting to join, then? Typically, we recruit from the MFI factories—they're the main employer of Reps in the galaxy and most effective source for growing our numbers quickly—but Perennial may make an exception."

PerennialPurpose4630 must be here too. I glance over at Bernard. "He just wants to listen."

"And are you his official spokesperson?" Ms. Curie asks, an eyebrow raised.

"I can speak for myself," Bernard says raggedly. "And I'm not here to join. Just observe."

"If you're looking for a performance, there are plenty on Venus," Ms. Curie replies stiffly. "You won't find one here, though." She shifts her focus to Hannah. "This was not approved."

"I didn't know," Hannah answers, her voice small. "They just showed up with him, and without the kid they brought before."

Ms. Curie frowns. "And where is this other boy?"

I shift my weight, trying to come up with a good answer.

"He didn't want to come," Lila says into the silence.

Ms. Curie eyes Bernard. "It doesn't seem like this gentleman wants to be here, either."

Bernard's expression darkens. "I can wait outside."

"It's too late for that," Ms. Curie says briskly, sweeping down the stairs without waiting for us to follow. "You're in this tangle of wires now, whether you want to be or not."

Hannah looks like she's ready to scratch my eyes out but says nothing.

The hallway at the base of the staircase is long and shadowed. Windows occasionally dot the walls, looking out over dark water. The voices grow louder as we turn the corner. Control panels and computer screens are mounted on desks all over the room. No one is paying them any attention. They're all staring at us.

"Would you like to introduce your guests to the rest of us, Charmhandler?" an authoritative female voice inquires from the back of the room. It belongs to an older woman with short, curly gray hair, who's perched on top of one of the desks like it's a throne.

Judging by Hannah's expression, that's the last thing in the galaxy she wants to do right now. I see her swallow as she steps away from us and moves to the center of the room. The dozen or so adults clustered around the control panels are silent, waiting.

"This is Myra," Hannah says, waving vaguely in my direction. "She contacted me because she managed to trace some of our meeting posts to my username."

The woman frowns. "How is that possible?"

"Myra and I grew up together. She's one of the few people in the galaxy who would connect my code name to me. I had no idea she was on Venus." Hannah shoots me a glare like my entire reason for coming was to irritate her. "Her friends Canter, Lila, and Bernard are with her."

"Uh, shouldn't we be using code names?" Canter asks.

"You don't get code names unless you're *in*," Hannah growls.

The woman hears her anyway. "And *that* remains an open question. Tell me," she says, turning to address me, "why are you here?"

I wring my hands. "We want to help. It isn't right that Reps are bound to contracts signed generations ago."

The woman narrows her dark eyes. "Some would say we did sign them, those of us here who began our lives as Repetitions"—she nods toward a handful of faces—"as we are the clones of those who did."

"But you're not a hive mind," I blurt out, echoing Bernie's words from what feels like so long ago. "Those people lived different lives from yours. Some of them even on different planets. It's not fair to hold new generations responsible." I feel my cheeks flush. "I've heard there are . . . implants that stop Reps from using their magic."

The woman nods. "That's true. There's a device that suppresses our magical talents, but we haven't been able to locate the facility where the injections occur to disable them."

"You know how to disable them?" Bernard steps in front of us, and the woman eyes him curiously.

"More or less. And who are you?"

"Just a Rep who wants to understand this group."

"What you are isn't who you are," says the woman

sharply. "I'm a fifth-generation Repetition, mostly assigned to data entry operations. The work instilled in me an appreciation for information, organization, and analysis— something that has come in handy this cycle." She winks at the group, and a few chuckle. "But *who* I am is much bigger than that. Your work is just one sliver of your being."

Bernard studies her as if trying to decipher something in her eyes. "My name's Bernard," he finally says.

The woman's eyes sparkle. "Perennial."

"How do you deactivate the implants?" Bernard presses. "Can you disable mine?"

"We have a device we believe can nullify the sensor," she says, "but we haven't perfected it. Originally, we'd planned to use it to deactivate the implants one by one, though it would be time-consuming. Given troubles with the technology, we've shifted our focus to finding the central location and dismantling the devices all at once."

My gaze is glued to Bernard, sensing an opportunity. "But you don't know where they're powered from."

"The facility is on Venus, but that only narrows down the search so much. We don't even know which waterway we're looking for."

"I do," Bernard says quietly.

Perennial shakes her head. "Impossible. No Rep retains those memories. It's part of the work integration process."

"I remember being there."

She studies Bernard, her eyes flickering over him like she's reading a complicated line of code. "How old are you?"

He crosses his arms. "Fourteen."

More than one adult in the room gasps. "How is that possible?" Ms. Curie asks.

"Director Weathers requested that my workforce entry be accelerated."

Canter crosses his arms. "Why would my dad do that?"

"I have no idea."

Somehow, I know Bernard's lying.

Perennial steps closer. "Where is the facility located?"

"I'll tell you exactly where it is," Bernard replies, "if you deactivate my implant."

She shakes her head. "As I said, the device isn't functioning properly." She exchanges a glance with Ms. Curie. "Our results have been . . . inconsistent."

"What does that mean?" Canter demands.

"The individual who volunteered for the test didn't survive."

The room is silent. "I've since modified the device to respond to the signal of the individual implant," Ms. Curie finally says, "but we haven't been confident enough to try again."

"Test it on me." Bernard's voice is low but firm. "In exchange, I'll tell you where the facility is."

"You're just a child," Perennial insists. "And it's not

ready. If you tell us where the facility is, we can focus our efforts there."

"You can't put all your wires in one circuit," Bernard argues, his face flushed. "If I direct you to the facility, and you can't deactivate the source or you get caught or a million other things go wrong, you're right back where you started. But if you know the individual deactivator works, you've still got a solid Plan B."

"It could kill you," Ms. Curie counters, her lips pressing into a thin line.

Bernard shrugs. "Then they'll just make another."

I stare at him, his dark hair falling into familiar blue eyes. I could see Bernie volunteering to test the device, too, but for the greater cause. With Bernard, there's another layer to it. Many others. Revenge. Rebellion. Retribution. Reasons and motivations Bernie would never have shared.

"But it won't be *you*." I reach out and touch his arm. I'm surprised when he doesn't shrug it off.

"It's worth the sacrifice." Bernard glances between Perennial and Ms. Curie. "If the device works, split into two teams. One to go to the facility, and the other to try to switch off as many blockers as you can, one by one."

"It'd be a good diversion," Hannah adds. "Even if the first group gets caught or it doesn't work, the Governing Council will be so focused there, they won't notice you're creating an army right under their noses."

Perennial frowns. "I can't justify the risk."

But Bernard is equally stubborn. "I'm not giving you the location unless you agree."

The adults descend into murmured conversations. It's hard to follow any single thread with so many voices speaking at once, but it seems like there are people on both sides.

After a few minutes, Perennial raises a hand and the chatter ends abruptly. She locks eyes with Ms. Curie. "How confident are you in the revamped device?"

She hesitates, then sets her jaw and nods. "Very."

"Then do it," commands Bernard.

Perennial paces the room. After a couple of minutes, she returns her attention to Bernard. "Reps have very little say in how our lives unfold. Sure, we can break our contracts, but the consequences are almost always too much of a deterrent. Fines, tarnished reputations, and the Governing Councils have never, to my knowledge, restored a Rep's magical potential. Though I'm sure that's buried somewhere in the fine print." She pauses. "Because of that, I'm going to give you a choice."

Bernard straightens, triumph gleaming in his eyes.

"You understand the risks," she says, and he nods.

"We need insurance about the location," a deep voice calls from the group. "In case he doesn't survive."

A man moves to the center of the room, hands tucked behind his back. The light catches on streaks of gray in his dark blond hair, which is pulled back in a low ponytail. I'm confident I've never met him, but he still looks familiar.

"Nathan, I don't think—"

"If this doesn't work, we'll be exactly where we started." He rubs at his beard, faded Inscriptions marking the back of his hand.

Canter notices at the same time as me. "Are those—"

"His magic was taken, too," Hannah says. "Just like my parents."

Nathan studies us with a look that reminds me of Ms. Goble. "Reps have suffered the most under this oppressive system, but they aren't the only ones affected. If this works, it will take a weapon from the Councils' arsenal. If it doesn't, nothing will have changed."

"We have another option," Ms. Curie adds quietly. "Public pressure."

"We've discussed this already," Perennial says, her voice tight.

I narrow my eyes. "What's she talking about?"

"Nothing that concerns you," Perennial snaps.

"A book," Ms. Curie says at the same time. "A list of people who've been stripped of their magic."

"An actual book?" Lila asks. "Like they had on the Old World?"

Ms. Curie nods. "The information can't be accessed by the open network."

"Where is it?" I ask. If we can find them, get them to come forward together, the Councils won't be able to deny what they've been up to.

"It's too well protected." Perennial glares in Ms. Curie's direction. "Besides, our efforts to broadcast Melfin and the Councils' abuse of power have been easily quashed."

"Your group posted that video of Melfin threatening the restaurant owner," I say.

Perennial nods. "The Council has been quite careful in covering up their activities, making them difficult to expose. But Melfin's ego is the size of an asteroid, and we thought we might be able to use his bragging to expose them all."

"Then why haven't you?" Canter asks.

"The Councils control the open network," Perennial explains. "That means they also control the public discourse."

"The book is hard evidence," Ms. Curie argues. "*Physical* evidence that can't simply be deleted if it becomes inconvenient."

"And there's still no guarantee it will make a kilobyte of difference."

"But if people knew—"

"In my life," Perennial says coolly, "I've found, both in this cycle and in my original's, that people rarely care about matters that don't directly affect them. Our focus is restoring magic, not stopping the oppression at the source. We need more resources before we can even think about going after that book." She turns back to Bernard. "We need our magic restored."

"And we need a fallback if this doesn't go well," Nathan adds.

Bernard nods. "I'll tell Myra exactly where it is. If the device . . . malfunctions, she can give you the information."

Perennial gestures at Ms. Curie, who turns and hurries from the room. While she's gone, Bernard whispers the details into my ear. All I can do is nod, confirming I understand. When Ms. Curie returns, she's carrying a strange device. Three bars form a large triangle with a metal plate mounted at each angle.

"Ready?" she asks.

"Bernard!" I blurt out. "Are you sure you want to do this?"

He grins. "Honestly, it feels incredible just to be asked that. And I'm sure."

Ms. Curie lays the machine across her palms. A soft crackle builds into the snap and hiss of electricity as the device floats into the air. "The implants aren't always in the same place," she explains, her eyes drifting shut. "This bounces the charge between the three plates so it deactivates it no matter where it's located." She directs the device over Bernard's head, and as it drifts down, the crackling ignites into sharp bursts, the electricity dancing between the three panels like lightning.

The machine drops, spitting sparks as it passes over Bernard, bathing him in a violet cloud of energy that condenses into a single beam, which explodes with a bang.

I scream at the same time as him, our voices lost in the sizzle of electricity.

CHAPTER THIRTY-EIGHT

"BERNARD!" I RUSH TO WHERE HE'S COLLAPSED. "ARE you all right?"

Lila drops to her knees, laying her hands over him. "He's alive."

I grab his shoulders and shake him. "Wake up. Wake up, Bernard! Please." Tears pool in my eyes as I look between Lila and Perennial, who's now hovering over Bernard, too. "Why won't he wake up?"

"The shock knocked him unconscious," Lila explains. "But his vital systems are normal."

Perennial touches her palm to Bernard's forehead just as his eyes fly open.

"You're okay," I choke out, still fighting back tears. "You're fine."

"I don't feel fine." He grunts, heaving up to his elbows, then squints at Perennial. "Did it work?"

"We won't know for a while," she says. "Your magic will still have to develop, just like anyone else's."

"But you're alive," Ms. Curie adds. "I'd call that a success."

"Maybe," Bernard says, rubbing his temple.

Perennial's concern melts back into steely resolve. "Our deal, then."

"It's on an oxbow lake off the upper branch of the River of Monet," Bernard replies, "about halfway up, but separated from the main waterway by a stretch of land so boats don't accidentally find it."

The room erupts into activity. A long line forms around Ms. Curie, others volunteering to have the device tested on them. One by one, she passes the machine over each, followed by the same spitting purple lighting. Many of the volunteers collapse like Bernard, but nothing worse happens. No one seems to know how long it could take for signs of magic to emerge, but it's more hope than most of them have had in a long time.

Finally, Nathan steps forward, and Ms. Curie directs the device over him. As the electricity dances around his broad shoulders he releases a whoop of excitement.

"What Creer were you?" Lila asks, beaming as he breaks into a jig after Ms. Curie moves on to the next person.

"Chemic." He stops to catch his breath. "I used to teach on the Mars Settlement until Jake Melfin cost me my job and my magic."

Recognition flashes through my mind and I gasp. "Are you Nathan Hackett?"

He rocks back on his heels. "How'd you know that?"

"I read an article about you last year. You predicted food cloning would break down if there weren't plants to reset the process."

"I did."

"Melfin got you fired for it?"

"Eventually, yes. But first he approached me to see if I had seeds to demonstrate my theory."

My mouth falls open.

"It must have been a trap, right?" Lila asks. "He was trying to see if you had a source?"

"I thought so, too, initially," Nathan says. "But it seemed like Melfin wanted the seeds himself. He kept saying if I could show him, he'd shield me from any consequences."

Canter glowers. "I bet he was trying to find a reason to send you to Mercury."

"Maybe." Nathan strokes his beard. "He seemed truly disappointed when I told him I didn't have seeds to share."

"And when you didn't, he ordered the Council to strip your powers?" I ask.

"Not the whole Council. Only a few members handle plant crimes."

"But you didn't commit any plant crimes," Lila argues.

"You'll find as you get older that there are the way things are supposed to work and the way they actually work," Nathan says grimly. "For those in power, things work whatever way they want."

"How does Melfin still have so much power?" Canter asks. "He's not even on the Council anymore."

"Even without his Council position, Jake Melfin has influence."

"Through his company?" I ask.

"I did a lot of reading once my Creer . . . Well, I had a lot of time on my hands after I lost my magic and before Perennial found me. I went down a black hole researching. MFI isn't just the biggest food production company in the galaxy; they're also one of the largest donors. And money talks."

"Donors? To what?"

"The Lunar Mending Institute. The Martian one, too. The company even has financial links to the Mercurian prison mines and an organization called A.R.C.S., though I haven't been able to find more information on them yet."

"That's the Rep facility!" I interject. "It stands for Advanced Repetition Cloning Services, or something like that. Bernard told me."

Nathan nods. "That makes sense."

"I don't understand."

"Let's just say sometimes power is earned, sometimes it's given, and quite often, it's purchased."

As I consider this new information, Nathan goes to test if his magic will work on a solution someone's dug out of a cabinet.

Two teams emerge, just as Bernard suggested—one armed with the device, discussing the most efficient way to continue unlocking the magic blockers, and the other plotting how to infiltrate the River of Monet facility.

"We want to come," I insist. "We can help."

"No," Perennial says. "You're too young."

"We're the same age as her!" I say, pointing at Hannah.

"Attending meetings is different than standing on the front lines. You've done more than enough." Perennial focuses on my ex–best friend. "We'll send someone to your home to help your parents."

Hannah's eyes light up, but her hope quickly dims. "Even if they get their magic back, they still won't be able to return to their Creers. Not with Jake Melfin around. Who would hire them?"

"I'm sure he's stripped a lot of people of their magic," I say, trying to sound reassuring. "There's got to be a way to find them and deactivate their devices, too."

"One problem at a time," Perennial replies.

"But—"

A hum fills the air, growing louder and louder, until the building itself starts to vibrate.

"What's that noise?" I ask.

Perennial crosses the room, pressing herself against a wall before peering out the window. When she turns back to us, she's as gray as moondust. "Another problem."

CHAPTER THIRTY-NINE

MS. CURIE HURRIES TO PERENNIAL'S SIDE. "GOVERN-ment ships approaching."

"Everyone, implement evacuation protocols," Perennial orders.

"We don't know any protocols!" Canter calls as the room dissolves into organized chaos. I rush over to the window. A half dozen sleek silver ships hover, circling the building.

"You kids can hide on the lower levels," Perennial replies as lights flash outside, bathing everyone in a crimson glow. "They aren't here for you."

"Come on." Ms. Curie shepherds us into the hall. "Hannah, you too."

"I don't want to hide!" Hannah argues. "I'm going with you."

"If you weren't going before, you certainly aren't now,"

Perennial scolds. "You'll stay where Indra shows you until we're gone and the government ships are, too. Don't come out, no matter what you see or hear."

When we don't move, Perennial's features turn to stone. "If you refuse to follow instructions, you'll be putting everyone in harm's way."

I don't make it more than a half dozen steps before a boom rocks the weather station and I slam into a wall.

"They're breaching the facility!" Nathan barks.

More blasts shake the building, pulsing like a heartbeat. They aren't as strong as the first one, but their frequency is unsettling.

"What's happening?" I whisper to Canter, whose brow is furrowed in concentration.

"The ships are trying to knock out the power to the station," Canter explains, still squinting. "But I feel some sort of countermeasure being launched from here. I don't know what it is. It has a lot of power, though." He nods over to where a few people are hunched over the consoles. "This place must have some sort of defense system. Most government buildings do. I bet they're using them to try to disable the ships."

I open my mouth to ask Ms. Curie more, but I don't get the chance.

"Let's go!" she snaps, the bracelet of wires around her wrist spitting sparks as she motions toward the hall.

"We can't just leave them!" Lila cries.

"You can't help them now." Ms. Curie leads us down one flight of stairs and then another. We must be at ground level now. I have to run to keep pace. "But maybe I can."

"How?" I ask. Another round of explosions rocks the building, sending us bouncing off the walls.

"The third option," Ms. Curie continues, trying to catch her breath. "I'm going after the book."

"Where is it?" Hannah asks.

"Hidden on Mercury."

Canter clenches his fists. "I'm going with you."

A triumphant spark flashes in Ms. Curie's eyes but quickly fades. She shakes her head. "No. It's too dangerous."

"I don't care," he says. "My mother's there."

"And my sister," Hannah says. "I'm coming, too."

"We're *all* going," I say. "We've come this far."

Voices echo in the hall behind us, angry and authoritative.

"They're inside," Ms. Curie calls, hurrying ahead. "We need to get—"

Another explosion rocks the building, knocking me off my feet. I throw my hands over my head as debris falls like rain. After a few seconds, everything is quiet again, and I heave to my feet, coughing. The ceiling and half the wall have collapsed, blocking our way forward.

Lila and Canter shove themselves free from the rubble, then stand shakily. "Where are the others?" Canter asks.

A groan to my right sends us digging. We find Hannah and Bernard half buried and fully bruised. It only takes Lila a nanosecond to patch them up.

"Ms. Curie?" I call.

"I'm back here," a faint voice answers from the other side of the wreckage. "I don't—I don't think I can get to you. Can you see another way out?"

I turn in a circle. Apart from a small window none of us could fit through, the only clear path is back the way we came.

I spot something moving out of the corner of my eye and spin toward the window, ducking just in time. A ship swoops past so close it looks like it's going to crash. Instead, the shuttle halts right outside. Thankfully, there's no government pilot behind the controls.

"Bin-ro!" Canter yelps. "Who taught him to fly?"

"Do we really need to vet his pilot training right now?" I snap. "We need to go!"

"Quickly," Bernard adds as more ships circle overhead.

I turn to Hannah. "Can you use your powers to get us out there?"

She studies the window. "Maybe I could stretch it—make it wider. I'll try."

"I think we're going to need more than try," Canter says,

sounding tense as he peers down the hall. The voices are clearer now, shouting orders.

Hannah rolls her shoulders and stands straighter. "You're right. I've got this." She stretches her arm toward the window and the wall surrounding it starts to morph, block by block, widening the window.

When it's big enough to squeeze through, I shove Bernard forward. "You've sacrificed enough."

Hannah's arms shake as she fights to hold the opening.

"I don't think Hannah will be able to shift the debris to get to you," I call to Ms. Curie. "Can you find another way through?"

"Not in time," she answers. "Just get yourselves out of here. Don't worry about me."

Canter swipes dirt from his forehead. "But what about—"

"Go! Take down Melfin," Ms. Curie calls through the debris. "It'll solve most of the problems you're trying to correct, and some you don't even know about yet."

"What other problems?" I demand as Bernard clears the opening and Lila follows.

Sweat beads on Hannah's forehead while explosions sound in the distance.

"It'll make sense when you find the book," Ms. Curie replies cryptically. "But it'll be dangerous. Anything to do with plants is dangerous."

My ears are ringing from the blasts—and more. "It has to do with the Botans?"

Her voice is stronger when she replies. "It has to do with everything."

"Myra, hurry," Hannah croaks as Lila breaks free and runs to the ship.

I twist through the tight space. The walls press in on me, the rough edges grabbing at my clothes, snagging my hair. I force myself not to think about what would happen if Hannah lost concentration while I was still inside.

Canter hovers outside the gap. "Did you really give my mother the seeds she used to start the garden?"

"Yes," Ms. Curie calls back. "And despite what your father thinks, I'm still glad I did. I regret a lot of things . . . but not that. Never that."

Cooler air hits my face as I stumble through to the other side. Hannah is slumped against the wall opposite her makeshift exit, her whole body trembling as she holds the blocks in place.

"Canter, let's go!"

"But why?" Canter calls frantically as he maneuvers through the opening, his cheeks pink with his need to know. "You couldn't have known she'd have Botan magic."

"I didn't even know Botan magic existed back then. I showed her because she was my best friend. As soon as she saw them, you could feel the magic in the air." Ms. Curie pauses. "I didn't get a chance to tell you last year, but I know your mother would have been proud you found the garden."

Canter emerges beside me, his eyes glassy.

"Come on!" I yell to Hannah.

She rushes into the gap, and as she moves forward, the blocks shift back together behind her. When she stumbles clear, the wall seals completely, except for the small window. She collapses to her knees, panting.

Supporting Hannah on either side, we race toward the shuttle.

"Where did you get the seeds from?" Canter calls over his shoulder as we reach the ship. We dive inside and I look back toward the building.

Ms. Curie's face is framed by another small window, her short black hair blowing in the wind. Just before we rocket into the sky, she calls out her answer, her voice proud. Triumphant.

"I stole them from Jake Melfin."

CHAPTER FORTY

AS THE SHUTTLE STREAKS THROUGH THE SKY, LASERS dance around us like lightning. Our ship rolls from side to side, dodging them, diving and twisting like a boat bobbing in stormy water. Bernard clutches his stomach, and my insides swirl dangerously as I fill in the others.

"Why would Jake Melfin have seeds?" Lila asks. "He's thrown more people into Mercurian prison for seed possession than anyone."

In the distance, over the cluster of lights I now recognize as the weather station, two silver blurs shoot in opposite directions like a mirror reflecting a shooting star. A flock of black ships zips after them. I can only hope both Perennial's teams escaped.

A lone government ship the color of onyx is on our tail. Bin-ro, plugged into the ship's console, whistles softly to himself as his evasive maneuvers make Lila's Mending powers increasingly necessary.

"I don't know." I clench and unclench my hands, trying to stay calm. "But I'm going to find out."

A whoosh followed by a sizzle rocks the ship, and I completely forget my nausea. Bin-ro lets out a string of beeps and chirps as the lights flicker—a barrage of robot curses. We swoop to the right, and I clutch the sides of my seat so I don't tumble to the floor.

"Canter?" I squeak. "Are we good?"

"Hang on." The air crackles with energy as he lifts a hand, panning it around in a circle. "Seems fine. The circuitry's a little singed, but functional. It'd be great if that didn't happen again, though."

"Beep!" Blue lights flash erratically on Bin-ro's hull.

"I *know* you didn't do it on purpose!" Canter replies. "You're doing a great job keeping us from getting cooked."

"Interstellar flying," Lila agrees.

"Let's try to lose this guy if we can," Hannah mutters as the black ship swoops closer. "And fast."

"I've got an idea." Bernard leans toward the front of the cockpit. "See those clouds over there?"

To my right, on the horizon, gray fog obscures the stars. Below us I see a sea of whitecaps. A storm's brewing.

"Beep boop!"

Bernard grimaces. "Fly straight through it."

I raise my eyebrows. "Is that a good idea?"

"No. But it's not a bad one, either. If we're quick and careful, we can barrel through the storm and change directions. By the time this guy gets out, hopefully we'll be long gone."

"Or," Hannah adds, "he'll be fried by lightning."

"At least we've got an Elector on board." Lila nudges Canter. "Think you can keep the electricity off us?"

"Storms are unpredictable." Canter ruffles his hair, then shoots us a crooked smile. "Good thing I am, too."

Bin-ro swerves us toward the storm. If I thought his evasive maneuvers were bad, flying straight into a storm makes this trip look like a Crawler to Apolloton. The ship bucks and jerks, sending us sprawling. As soon as we cross into the slate clouds, Canter's eyes snap shut. His hands hover just above his knees. He doesn't move or speak, but sweat soaks his hair, trickling down his temple.

"So assuming we don't die," I say, trying to distract the others, "how are we getting off Venus and all the way to Mercury?"

"My parents work at the MFI factory that supplies the Mercurian prison with food," Hannah says slowly. "We can hide on the shuttle when it leaves for its next delivery."

"How will we know which one to stow away on?" I ask. "There must be tons of supply ships coming and going."

"I'll know," Hannah insists. "I've been there plenty of times, bringing my parents lunch or dinner—sometimes both in one shift. If we play it right, no one will even question us."

I grip the edges my seat so hard my knuckles are as white as jasmine. Lightning slices the air in front of us, and I bite back a scream. Or at least I think I do. It could have been drowned out by the earsplitting rumble of thunder that followed.

After what feels like a century, we burst from the clouds. A scattering of stars twinkle in greeting.

"Is he still behind us?" Lila asks, twisting around.

Hannah peers through a window. "I don't see him. Good plan, Bernard."

"We're not clear yet," he says grimly. "The farther we get from here, the better."

"Head east," Hannah orders, and the ship dips into a turn. "The MFI factory shouldn't be far." She inputs the coordinates into the dashboard.

We're mostly silent as the ship skims over the indigo sea. Thankfully, no one seems to be pursuing us. Lights glitter in the distance, close to the water. That must be the factory.

The dock is deserted when we land, but inside is ablaze. "Lots of people work here," Hannah explains. "If we act like we belong, no one should question us."

I grin. "Follow my lead. I'm an expert at looking like I'm where I'm supposed to be, even when I'm not."

Hannah and I are the first off the shuttle. "Just like old times," she murmurs.

"Remember how we used to sneak down to the Crater Café in the middle of the night to get turbocharged chocolate drinks?" I ask, my mouth watering at the memory. Behind us, Bin-ro whistles a song that sounds just like the jingle the café used in its advertisements.

Hannah grins and hums along for a few bars. "Then we'd be up all night messaging each other because neither of us could sleep."

"I still can't believe the girl who worked there thought we were university students on a study break."

The doors slide open, revealing machinery stretching in neat rows as far as the eye can see. A handful of workers go about their business, bent over equipment or chattering in groups. They don't even glance our way. I notice some of them don't look much older than us.

"She didn't," Hannah answers. "I never told you. It was after . . . Anyway, I ran into her in the lobby, and she asked how my studies were going, and then *winked*."

"Crashing comets! I really thought we'd fooled her."

"Me too." Hannah giggles. "The worst part was my mom was with me, and I had to launch into a galactic space ballad about how I went to the café to study for a Mender theory test."

"Did she buy it?" I ask as I follow Hannah around a corner. I can hear the others behind us, but I don't turn around to check. The more natural we look, the less likely we are to draw unwanted attention.

"No. But I put together such a convincing story, I don't think she even wanted to know what was really going on."

"That sounds like your mom." An unexpected wave of sadness washes over me. I'd forgotten how much I missed Hannah. Canter and Lila are interstellar best friends. Still, there's nothing like the easy feeling of being around someone you've been through so much with.

But as soon as the thought crosses my mind, the warmth between us shifts like it was hit with liquid nitrogen.

"Myra," Hannah says quietly.

"I know." I shake my head and stare straight ahead, where a packaging machine is being supervised by a man and a woman. The woman presses buttons while her partner makes notes on a holo-pad. "It's strange being together again after all this time. Not *bad* strange. Just different." Then, in a quieter voice, I add, "I really am sorry. For everything."

Hannah doesn't answer. I risk a glance and realize I'm alone. But not for long. A portly man with a red face and aggressive sideburns stomps toward me, a sleek factory robot whizzing along beside him. His gaze is locked on my face, and there is no escape. There's only lying. And hoping it works.

"You!" he barks. "You're the new trainee. Cynthia." The way he says it, it isn't a question. "You were supposed to be here ten minutes ago." If possible, his face gets redder as he presses a series of buttons on the robot's complicated-looking control panel. Lights flash on its screen and it chirps in response. The man nods and points to the far corner of the factory. "They need help stocking the next delivery. And where's your uniform?" He doesn't wait for an answer. "Wear it next time." Spit flies from his mouth. I try not to flinch. "And for Jupiter's sake, be on time!" he calls over his shoulder as he marches away, the robot buzzing after him.

Once they round the corner, my friends seep out of the aisles and from behind machines like water trickling downstream. "Some help you all were," I grumble.

"You were interstellar!" Hannah says, thumping me on the shoulder. "And you just got the perfect assignment! That ship you're supposed to help load? I think it's one of the Mercury food delivery shuttles. They always park in that corner."

Hannah and I cross the floor with our chins high and our pace purposeful. The others trail behind us, pausing here and there to check a setting or pretend to read something on the screen of a nearby robot.

We reach a team of three people, two men and one woman, loading a beige shuttle. One of them looks around Bernard's age. The other two could pass for peers of my parents.

"You're supposed to go on break," Hannah announces, and I struggle to suppress the surprise I'm sure is rippling across my face. "We're finishing up this shipment."

"Thank the stars," the older man says, swiping a sleeve across his forehead. "I thought they'd never call us in."

"Convenient they wait until we're nearly done," the teenage boy sneers. "Are you sure you weren't supposed to come over ten minutes ago?"

"Actually, they said we could wait for this delivery to be complete," Hannah snaps back. "We can just go lounge over there while you finish up if you want."

"Ignore him," the woman says. "He's just grumpy because we missed our lunch block. C'mon." She gestures for the other two to follow her. "Let's go before management decides our metrics are behind."

The three workers disappear into an aisle, and my friends and I slip up the ramp onto the shuttle, Bin-ro whistling behind us.

CHAPTER FORTY-ONE

NONE OF US DARE SPEAK WHILE WE'RE HUDDLED among the crates in the back of the shuttle, Bin-ro cradled in my lap. The ship comes equipped with two human drivers to unload it, and they won't be pleased to find five stowaways crowded in the back.

The ride to Mercury is long on the slow delivery shuttle, and I fight the urge to doze as we cross the distance between Venus and the planet scorchingly close to the sun.

I didn't get a chance to see Mercury as we approached, but close up, I can't imagine the view was interstellar. Mountains of crimson rock stretch as far as I can see. Buildings carved into the landscape by centuries of prisoners stationed here. The whole scene is charred and ugly and miserable.

While the workers from MFI guide the first row of crates

inside on hover carts, the doors are left wide open, with no security in sight. My friends and I creep inside the building, quickly crossing into another corridor before winding our way through the maze of tunnels.

Despite climate-control technology, the floors and walls radiate heat. We pass into another hallway, this one lined with rows and rows of doors with complicated locking mechanisms. Canter and Hannah slow, their eyes lingering on each cell we pass.

"We don't have time to check them all," I remind them. "There could be a hundred hallways like this one."

"I know," Canter replies tightly.

"Once we figure out where they are, can you use your Elector magic to short-circuit the locks?" I ask.

Canter pauses to study one of the devices. "I don't know. They may have an insulation mechanism that stops Elector magic from interference."

"Let me check." Hannah lays her hands over the lock and closes her eyes. "There are layers and layers of equipment inside," she says, her eyes fluttering open. "Circuits, thick buffering material, and some sort of trigger."

Canter sighs. "An alarm."

"Probably." Hannah grimaces. "Without training, I can't say for sure."

I put a hand on her shoulder. "We can work together to figure it out once we find them."

"That's not going to be easy," Canter replies. "There isn't much on the open network about this place, and everything I could find said it's laid out like a maze."

"Interstellar." I fiddle with my glasses. "We need to find the control center. From there, we should be able to figure out where they're keeping Fiona and Meredith."

Bin-ro gives a sharp beep, and a hatch opens in his metal shell. A small round plate emerges and spins 360 degrees.

I raise my eyebrows. "Have you seen that tool before?" I ask Canter.

"Never. Maybe it's letting him scan the layout of this place?"

"*Beep!*" the small robot chirps, then speeds off down the hall. When none of us follow, he turns and releases a low whistle, like someone calling their dog, before continuing on.

I glance over at Canter and he shrugs. "He's never steered us wrong before."

We hurry after Bin-ro without another word.

Hannah twists her hair through her fingers as we pass from one hallway into the next. "It's going to be tricky if we bump into someone. There's nowhere to hide."

Lila bites her lip. "I may be able to help with that." She pauses and covers her face with both hands, like a kid playing hide-and-seek. My mouth drops open as her hair, long, dark, and curly, shortens until it's barely skimming her ears. When she removes her hands, I reel back. Her entire face has changed. In Lila's place is a middle-aged man who's oddly familiar.

"You look like the shuttle delivery worker," Hannah marvels. "How'd you do that?"

"It's a trick the Menders at V.A.M.A. use when they get into character," she explains, then turns to me. "I told you I'd learned how to switch my hair and eye color."

"Yeah, but this is on a whole other level. It's really strange hearing your voice coming from that face."

"Well, it'll be worth it if it keeps us from getting caught."

"This is scarier than when you made my skin absorb the seeds," I tell her. "Can you change back now? It's creeping me out."

She laughs and the delivery worker's face fades away, replaced once more by Lila's.

"That's better," Bernard says, shaking his head.

"*Beep boop!*" Bin-ro chirps from the end of the hall and we hurry to catch up.

Eventually, we round a corner, and instead of more doors, face a glass-enclosed room. Inside, computer screens, flashing control panels, and a half dozen guards fill the space.

"What do we do?" I whisper as we crouch just out of sight. "Canter, can you fry the circuits?"

"If I do, I might not be able to get them back online

again. But maybe I can create a diversion." He glances behind us. "I'll be right back."

Before I can stop him, he disappears back down the corridor we came from. I exchange a worried look with Lila.

A few minutes later, an alarm blares from inside the control room. I jump, my head swiveling as I listen for the sounds of someone coming. I risk a peek and see the guards clustered around a console, pointing frantically. All at once, three of them rush out, disappearing down another hall.

Footsteps echo behind us, and we all freeze. But it's just Canter, looking smug.

"How'd it go?" he asks.

"Pretty well," I say. "There're only three more in there. What'd you do?"

"Short-circuited one of the lock panels a floor below."

"Won't they be suspicious?" Hannah asks, chewing her lip.

He shakes his head. "I was careful, and it was just one. It'll look like it overheated."

"My turn, then," Lila says, her eyes sparkling. "Let's try this again." She turns back to the control room, where the remaining guards are hunched over computers.

I hold my breath as Lila morphs back into the delivery driver. She turns, winks, and hurries down the hall, rapping on the control room door.

The guard closest to the glass startles, then presses a

button on the console, and the door slides open. "I think they need you one level down," she says, her voice low and even. "There's some sort of commotion."

The guards exchange a look. "All of us?" the first one asks.

Lila leans back against the counter, her hands tucked behind her back. "They didn't say, but you might want to go check."

The still-blaring alarm must convince them. They push to their feet, usher Lila out, and shut the door behind them. "Where are you supposed to be?" the last guard out asks, his eyes narrowing slightly.

"Just finished unloading a delivery from MFI," she says, running a hand over her closely cropped hair. "Hoping to get back home in time for my dinner break."

That seems to satisfy them. Without another word, they hurry away, down the same corridor the first group disappeared into.

"Good job getting rid of them," I murmur as Lila's features melt back into her usual ones. "Too bad they shut the door behind them, though. It must've locked."

"Oh, I'm sure it did," she says. "Good thing one of them left their ID card on the counter." She turns her hand over, where a small metal rectangle rests on her palm.

"Crashing comets!" Canter looks like he could hug her. "That should help with the computers, too. Let's go!"

Lila scans the card on a panel and the control room door slides open.

"Wait!" Canter throws out an arm. "Something's wrong."

I scan the hall. "Is someone coming?"

"There's more electrical charge in that room than there should be." He scrunches his forehead. "It feels familiar . . . like the S.L.A.M. halls after curfew."

My eyes widen. "Curfew trackers."

Canter grunts. "Something like that."

"There must be another security measure we need to disable," Hannah says.

"It'll take too long to find, and who knows if the ID card will work. It might need a password." Canter reaches into his pocket, pulling out a wad of something shiny. "Good thing I came prepared."

We each wrap reflector paper around our shoes and tiptoe toward the room. I cringe as I pass the threshold, pausing, but nothing happens.

"Nice job, hotshot."

Canter sweeps into a low bow as the rest of our crew files in.

Hannah slides behind a computer console, and we cluster around as Lila passes her the card. She pulls up a map of the planet. "It looks like the MFI offices are linked to the prison by a tunnel." As Hannah types, the screen flashes with text, files, and folders. "I can't access their network from the prison's system, but it doesn't look that large on the map."

"Why would MFI be connected?" I wonder aloud.

"Looks like all the buildings on Mercury are." Hannah points to something on the screen. "I remember reading something about a planetary heat shield. It's easier to power with the buildings clustered together."

"What about the prisoner list?" Canter asks hesitantly.

"Hang on." Hannah's fingers fly over the projected keyboard.

How is she doing that? I wonder. "I can't even read what's on the screen. How fast would you be with proper Tekkie training?"

"We'd already be gone." She flashes me a smile—a genuine one—then gasps as her eyes return to the screen. "Jupiter Jackpot!"

"Shh!" Lila hisses, glancing behind us.

"Did you find them?" Canter demands.

"I found Meredith. Just give me a second. . . ." She squints, scrolling across the screen, before tapping a square. "Yup. Fiona Weathers. Same block as my sister."

Canter doesn't move, but I can see his mom's name in tiny type reflected in his eyes.

"Do you think there are other Botans in that section, too?" I ask eagerly.

Hannah taps a few more buttons and nods. "The charges against Fiona and Meredith are listed as P.O."

331

"Plant offender," Lila translates.

Hannah taps a few more keys. "The others in that block have the same charges."

I take a slow breath, trying to swallow the excitement bubbling up in my chest. "How do we get them out?"

"I can disengage the locks in that hallway from here," Hannah says. "That way, we can check the other cells without an alarm going off."

"What about the book Curie mentioned?" Bernard asks. "It could be anywhere. The prison warden's office, a supply room . . ."

"Hold on," Hannah says. The computer screen's a blur. She scoops Bin-ro up and places him on the counter. "Can you store the map?"

"Beep!" Bin-ro plugs himself into the computer console.

"Did it work?" Hannah asks.

A blue light gleams on Bin-ro's hull until the entire floor is bathed in a cobalt projection of the map of Mercury.

Hannah turns to face us. "We should break into two teams."

"I'm going with you and Canter to the Botan cellblock." No one argues.

"Then Lila and I can search for the book," Bernard offers.

"Beep boop beep!" Bin-ro chirps, spinning in a circle.

"We didn't forget you, buddy," Canter replies. "You go

with Lila and Bernard. Help them check all the rooms."

"We'll need to keep in touch," Lila insists. "I have my messenger and Myra has hers. If anyone finds anything or runs into trouble, ping the others."

"Are we at all worried about the shuttle leaving us behind when it heads back to Venus?" Bernard asks.

"It makes a run every day," Hannah replies with a shrug. "If it leaves, we'll hide out until tomorrow and take the next one."

"Still, let's not waste any time." I glance back at the empty room. "The guards will be back any minute. The longer we're out in the open, the greater the chance we'll get caught."

We're all quiet for a moment, and I wish on every lucky meteor I've ever had that we make it back. And with everything we came for.

"Be careful," Lila whispers as she heads down the hall with Bernard.

"You too," I say quietly. "Good luck."

"Keep an eye on your messenger," Hannah reminds them. Bernard nods, then disappears around the corner. Canter and Hannah are already halfway down the hall. I hurry to catch up.

"We shouldn't be moving this fast," I whisper. "We don't have Bin-ro to tell us when someone's coming."

"We have ears," Canter says without slowing.

"And I can't use them with the racket you're making," I hiss.

Hannah slows her pace. "Myra's right. If we get caught when we're this close, I'll throw myself into the sun."

"It's not much farther, anyway," I add. "The cellblock was two levels down."

We're still moving quickly, but our footfalls are much lighter now, and it's a good thing, or I'd never have caught the voices coming from up ahead. I grab Hannah's and Canter's shirts, yanking them back, then put a finger to my lips.

We backtrack. Hannah motions to a door on my right, but when I try the handle, it's locked. I nod at Canter, stepping aside so he can get closer. Lightning flashes from his fingertips, and then Hannah eases the door open so we can slip inside, slapping a button to close it behind us. Just in time. The voices outside grow louder, then stop right outside.

I glance around. We're in an office, but not an abandoned one. A name glows over the far corner of the desk: WARDEN CASSANDRA VANDER. My heart leaps. *Maybe the book is here!*

"I've told you, Mr. Melfin. We've had absolutely nothing unusual happen today." I stare into Canter's and Hannah's pale faces, even as I can feel the blood draining from my own. "Besides your transport, the only other traffic was the shuttle from your factory, and you searched that ship yourself before it headed back to Venus."

"I know they're here," growls Mr. Melfin.

Who could have told him? Someone from Perennial's group? No. No one there would betray the mission. Someone from the factory?

"Why don't we step into my office, and we can discuss your concerns further."

"They aren't hiding in your office!" Mr. Melfin barks. "They're here, somewhere. I know what they're after, and it's not in that room!"

"We already checked your offices and the cellblock you were concerned about," Warden Vander replies, irritation creeping into her voice. "And, truthfully, I can't imagine a few kids could've found out about those records. Or why you're so concerned."

"I pay you handsomely to not worry about what my concerns are," Mr. Melfin snaps, though his voice sounds farther away. "I want to be alerted the moment they're located."

Footsteps sound down the hall and disappear. I whip out my messenger:

Melfin here. Knows someone is searching for Botans and the book. Sounds like it's in the MFI offices. Be careful.

"How did he find out?" Hannah asks, her eyes wide.

Slowly, I release a breath. "I don't know, but we'd better go."

Canter nods and cautiously steps into the hall, Hannah right behind him. "Melfin said they'd already searched the cellblock. We'll never get a better chance."

He's right, but how we'll be able to break his mother and Meredith out, find the book, and get out of here with the shuttle gone and Melfin on our trail, I have no idea. One thing at a time. First up: the Botans.

Moving faster than we dared earlier, we skid down the hallway Hannah pinpointed.

"Which rooms are they in?" Canter asks, his face paler than I've ever seen it.

Without thinking, I reach out and grab his hand, squeezing tight. I tell myself it's to comfort him, but it helps me steady myself, too. "Are you okay?"

"No." When he looks at me, a storm of emotions crashes in his eyes. "Everything's going to be different when we open that door."

"Good different, though," I say. "But yeah, still different." I grip his hand harder. I know it's too tight, but I also don't think he minds. "No matter what, you've got me. And in a few minutes, you'll have your mom back. And it'll be amazing."

He smiles. "Thanks." He turns to Hannah, releasing my hand. "Which cell?" he asks again.

Hannah points down the corridor. "Your mom's in that one on the end." Canter approaches the door slowly, as if afraid it might transform into a monster at any moment. "And Meredith's here," she quietly adds. Anxiousness churns through me as I wonder how Hannah's sister will react when she sees me. All I can do is hope she can find a way to forgive me as well. Hannah's hands shake as she passes by a few doors, stopping at one in the middle of the hall.

"I'll check the others," I offer, wiping my sweaty palms on my pants before pressing an access button. It slides open and I squint into the darkness. And then a wave of ice washes over me. "There's no one here."

Hannah and Canter stand frozen in the open doorways.

I can hear Canter fighting against a sob. "They're all empty."

CHAPTER FORTY-TWO

"THAT'S IMPOSSIBLE," HANNAH SAYS, STILL STARING into the empty cell. "Maybe the numbering was wrong." She hurries up the hall, opening each door she passes. Canter pushes his way into cell after cell, each one empty.

As the last panel slides shut, Hannah slumps against it, slipping down to the floor.

Canter's hands are fists at his sides. "Where can they be?"

Hannah doesn't even look up. "Not here. Not anywhere."

"That's not true!" My heart's pounding. "They've got to be somewhere. Maybe . . . maybe the book will have a clue."

Canter doesn't say anything as he follows me, red-faced, eyes hollow. Hannah climbs slowly to her feet.

I'm relieved when I message Lila and she responds right

away. "No luck yet," I relay, forcing positivity I don't feel into my voice. "They dodged Melfin and have searched four of the six rooms in the MFI headquarters. We're meeting them at the fifth one." I glance down at the screen again. "This way," I say.

There's no sign of Melfin or Warden Vander as we navigate the halls to a long, sloping tunnel. The entrance to the MFI offices is marked with a simple sign. "Bin-ro detected you," Lila says when she steps out to meet us. "It's not over yet," she murmurs to Canter and Hannah as we pass inside. "Ms. Curie said the book had something to do with plants. We might find an answer there."

"And if we don't?" Canter asks, his voice bitter.

"We keep trying," I reply firmly. "We won't stop until we find them. I promise."

"Then we'd better be quick," Bernard insists, eyeing the closed door anxiously.

We surround the desk in the corner. A small projection swirls above it—the name Jake P. Melfin glowing midair. My stomach swoops.

The obvious drawers are mostly empty. Moving on, we scour the desk for signs of a secret compartment.

"It's not here, either," Lila says, rubbing her eyes.

"Bin-ro, can you show us the projection again?" Bernard requests. The little robot scoots forward and shines the map on the side of the desk.

"Wait!" I glance up at the overhead lighting, then back. "I've got an idea." I lie down next to the desk, peering up.

"Uh, Myra. Are you okay?" Canter steps closer, worry in his eyes. "Did you accidentally use your Mender magic to put her to sleep?" he asks Lila.

Ignoring him, I shift, twisting my head from side to side, and that's when I see it. A perfect *X* reflecting off the side of the desk.

"I've got it!" I exclaim, clambering to my feet, careful not to lose sight of the spot.

Canter frowns. "What are you talking about?"

"Did I ever tell you how I found the entrance from the hidden lab into the moongarden?" I brush my fingertips against the desk's smooth side. "Bin-ro showed me. A light panel glinted off the side of the counter, and the reflection formed a triangle. That's how I knew where the button was." I press my fingertips into the metal. A soft click sounds somewhere inside the workstation, and then a panel slides out, no wider than the space from my wrist to my forearm. Inside rests a box.

Lila gasps. "Is that box made of *wood*?"

I gently lift the container from the drawer. It looks just like the material Mr. Finch's violin was carved from. It even has four thin cords strung across the top. "I think so," I reply, turning the box carefully in my hands. "There's no latch or hinge. There aren't even seams."

Canter leans in closer. "Is it just a solid block?"

I shake my head. "It's too light." I scrutinize every inch, tracing the lines and swirls, and that's when I see them—faint words carved into the bottom.

DO WHAT IS ESSENTIAL AND NOT WHAT IS GOOD.

"What does it mean?" Canter asks.

I wish I knew.

I look up, and Lila's pacing the room. "Sounds like something Melfin would believe. Do what you think will get you ahead . . ."

"And the rest of the galaxy can kick Moon rocks," Canter growls.

That does seem on-brand for Melfin, but I can't help thinking we're missing something. "Why are the *D, E, A,* and *G* darker than the rest?"

"And what are those strings on top for?" Bernard adds.

"The four main strings on a violin," I yelp as I flip the box over again. "What if those are notes?"

"How do you know that?" Canter asks. "And what does that have to do with anything?"

"Maybe if I play the strings in the order of the high-lighted letters, maybe that's what opens the box."

"Why would Melfin use musical notes as a code?" Lila asks.

"The Melfins are originally from Venus. Kyle told me his dad sent him to V.A.M.A. to develop his musical skills."

Canter doesn't seem convinced. "That seems too easy."

I quickly run the calculation in my head. "Four digits translates into ten thousand possible combinations. If you don't know the names of the strings of a violin, the letters on the back wouldn't mean anything. And what are the odds a musician from Venus would be searching the Mercurian prison for this box?"

"All right, all right." Canter holds up his hands. "Try it already."

I double-check the order of notes again. For all I know, playing the strings in the wrong order will set off an alarm or seal the box for good. I take a breath, then pluck the strings. Each note rings out clear and bright, resonating in my bones. When I play the last one, something clicks and the box opens, revealing a small, very worn book inside.

Gaping, Lila gently picks it up. The black cover appears to be made of some kind of sturdy, flexible fabric, though it's very worn and faded. Inside, the frail pages—paper!— whisper and crinkle. She gasps. "It's a log of Botans."

"Is my mother in there?" Canter asks quickly.

Lila turns page after page, scanning the contents. About halfway through, her eyes settle on something. Without a word, she passes the book to him.

The color drains from Canter's face. "She was exiled? Exiled where?"

"It doesn't say." Lila's voice sounds like she's choking back tears.

"What else does it say?" Hannah asks anxiously.

"It's a record of her capture," Canter explains, his forehead creasing as he scans the pages. His grip tightens, and when he looks up again, his face is a war of shock and fury. "It was him."

"Who?" Lila asks. My stomach sinks.

I know what's coming.

"My dad," Canter says. *"Mrs. Fiona Weathers was caught with seeds by the Chemic representative on the Governing Council, Bradford Melfin, who was informed by his son that the illegal materials were in her possession. The informant, Jake Melfin, received a tip from Mr. Robert Weathers that his wife had come into possession of illegal seed paraphernalia with intent to grow."* Canter lowers the book to the desk, then covers his face with his hands. "Lies on top of lies inside of lies. Not only did he know she was alive— imprisoned, or exiled, or wherever the meteor she is. *He* was the one who turned her in."

I wish I could rewind myself into the smallest of specks as easily as I reversed my plants back to seeds. "That's not what happened," I whisper, so quietly I can barely hear my own voice. "He told Jake Melfin because they were friends, and Jake was supposed to take over MFI when his father retired. Your dad thought Jake would help her. Use his influence to make Botan powers acceptable again. Jake wasn't supposed to tell his father. That's why your mother was taken away."

"How do you know that?" Canter asks.

I shift from foot to foot. "I overheard Ms. Goble telling my mother."

"You knew," Canter says, his voice strained. "You knew, and you didn't tell me?"

I look anywhere, everywhere, but at Canter. Lila stares at me, wide-eyed. Hannah and Bernard are studying the floor. "I didn't think it would do any good."

"It doesn't matter what good it would do! She's *my* mother. I had a *right* to know. How can you call yourself my friend when you've been keeping something so big from me?"

"When I found out, you were in such a bad place. I thought telling you would make things worse."

"What does that even mean?"

"Every other week you had some wild plan for contacting your mom, each one riskier than the last." I fight against the wave of guilt and anger threatening to crash over me, striving to keep my voice steady. "I didn't know

what you would do. What you might say to your dad . . .
I wasn't sure you'd let me explain before you raced off to
confront him."

"You've known since we were at S.L.A.M.?" I nod. "So
why not tell me when we got to V.A.M.A.?" Canter asks,
his voice rising. "My dad wasn't there. What's your excuse
for that?"

"It's not an excuse!" My glasses slip in my sweaty fingers.
"After we got to Venus, you stopped talking about contacting the prison, and I didn't want to ruin it. You seemed so
happy. When I saw you, anyway."

I didn't mean to say that last bit, but now that the words
are out, there's no taking them back.

"*That's* why? I wasn't paying enough attention to you,
so you decided to punish me." I've never seen Canter this
angry. "It's not my fault you couldn't fit in, Myra."

Lila gasps. "Canter!"

"That's not true." Tears burn my eyes, but I blink them
back, refusing to let them fall. I realize I'm clenching my
hands so tight, my fingernails are digging into my palms.
"If I wanted to, I could've."

"You didn't even try."

"Yes, I did!" I fire back, my voice shaking. "I tried to
show you."

"What are you talking about?" Lila asks quietly.

"That night we were supposed to have dinner on the dock," I say around the lump forming in my throat. "I'd been learning to play music. I was going to show you both. Surprise you. But . . ."

"But what, Myra?" Lila prods.

"You didn't show up." I try to keep the note of accusation from seeping into my voice. I almost succeed. "After that I stopped playing."

Canter snarls. "And to get back at me, you decided to keep what you learned about my parents a secret! I don't get it. You can't stand my dad, but you'd protect him instead of telling me."

"No. I'd never do that! I didn't want you to get hurt again. And nothing in there"—I jab my finger at the book—"says anything that contradicts what I told you."

Lila picks up the book, shuffling through the pages until she finds the passage about Fiona. Her gaze flicks across the page. "She's right, Canter."

"It wasn't your dad's fault," I repeat. "You're my best friend. Why would I purposely hurt you?"

Canter leans back against the desk. "Because you're jealous and pathetic," he replies coldly.

Bin-ro whistles so loudly it's more like a shriek.

"Canter!" Hannah says from somewhere behind me. "That's out of line."

"I'm not pathetic." I rub my eyes with the back of my

fists. "You wouldn't even have found the moongarden without me. You wouldn't know anything about your mother. Or Botans. Or any of it."

Lila's still frantically flipping, lost in the pages.

"So I'm an idiot, then?" Canter sneers. "Only *you* can solve the galaxy's problems."

"I never said that!"

"You guys!" Lila says.

"You may as well have!" he yells. "You don't think I can handle the truth about my own parents. You don't tell me about the new garden. Or that you shared secrets that could get us thrown in prison with some kid you've known for a nanosecond. You cut me out a long time ago. Maybe I am an idiot, since it took me this long to notice."

"You guys!" Lila repeats, louder.

"That's not what happened," I choke out through a sob. "And this isn't all my fault. I've barely even seen you since we got to V.A.M.A. You *did* ditch me. Maybe you didn't mean to, but you did. And maybe I was jealous. And hurt. But I didn't keep everything from you because of that. I just didn't know how to tell you."

"See?" Canter snaps. "Like I said. Pathetic."

"*Be quiet, both of you!*" Lila shouts. "Listen! You need to hear this."

"Hear what?" a deep voice says from behind us.

CHAPTER FORTY-THREE

"NEVER MIND," MR. MELFIN SAYS, STROLLING INTO THE room. "I've read it." A tall, thin woman with a severe bob and harsh eyes follows him inside, closing the door behind her. "Warden, would you mind?"

She nods and plucks the book out of Lila's hands, tucking it into the box and snapping it shut. Something buzzes in her pocket, and she pulls out a messenger. "The informant has arrived. And your other guest is on the way."

"Good," Melfin says. "Where should we receive them?"

"The prison's control room," she replies, unclipping some metal cylinders from her belt. "But first, let's make sure our intruders don't get any foolish ideas."

Warden Vander clamps restraints on our wrists, linking them closely together, and marches us out into the hall. She plucks Bin-ro off the floor, tucking him under one arm, ignoring his stream of beeped and whistled curses. "We'll want to see what sort of data this machine has recorded, too."

In what seems like no time at all, we're back in the control room, the guards all returned and alert. The warden sets Bin-ro on the floor, then turns her attention to something on a screen.

"Informant?" Hannah whispers beside me.

"Could be someone from Perennial's group," I say miserably.

Hannah's eyes flash. "Never. What about that kid you brought to my apartment the first time?"

"Noah wouldn't do that."

"Maybe it *was* him," Canter says, glaring at me.

"He's my friend."

"Sorry if I don't trust your judgment these days."

"Both of you, stop it!" Lila whispers. "Whoever told them, there wasn't anything we could have done to stop it."

"We'll find out who they are soon enough, anyway," Bernard adds softly as footsteps echo down the hall.

A pale, dark-haired figure steps into the room, and a chill runs through me.

Canter gasps. "Ms. Curie?"

"Indra?" Hannah says, her mouth hanging open.

Ms. Curie glances at us coolly, then turns to the warden. "I assume they've been searched?"

"They're just children," the warden replies. "You don't really think they have anything dangerous on them?"

"Children who've been meddling in adult affairs," Mr. Melfin says icily. "Why should they receive special treatment?"

The warden sighs, then motions to one of the guards. He hurries over and pats down each of us, wrenching out our pockets, swiping his hands through our hair, shaking out every fold of our clothes. When he reaches Canter and turns out his pockets, something spills to the floor like a handful of pebbles. Except they aren't pebbles. . . .

Warden Vander's eyes bulge. "Are those—"

"*Seeds,*" Ms. Curie hisses, bending to scoop them into her palm.

"How in the name of Pluto . . ." Mr. Melfin rubs his jaw, eyeing the seeds like someone might look at a handful of jewels.

"Apparently, the apple seed doesn't fall too far from the tree," Ms. Curie says, her icy gaze lingering on Canter's face as she deposits the contraband on a table.

"This changes things," Warden Vander says stiffly.

"Check them for Inscriptions," Mr. Melfin demands.

"I don't. I didn't. Those aren't mine!" Canter insists, his eyes wide as a guard closes in.

The guard grabs Lila's wrist and yanks up her sleeve,

then nods to another guard at one of the consoles. "Mender," he says, releasing her and shoving her away.

Canter turns toward me. "They aren't mine," he repeats.

The guard steps toward Bernard, reaching out for his arm. His gaze lingers on the gray Rep uniform and his eyes seem to glaze over, dismissing Bernard as easily as he would a piece of furniture. He quickly drops Bernard's sleeve and sidesteps to Hannah. He inspects her arm, frowns, then checks the other arm. "Non-Creer."

Rage swirls through me, but I swallow it down. When he turns to me, I try to yank out of his grip, but he holds firm, ripping up my sleeve, and then his face goes pale. "Botan," he whispers.

"Don't record that!" the warden barks at the guard typing notes. "I'll take care of it later."

In the book. With the rest of the Botans. The exiled Botans. I wonder how many of them were betrayed this way. Maybe all of them.

How did seeds make their way to Canter's pockets? The only ones in the room with access to plants are me, Lila, and Canter, and none of us took them.

Except there's another person in this room who's admitted to having seeds. "You!" I shriek, lunging toward Ms. Curie. A guard catches me around my waist and hauls me back. "You planted them on Canter when you hugged him!"

Ms. Curie gave Fiona the seeds she stole, but she never said she gave them all to her.

"Ridiculous," Ms. Curie scoffs. "Why in the galaxy would I do that?"

"To get back at me," another voice says bitterly. Director Weathers stands in the door, his face twisted with fury.

"Robert," Mr. Melfin croaks, running his hands through his hair. "When I called you, it was because I thought your son had gotten mixed up with the wrong crowd. But given what we've caught him with . . . there's nothing I can do."

"There is," Director Weathers growls, nodding at Canter's still-pushed-up sleeve. "He's not a Botan. You've seen his Inscriptions."

"Elector," the guard in the corner confirms, and I breathe a sigh of relief. Canter's been spending so much time using his Elector powers at V.A.M.A., his Botan Inscriptions have mostly been covered.

"There are consequences for being caught with seeds," Warden Vander says grimly. "Severe consequences."

"I'm aware," Director Weathers replies, his voice sharp. "I'd like a word with you two. Alone."

Mr. Melfin and the warden exchange a glance.

"Keep a close eye on them," the warden directs before she and Melfin follow Director Weathers out into the hall and the door slides shut behind them.

"How could you do this?" Hannah hisses.

"Be careful trusting someone when you can't understand their motivations," Ms. Curie replies, sparks flickering between her fingers. "They might not be what you think."

After a few minutes, Director Weathers returns, looking grimmer than when he left. Mr. Melfin and the warden file in behind him.

"I'm taking these two home," the director says, motioning to Canter and Lila. Two guards cross the room and remove their restraints.

"What about the rest of my friends?"

"A proven Botan and a Botan relation, both intent on involving themselves with dangerous, illegal plant materials," says Warden Vander, nodding at me and Hannah. "Allowing them to walk free would be too great a risk to the Settlements."

"But he had seeds," Ms. Curie barks, pointing at Canter. "He's just as meddlesome as the rest, if not more so!"

"We have reason to believe the Botan girl planted them on him," the warden says coolly.

"It wasn't me!" I counter. "And Hannah isn't a Botan! You can't keep her here just because her sister is."

Warden Vander's eyes glint. "Who said anything about keeping you here?"

"What do you mean?" I ask.

"Come now," Mr. Melfin chides. "You were clever enough to get here, and I know you saw those empty cells."

"But—"

"Hardly anyone in the Settlements knows about Botans nowadays," he continues. "Only the Governing Councils, and the members believe that those few Botans apprehended are sent here, locked away with the plant offenders to keep the rest of society safe." He smirks. "Even fewer people realize that keeping them here among us is too great a risk. What would happen if they escaped? No, the safest option is to remove them from the Settlements altogether."

"Where are you taking us?" Hannah demands. "Where's my sister?"

Mr. Melfin blinks at her. "With the rest of her precious plants. Back on the Old World."

CHAPTER FORTY-FOUR

I CAN SEE THE OLD WORLD THROUGH THE CONTROL room window, glowing millions of miles away like a particularly bright star. Next to it, hardly larger than the stars scattered around it, shines the Moon. My home. And I'll never see it again. I may never see anything again.

"The Old World is toxic," I say slowly.

Melfin shrugs.

"Perhaps with your powers, you can convince the plants to stop spewing poison into the atmosphere."

"Dad, you can't let them do this!" Canter yells. The warden nods, and a guard crosses the room and grabs his arm, hauling him toward the door. "Get off me!"

Lila, who until now has been frozen with shock, breaks free of the guard holding her arm and rushes at Melfin. "Please. You can't send them away. Keep them here. Or . . . or put them to work in one of your factories."

"I don't need Botan magic in my factories," he snaps, like Lila suggested something revolting.

"Yes, you do!" Canter bellows, still struggling. "The Settlements aren't going to tolerate that slime you call food forever."

"I'm afraid, Mr. Weathers, they don't have much of a choice."

"Call Myra's parents," Lila pleads. "Maybe you can come up with some sort of deal."

"Her father"—he juts his chin at me—"was the main voice advocating for my removal from the Governing Council. I won't be making any deals with *him*."

The floor seems to fall away under my feet. One of the prison guards catches and steadies me, then backs away, as if I'm contagious.

"If not the Hodgers, then Hannah's parents," Lila presses. "Maybe they could—"

"I don't deal with non-Creers."

"They aren't non-Creers!" Hannah and I say at the same time.

A desperate idea occurs to me, and at this point, I don't have anything else to lose. "Melfin's stripping away people's powers," I tell the warden. "He's using the same technology that blocks Reps from accessing their magic to get back at anyone who crosses him or his company."

Director Weathers frowns. "What is this, Jake?"

"The girl is a Botan." Melfin shakes his head. "You can't trust a thing she says."

Warden Vander's expression is unreadable. "If that were true, it would be a very serious offense. Do you have any proof?"

"There's a video of him threatening to take a restaurant owner's powers."

"And where is this video?" the warden asks.

I swallow. "Gone."

Melfin looks triumphant.

"My parents used to have Creers, but ever since my sister got caught with seeds, they've lost their magic, and now he has them working in his factory," Hannah blurts out.

"Alas, emotional strain can impact a person's abilities," Melfin says, his voice laced with false sympathy. "Your family suffered a great loss. I was glad to offer them employment after learning of their circumstance. It was the least I could do."

"That's a lie!" Hannah spits. "The Council did something to them."

"The Governing Councils don't have that kind of power," Director Weathers says slowly.

"They do," I insist. "And I heard Melfin tell Hannah he could give her parents their Creers back *if* she told him where her sister got the seeds."

The warden studies Melfin, then says, "The word of a Botan is hardly credible."

"*Beep!*" Bin-ro rolls to the center of the room.

"I'll deal with you later," the warden snaps. "A memory wipe should do the trick."

"No!" I'm not sure which of us says it. Maybe all of us.

A blue light glows on Bin-ro's hull, and I wonder why he's projecting the map again. But it's not blueprints. It's a recording.

A small hologram of Melfin outside Hannah's apartment beams into the air, his words, tinny but audible, playing on Bin-ro speakers: "*Oh, I don't know about that. Just imagine it, Hannah. You and your family move into an apartment not at risk of being swallowed by the sea. Your parents' magic,* snap, *returned. You could enroll at the school of your choosing. Weren't you supposed to attend the Scientific Lunar Academy of Magic? You know, the director's an old friend of mine.*"

Melfin freezes.

"*I could easily make arrangements for you to be reenrolled. All you need to do is tell me what I want to know.*"

I watch as Hannah steps into view, stopping next to where we all hid in the stairway. "*I've told you thousands of times. I don't know where Meredith got the seeds.*"

"That sounds like proof to me," Director Weathers murmurs as Bin-ro's light dims and the hologram fades.

"It seems it is." Melfin is frozen, still staring at the spot where the projection was moments before. "Do you agree, Warden?"

"I do." She hesitates, then turns toward the center of the room. "It's unfortunate that the robot appears to have malfunctioned." She thrusts out a hand, indigo lightning exploding from her fingertips toward Bin-ro.

The tiny robot shrieks so loudly, I hunch my shoulders to cover my ears. Before I can move toward him—before I can do anything—electricity surges around him, the currents dancing like a violent storm. Bin-ro shudders and jerks, as if his small robot body is rolling in an angry sea. There's shouting, but I barely hear it. I fling myself forward, trying to shield his metal body with my own, but hands seize me, and I crash to my knees at Bin-ro's side.

Or what used to be Bin-ro. All that remains of my first friend, my most trusted companion, are singed wires inside a blackened shell.

CHAPTER FORTY-FIVE

"NO!" I SOB, MY HEART SPLINTERING LIKE GLASS. I look up, searching for Canter. "Fix him. Please, Canter. Can't you fix him?"

Canter twists free, falling to the floor beside me, and scoops Bin-ro up in his arms. Holding a hand over his hull, Canter creases his brow in concentration; then his face crumples as he shakes his head. "There's nothing to fix. He's gone."

I push to my feet, the guard's grip still tight on my arm. "How could you do that?"

"The warden and I have a mutual understanding," Melfin answers, his voice hissing in my ears. "I have many such arrangements. One of which may be of particular interest to you. Yes, I'd like a private word with this one," he says, motioning toward me.

"I don't have anything to say to you," I spit.

"Who said you had a choice?"

Warden Vander herds everyone else out of the room. Canter bellows as he's dragged away, tears streaming down his face. Hannah's cursing and struggling. Lila's sobs are so painful, they seem to slice through the air and cut into my chest. Bernard is the last to go. He's doesn't make a sound, and his eyes never leave the speck of light glowing blue in the sky.

"What do you want?" I growl when the door closes.

"Let's call it a parting gift . . . to thank you for that *seed* of publicity you provided my company last year. I always repay my debts. You see, there were only a handful of people who knew about our food cloning difficulties." He toys with buttons on the control panel, considering his next words. "My gut told me Robert Weathers was the source. I've always suspected he might harbor some lingering bitterness toward me, though we'd seemed to have moved past it in recent years. Still, you never know when it comes to family. Grudges can be long and cold."

"Get to the point."

He presses a button and a blinking light activates on the console. "However, I was surprised to find out recently that it wasn't him. And with my favor back there"—he nods toward the door Canter and the others vanished through—"I'd say I've made amends and won't need to worry about the Weathers family in the future. Though now I have a little extra leverage—thank you for that—and Robert is fully aware of the consequences of crossing me. . . . But that's not what I wanted to talk to you about."

The screen on the wall flickers, and then some sort of video feed fills it. Sitting outside with his back to the garden—*my seagarden*—is Noah.

"Wh-what?" I stammer. "What is this?"

"I believe you know my newest employee," Melfin answers with a Cheshire cat grin. On the screen, Noah grimaces but says nothing.

"*WHAT IS THIS?*" My gaze shifts from Noah's face to Mr. Melfin's. I'm twisting the metal rings around my wrist so hard, I can feel them cutting into my skin.

"When I suspected Robert of being the source, I directed my son to get close to Canter to confirm as much, but unfortunately Kyle failed. Miserably. And so I looked to our mutual friend here. Turns out, he was much more successful."

Noah shifts uncomfortably, looking everywhere but at my face. "You told him about me?" I demand, my throat hoarse. "About the garden?"

"I thought Mr. Melfin would be able to help you," Noah mumbles, still avoiding my eyes. "I figured he'd want to use your abilities to help his company. I didn't expect . . . I never believed . . ."

A memory slips into my mind: Noah suggesting I partner with MFI. Rage isn't far behind. I feel like my whole body is on fire. "This whole time, you were a spy. For *him*."

"N-no," Noah insists. "I'm your friend. I only wanted to help."

"And what'd you get out of it, Noah?" I round on Melfin. "You said he was your employee. What does that mean?"

"I told you I worked for MFI," Noah says, his voice pathetic. "Unloading their shipments."

"That's not what you meant, though, is it?"

Melfin leers. "Clever girl. Under other circumstances, I might have found a place for you within my company."

"Not in this solar system."

"I've invited young Noah here to join MFI's culinary department."

"What are you talking about?" I snap. "You only make slime squares."

"Not anymore." Melfin nods at the screen, where my garden sprawls into the sea.

"You're—you're going to use my garden?"

"Not for everyone. The general public's already accepted my imitation product. Why would I change course?"

"Because it has almost no nutritional value! People will starve."

He shrugs. "Not for a long time. And not everyone."

And then his meaning becomes clear. "You're going to keep my garden for yourself. You're going to use it to clone your own food."

"And for select others. Those who can afford it. Or who can give me what I want. I should thank you. You've given me the galaxy's best bargaining chip."

I'm rooted to the spot, staring at the screen and my garden and my friend. Except it's not my garden, and Noah isn't my friend. Not anymore. "How could you?" I whisper.

"You said you were going to meet with that group," he pleads. "When I told him, I didn't know you had gone . . . that the plan had changed." He looks sick when he finally meets my gaze. "I had to tell him something. You heard what he did to your friend's family. I couldn't—I can't risk that. Not having any magic at all." He shudders. "I thought they'd just arrest the Reps."

"And that was okay with you?" I ask coldly, stepping closer to the monitor.

Noah flinches, like I'm about to hit him, and if he weren't millions of miles away, maybe I would.

"I thought I was about to squash a small movement that could potentially become irksome to me," Melfin interjects. "If people can undo their magical suppression, what sort of leverage will I have? How do you think I've kept other companies from competing with MFI?"

I remember the competitors I'd read about on the open

network—the ones that launched, then suddenly shut down. "You took their Creers."

"I had to put a stop to it. And we did. When I arrived, government patrols had already intercepted one ship and were about to capture the other."

I can only hope one of Perennial's teams was successful.

"The twinkle on the star, though, was finding Sandra Curie there."

"Because she told you where we went."

"Here I thought you were only meddling with plants and Reps—serious enough mischief to be sure. But Sandra said you had your sights on me personally. Looks like we'll clean that up now. For good."

"What's happening?" Noah asks, miserable. "Will Myra be locked up with the other Botans?"

"What do you care?" I spit.

Noah's near tears. "I didn't mean for this to happen. You've got to believe me."

"I don't trust anything that comes out of your mouth."

"What you believe or don't is of little consequence. I have big plans for Miss Hodger. And they don't involve keeping her here." Melfin glances sideways at me, a self-satisfied smile spreading across his face. "You see, she's going back to the source."

"The source?" Noah's brow furrows. "You can't mean—"

"All you need to concern yourself with," Mr. Melfin says

coldly as he walks over to the console, "is showing up on time for work tomorrow."

"But wait! Myra, please—"

Melfin flicks a switch, and the screen goes black. "I wanted to thank you for the gift of the garden. I've been searching for something like it for a long, long time."

I glare at him. "I know. Ms. Curie told me she took Fiona's seeds from you."

He raises his eyebrows, but just as quickly, his smug mask drops back into place. "Did she? What else did she tell you?"

I'm silent. I don't want to admit that I don't know any more.

"My family's company has been around since the days of the Old World. When humanity moved to the Settlements, we were one of many food producers. Today, we're the only one left of any significance. One by one, the rest developed . . . production issues. You seem like a clever girl. Why do you think that is?"

The pieces click together in my mind. "You were growing plants to replace the cloned material."

"At best, plant cloning can only last a few decades."

Back in Apolloton Ms. Goble had reminded my mother about their upcoming reunion. Their *twenty-fifth* reunion. And my father had mentioned Mr. Melfin prosecuting more plant offenders than anyone since Fiona was captured. "You've been searching for new seeds to restart the cloning process."

"Magical suppression technology worked well to keep new competitors from growing, but it didn't solve the problems with the formulas. For years, I've been trying to replace what was stolen from my family. I've tried to confiscate seeds from every plant offender I've identified. They pop up more than you'd think. The Governing Councils don't like too much publicity around the arrests, of course. They don't want others getting any wild ideas. I even questioned some of the restaurants I supply, trying to locate an underground market, but I only hit dead ends." His eyes gleam. "Until you came along."

Nausea floods through me, and I steady myself on the console. "Why are you telling me all this?"

"I hoped you'd be comforted knowing the garden will be put to good use." He leans closer, as if sharing a secret. "Don't worry. I'll take wonderful care of your plants."

Before I can answer, or throw myself at him, or scratch out his eyes, he crosses to the door and opens it. "I believe it's time to board your shuttle."

I open my mouth to shout Melfin's plans. What he's been up to. But I swallow it all down as the others file back inside. Who would believe me, anyway?

"My parents?" I whisper.

Melfin licks his lips. "I can only imagine the horror of

discovering that your only daughter was caught with illegal seeds, practicing forbidden magic. Such a shock. I hope it doesn't take a toll on their own abilities. Like Miss Lee's parents."

"You can't!"

"Don't worry. I'll personally call them to explain everything once we're finished here."

"No," Director Weathers says gravely, locking eyes with me. "I'll tell them." He turns to Canter and Lila. "Come on. We're leaving."

"No!" Lila shrieks.

"I'll never forgive you for this!" Canter shouts at his father, trying to wrench himself free of the guards' grip, the darkened shell of Bin-ro still clutched under his arm. "Never!"

As Canter struggles, something stirs in the air. A vibration. A shuddering. *Magic.* My eyes scan the room, stopping on the pile of confiscated seeds Curie deposited on the counter. They're shaking like someone's jostled the table. My eyes widen as I realize what's about to happen.

I throw my hands out a nanosecond after Canter's magic bursts from him. Thankfully, no one notices the timing. They're too focused on my outstretched shackled hands and the vines whipping around the room.

Flowers the size of dinner plates erupt like bombs. Branches covered in razor-sharp thorns crisscross the space, tangling around the guards' legs, sending them crashing to the floor. I try to overwhelm Canter's magic, rewind the plants back to seeds, or at least stop more from sprouting, but instead more and more burst to life.

"Stop her!" the warden shouts, ducking as a particularly lethal-looking vine lashes over her head.

"It's not her!" Canter tries again to twist free.

Director Weathers's gaze shifts from the hostile plants to his son's clenched fists to me.

"It *is* me," I insist, flicking my wrist. More plants burst to life—rose hips and starflowers and comfrey and every other rash-causing species I can summon from the pile. The flowers wrap themselves around necks, faces, and arms. The warden rips one that's wound its way into her hair, her cheeks already scarlet where the leaves brushed against her skin. Melfin has the most luck disentangling himself, but even he can't escape the hives blossoming across his neck and face.

"Enough!" the warden shouts. "Stop this, or I'll send all your friends with you."

I catch Director Weathers's eye, then jut my chin toward the door. He has to get Canter out of here.

"We're leaving before she can do any more damage," the director blusters, grabbing Canter and hauling him toward the exit. Vines tangle around Canter's feet, holding him in place.

I counter his magic with my own, struggling to convince the plants to release him before anyone notices that the Botan magic in the room isn't just coming from me.

"Stop it, Myra!" Canter yells.

"Let him go!" the warden snaps at me as she sweeps her arms in a circle. A ball of energy shoots from her hands, sizzling as it connects with one of the vines. It burns and withers, but two more shoots sprout from the ashes.

"This is why we can't risk Botans in the Settlements." Melfin's eyes glint as he digs in his pocket. "They're too dangerous."

"Myra!" Lila sobs. Her Mender powers are useless right now and she knows it. "You've got to do something."

Melfin extracts a vial, snapping off the cork. Amber liquid boils inside, steam seeping into the air and winding toward me like a red river. As I breathe in the fumes, my eyelids droop. I focus all my energy on a massive bloom at my feet. Petals fly through the air like a flock of birds, dispersing the gas, and my mind instantly clears.

With every ounce of my magic, I try to break the plants' hold on Canter, and his on them, but it's not enough. His emotion is too strong—too desperate. I can't match it. Not alone.

"Release the boy!" Melfin barks, digging in his pockets for more Chemic weapons.

I strain against Canter's magic and the army of plants

he's conscripted. More and more sprout around him. I can barely contain one before five others take its place. The warden is shouting at me again, though I have no idea what she's saying. I'm drowning, looking for a crack, an opening. The growth is so thick, I can barely see Canter and his father anymore.

Then all at once, the vines start to unwind and retract.

Baffled, I search around the room. Bernard stands very still in the corner. His eyes are shut, and his hands are slightly outstretched. Joy blooms in my chest. *Bernard's found his magic!*

Together, we push against the flood of Canter's sorrow. Some of the plants wilt, curling into gray ash, while the others revert to seeds.

"No!" Canter sobs as his father drags him away, crunching withered leaves and branches beneath their feet. "Stop!"

And though I'm the one who's been delivered a death sentence, I can't help the wave of heartache I feel for Canter. He lost his mom, found her, then lost her again. I want to say something comforting, but before I can find the words, he's wrenched through the door. Just before he disappears down the hall, Director Weathers glances back, gives me a small nod, and then he's gone, too.

I never even had a chance to tell Canter I'm sorry. For not telling him about his father. For all the things I said that I didn't mean.

And now I never will.

"Myra!" Lila shrieks as she's pulled after him. "I'll find a way. I promise, I—"

"It's okay, Lila," I say softly. But the hall's already empty.

And then it's just me, Hannah, and Bernard standing in the control room, surrounded by guards and the remnants of a million plants.

Bernard!

"Wait!" I say, frantically gesturing to him. "He's supposed to go with them."

Warden Vander shakes her head. "He'd have to be retired anyway. May as well send him with you and spare me the paperwork."

"You vile, disgusting scrap of space junk—"

"It's all right, Myra," Bernard interrupts, matching the warden's detachment with a cold, firm gaze. "I guess you were right all along."

"About what?" I'm sobbing, fighting to shake off my guards, to loosen my restraints.

"About me being like Bernie. Maybe I am like my prior Repetition. And hopefully, my future ones will be, too." He smiles. "I hope they cause all sorts of trouble. Just like we did."

Mr. Melfin frowns. "I'll ensure there are no future Repetitions of you scheduled." As he makes a note on his messenger, Bernard catches my eye. And winks.

At least Bernard—Bernie—will finally be free.

I don't have time to celebrate the small victory. The guards drag us out of the room, hauling us through the maze of the prison, and before I know it, we're back on the dock, where a battered old shuttle sits waiting.

"Why waste a new transport on a one-way mission?" Melfin says.

Warden Vander checks her messenger and frowns. "Let's make this quick. There's an unfolding situation on Venus that needs my attention."

Maybe Perennial's group managed to infiltrate the Rep facility after all. Maybe Reps across the galaxy are suddenly finding they have magic.

We're shoved across the landing pad, our restraints are unhooked, and then we're pushed through the open shuttle door.

"On the bright side of the Moon," Melfin adds, "at least you'll be able to use your magic freely. For however long you survive."

The door seals shut, the engine hums to life, and then the shuttle lifts into the air, zipping through the artificially enhanced atmosphere.

"Hannah, use your Tekkie powers!" I call. "Take over the controls."

She scrambles up and throws herself behind the console. Bernard and I hover over her shoulder. Through the nav-screen, the orb of light that is the Old World grows bigger and brighter.

"Hurry!" I plead.

"I'm trying!" She slams buttons and spins dials. She even rips open a hatch in the control panel, exposing a nest of wires, then digs through them, splicing and reconnecting them. Finally, she slumps back. "It's dead."

"What?" Bernard demands. "How's the ship flying, then?"

"The *control panel* is dead," Hannah says, her voice bitter. She squeezes her eyes shut. "They must be guiding it from the control room."

"Can't you fix it?" I ask frantically. We're near enough now that I can make out the landmasses on the Old World clustered between cobalt seas. The Moon sparkles silver beside it. "Give it a charge?"

"I'm not an Elector," Hannah snaps. "There's nothing I can do."

In silence, we watch as the Old World, and certain death, speed closer and closer.

"I'm sorry," I whisper. Hannah and Bernard turn to face me. "This is all my fault."

"It's not." Hannah squeezes my shoulder. "Just because we failed doesn't mean we shouldn't have tried."

Bernard leans back in his seat, staring out at the stars. "Maybe Canter and Lila can bring Melfin down once and for all."

"I wish I'd had time to tell Canter I'm sorry," I whisper into the quiet. "I should have told him about his parents a long time ago.

"You're not the only one who kept things to yourself," answers Bernard, still focusing into space. "I never told you why Director Weathers pulled me into the workforce so early."

"I thought you didn't know."

"I lied." Bernard stares out the window. "When he assigned me to V.A.M.A., he told me to befriend his son. That Canter had been close to my prior Repetition and missed him. I thought it was strange. Half our Rep training is having it drilled into us that we're not supposed to form relationships with anyone, especially non-Reps. But the other half is not asking questions, so . . ." He shrugs.

"I don't understand. You didn't want to be our friend."

Bernard grimaces. "It's bad enough we're bound to our jobs, lifetime after lifetime. I didn't want to be forced to be someone's friend, too." He glances at me from the corner of his eye. "I have to admit it was sometimes tempting." He sighs. "I guess I'm not a very good Rep."

"But you're a great friend." I smile at him. "Whether you wanted to be or not."

He grins back at me, and we both turn to the nav-screen.

We're near enough that I can see mountains creeping up to touch the low-hanging clouds. Golden sand dunes.

Branches of river systems resemble the roots I've grown so fond of. Forests sprawling from coast to coast.

"I still wish Canter knew," Bernard says softly.

"Me too." I grip the handrails on my chair. "But he'll be okay." I'm not sure if I'm trying to reassure Bernard or myself. "He has Lila." *But not Bin-ro.* I fight through the fresh wave of grief, focusing on the cobalt oceans and emerald forests filling the nav-screen.

The windshield tinges crimson as we cross into the Old World's atmosphere.

"What are the odds we land in one piece?" I ask Hannah.

"Better than the plants not killing us if we do." She turns to Bernard. "How long did it take for the Old World plants to poison people?"

He's quiet for a moment, concentrating, then shakes his head. "I can't remember. Not long, I don't think."

There's nothing else to say. No plans to be made. No magic to save us. I reach out one hand and clasp Bernard's and take Hannah's in my other. Neither of them pulls away.

I squeeze my eyes shut, bracing for the inevitable impact.

Even though it's the last thing I should want—even though I know I probably won't live long enough to appreciate it—I'm sort of glad. If it has to end, at least it'll be surrounded by plants. On the Old World. Home.

For however long we survive.

ACKNOWLEDGMENTS

THEY SAY IT TAKES A VILLAGE TO RAISE A CHILD (IT'S TRUE), but it also takes one to create a book, and so I first want to thank my local community. Thank you to my children's school, teachers, and librarian, my town library, the local bookstores and booksellers, the beautiful town I am lucky to live in, filled with so much open space (and garden inspirations), and especially to my parents, friends, and extended family. Your encouragement has been a beacon of light for me throughout this journey, and I would have never found my way without you all.

And when it comes to navigating this strange world of publishing, find yourself an agent who will support you, advocate for you, send you gifs when you need a laugh . . . and Zoom you with an impromptu violin demonstration to help you work out the details for a musical scene. Thank you from the bottom of my heart to Moe Ferrara for all these things and more. I am so thrilled to be on this journey with you.

To Derek Stordahl, Bethany Buck, and the rest of the Pixel+Ink team—Terry Borzumato-Greenberg, K Dishmon, Lindsay Warren, Michelle Montague, Miriam Miller, Erin Mathis, Annie Rosenbladt, Mary Joyce Perry, Melissa See, Elyse Vincenty, Alison Tarnofsky, Sara DiSalvo, Kayla Phillips,

Melanie McMahon Ives, Courtney Hood, Jamie Evans, Jill Freshney, Raina Putter, Melissa Kavonic, Regina M. Castillo, Jay Colvin, Kerry Martin, and Arlene Goldberg—thank you for all you do to bring Myra's story to life and into the hands of readers. The talent, passion, and expertise of the Pixel+Ink team is out of this universe, and I feel so grateful to have this series with such a remarkable publisher.

Deepest thanks to my editor, Alison Weiss, who is a treasure trove of brilliant ideas, storytelling insights, and editing excellence. I could not imagine a better champion for this story or a better partner for honing how to tell it.

To Sarah Coleman (a.k.a. Inkymole) and Sammy Yuen— thank you for putting your magic into yet another stunning cover. It never gets old seeing Myra's adventures come to life through your artistry.

Thank you to my critique partners who have become friends, and friends who have become critique partners. To Maura, Tracy, Jen, and Melissa—I'm so lucky to be able to swap pages with you from our imaginary worlds and to have your friendships in this one. And to Victoria, I have the deepest admiration for who you are as a writer and who you are as a person and am so grateful to share some of this journey with you. Fingers crossed we can be at the same event at the same time in the near future!

And for my husband and children, who endure my late nights and early (and sometimes grumpy) mornings, with special thanks to Jensen, my galactic battle coordinator; Julia, my trombone musical advisor; and Jared, my go-to confidant, resident comedian, and favorite photographer. I hope each of these books is further proof to you all that any of your dreams are possible, and I hope you always reach for the stars with your own.